MW01175024

The Pursuit of
Miss Charlotte Edwards

KELSEY GREYE

WESTBOW
PRESS

A DIVISION OF THOMAS NELSON

WestBow Press books may be ordered through booksellers or by contacting:

WestBow Press
A Division of Thomas Nelson
1663 Liberty Drive
Bloomington, IN 47403
www.westbowpress.com
1-(866) 928-1240

Because of the dynamic nature of the Internet, any Web addresses or links contained in this book may have changed since publication and may no longer be valid. The views expressed in this work are solely those of the author and do not necessarily reflect the views of the publisher, and the publisher hereby disclaims any responsibility for them.

ISBN: 978-1-4497-0418-6 (sc)
ISBN: 978-1-4497-0417-9 (dj)
ISBN: 978-1-4497-0495-7 (e)

Library of Congress Control Number: 2010933035

Printed in the United States of America

WestBow Press rev. date: 8/9/2010

For Bonnie, whose support, creativity and excellent eye for murder were instrumental in every area of this book. Thank you for everything.

Acknowledgements

Mom and Dad: for all of the support you've given me and for being such incredible examples of Jesus Christ throughout my life, I can never thank you enough. Graeme, encouraging me and actually wanting to read this just because I wrote it pretty much makes you the best brother ever. Steph, Sara and Jolene – parts of this book are the culmination of things we imagined, discussed or mocked during our college years together. Frightening, isn't it? Michelle, you inspire me every day with your God-centered view of life. Thanks for understanding me so well. Kathryn, Rochelle, Christine and Lisa, you have all been such blessings to me, particularly when I need a reality check. Mandy – thank you, first, for all the time you spend working on my muscles because, let's face it, they're troubled, and second, thank you so much for all the encouragement, support, ideas and common sense. My Southridge family – what an honour it is to be part of a church that continually declares Jesus Christ as Lord and seeks to impact the world for Him. To the staff and faculty at Millar College of the Bible – thank you for teaching me to handle the word of God with reverence and challenging me to live a life worthy of the Lord; and to the students – you are so much fun to teach! And finally, the Greens: Jorin, Dorothy, Michael and Kathy, my Pambrun family. Words are not enough to express how grateful I am to God for bringing you into my life at a time when my world looked rather bleak and making you and your home a sanctuary for me.

Contents

Chapter
1

*A*ny number of the terrifying and exhilarating scenes from recently read novels that were running through her mind would have been preferable to the reality that Charlotte Edwards encountered on the morning of her twenty-seventh birthday. Perhaps this opinion seemed to be overly melodramatic; but as she peered out at a gloomy day through the small window next to her writing desk, Charlotte felt entitled to be a little melodramatic.

She was well past marriageable age and was utterly dependent on what little family she possessed. This was, indeed, quite the source of her angst—not so much the lack of husband, though she admitted to herself that acquiring one would likely be pleasant—but it was depressing to know that she was intrinsically tied to her relatives for what was likely to be the rest of her life. It was this thought that brought her to the brink of tears in the weak light of the early dawn.

Charlotte's parents had died together in a carriage accident when she was only a toddler, leaving her to be raised by her extended family. Though it actually consisted of two aunts, two uncles, and over the course of the following years, four cousins, she made her home, if it could be called that, with her Aunt Beatrice, Uncle Roland and cousin, Louisa. This would not have been so bad if her relatives had had anything at all in common with their young charge. However, she grew up a quiet and thoughtful child, preferring reading and solitude in the midst of children and adults who thrived on noise and foolish conversation. As a result, not only was

Charlotte lonely and oft-ignored, but her quiet nature caused her family to think her rather stupid, and they considered her a burden on both their time and finances. She learned this at a fairly young age due to the fact that her aunts and uncles had never quite grasped the concept of lowering their voices when discussing serious matters; oblivious that children did, in fact, have ears and knew how to use them.

From her earliest moments, Charlotte had known that she was not wanted. This could have crushed her spirit had she not possessed a remarkable ability to escape into her own thoughts and worlds for hours on end. While she felt the lack of love keenly, she managed to use her imagination not only to build, in her mind, a life she desired, but to entertain herself with the precise and witty insults she would unleash on her relatives should she ever cease to rely on their goodwill for survival. It was this that kept her sane as she grew to adulthood among her silly, mean-spirited cousins and increasingly irritating, overbearing aunts and uncles.

As she stared out her window, Charlotte felt herself smile as she thought of the one secret she had managed to keep from her nosy, intrusive relatives. As soon as she had learned the art, she began to write, allowing all the thoughts and dreams she had stored up to flow from her mind to the page. The results were astounding: short stories and essays in childhood, then serial stories, and finally a complete novel, finished just two weeks prior to the birthday she was now celebrating. She had no idea if her writing was any good or not, but she found it satisfying that she had not simply drifted into a mindless, bitter oblivion as she grew older, but had sought to transfer her unique perspective on the world onto paper.

Upon the arrival of her eighteenth birthday, Charlotte had gathered up the best of her "horrid" short stories (for she truly did have a gift for the macabre and dramatic lurking under her quiet exterior), and had snuck out to the dingy offices of one of the gossip-oriented newspapers in town. Though she did not consider it fine literature, the revenue from her secret submissions that the butler, her trusted friend, Graves, had steadily collected for her served to cover the cost of more writing material. She had Graves bank the rest for her under an assumed male name in hopes of someday having enough to live independent from her family. Thus far, the amount was respectable and growing slowly but was not nearly enough to secure her freedom.

The trunk that contained her manuscript was in the corner of her dark little second-story room. Her family believed that all it housed were the books she'd collected over the years. They had little use for any type of literature. However, Charlotte had spent the better portion of a month during her thirteenth year constructing the false bottom under which she hid all her writings. It would never do for her aunts, uncles, or cousins to find them, for most of what she'd written had been inspired by her own life, often including the foolish behavior of her family told from her own dry perspective. She doubted that they would recognize themselves as the villains in the gothic romances and horrors she'd composed, but one never knew; thus, it was safer for all involved that her manuscripts lay hidden from prying eyes. Besides, if they knew she wrote, it would just give them one more thing about her to mock and belittle.

The light was gradually growing more pronounced, and she knew that the early morning time she treasured for reflection and writing was drawing to a close. Soon she would have to face her family and a day filled with comments on her age, her unsatisfactory appearance, her lack of suitors, and the burden she was on her family. With the last of her tears still shining on her cheeks, Charlotte rose from her desk and walked to the little basin and pitcher sitting on her bureau. She washed her face briskly, trying to erase the evidence of her pain, dressed her thick light-brown hair simply in a chignon at the nape of her neck, and chose a plain muslin day gown that had been made over from one of her cousin Louisa's dresses from the previous year.

The slight figure that stared back at her in the cracked mirror was a little pitiful, she thought. Big, expressive green eyes looked out from a pale oval face with a lovely Cupid's bow mouth that rarely had reason to smile. Better not stare too long, she thought, or she would become even more depressed than she already was.

Having finished washing and dressing, she knelt by the edge of her bed and lifted her face to heaven, praying the same prayer she'd prayed every birthday since she was a little girl. "Lord, I thank you for this new day and give it back to you. I'm only asking for one thing again this year. Please, God, could you send me someone to love who will love me back? That's all I want. And please help me make it through today with your grace and your strength. Amen."

Rising, she picked up the worn, fine copy of the Book of Common Prayer that had belonged to her father and rubbed her fingers lightly along the spine. She couldn't remember much of him or her mother, but it always made her feel closer to him when she read the sweet, steadfast truths that were so dear to him. After a few seconds, she replaced it on the shaky narrow table next to her bed. She took the locket lying next to it there and

3

slipped it over her head, tucking it into her dress. Though her mother's locket was undeniably Charlotte's by rights, it was never a good idea to flaunt her few possessions—particularly good-quality jewelry—in front of her greedy family. With a sigh, Charlotte steeled herself and opened the door to face another day.

Chapter

2

There are certain individuals who find their pleasure in belittling others—particularly those less fortunate than themselves—and are exceedingly good at it. Mrs. Beatrice Smythe-Poole was one of these individuals. Long practice and a naturally shrewish temperament made her ability truly remarkable. The unfortunate target of her attention was most often her niece, and Beatrice took great pains to call attention to every failing she felt Charlotte displayed, regardless of whether or not it actually existed. One of her favorite pastimes was going into a stage-worthy soliloquy on the burden of Charlotte—and her own benevolence and long-suffering in continuing to look after her useless niece. To Charlotte's mind, Aunt Beatrice's understanding of benevolence differed vastly from everyone else's.

Charlotte recalled, with vivid clarity, overhearing a conversation between her Aunt Beatrice and Uncle Roland when she was only ten years old. On this particular occasion, she had grown tired of the incessant whining, teasing, and general idiocy of her cousin, and had snuck away down a little-used hallway that happened to wind past her uncle's den.

"What do you mean, we can't send her away?" cried Aunt Beatrice. "You promised that once she got a little older, we could send her to boarding school until she could earn her keep as a governess. Roland, I don't understand what's going on!"

Charlotte's ears perked up. Boarding school had the potential to be infinitely more enjoyable than life with the Smythe-Pooles. She edged closer and listened intently.

"Beatrice, calm down. I know what I said, but things have changed. We can't send her away. What if she said something? To the wrong person? It could mean disaster for us if someone looked too closely!"

"Don't be silly, Roland. She doesn't know anything, and besides, she's a very stupid girl. Who would believe it if she did say anything revealing? You know she hardly says two words in a week. There's something very odd about that child. I don't want her in our home. Please, Roland, get rid of her for me?"

Charlotte tried to piece together what they were talking about, but it was all too vague. Something she was supposed to know about? A secret? But what? She knew they were discussing her. Aunt Beatrice had often informed her that she was indeed a very odd child. She also informed her often that she was remarkably stupid—so often that Charlotte had ceased to pay much attention to what was said directly to her, and instead focused her attention on observing what was said and done around her. She gleaned an alarming amount of information that way and quite enjoyed her secret store of knowledge.

Little more was said between her aunt and uncle after that about boarding school, and the idea was soon abandoned. Charlotte had instead been educated by a series of indifferent tutors that she shared with her cousin, Louisa.

It was fortunate that Charlotte was both intelligent and ambitious, or she would have had no education to speak of. As it was, she not only managed to gain a proper education, despite the lack of attention and encouragement, but she also trained herself in Latin and German. The languages were introduced to her by a tutor fresh out of university, an idealistic young man with strong ideas on the equality of the sexes. He was soon dismissed, after Louisa took a fancy to the poor fellow and had been unrepentantly indiscreet in dress and manner to try to gain his attention for distinctly nonacademic activities. Nothing short of scandal would have been the result, had the young man succumbed, but as it was, Charlotte's aunt and uncle stepped in and threw him out of the house. After that memorable occurrence, which she had greatly enjoyed watching, she was forced to learn and study on the sly. Over the years, she found a knack for hiding her knowledge, playing the role of the plain, poor, and worthless relation so as not to draw any undue attention to herself.

And so it was that when Charlotte emerged from the sanctuary of her little room on her birthday morning, her first encounter was, inevitably, a bad one.

"Why, Charlotte, I see that you have slept in again!" cried Aunt Beatrice, as though her niece were a lazy sluggard instead of the most industrious of the lot.

"Don't you realize that, even though it is your twenty-seventh birthday—a fact I should think you would not want to acknowledge—this family cannot and will not abide by your every whim? You are still expected to pull your weight around here, regardless of what day it is. You know very well that breakfast is served precisely at eight."

It was a quarter to eight, the grandfather clock announced, just as Beatrice finished speaking, but she conveniently ignored this. Charlotte realized that she shouldn't have expected anything better, considering past history, but somehow she always felt her birthday should bring some sort of truce. Aunt Beatrice had a real gift for making her feel like an outsider and for making her think, for a brief moment, that she really had slept in to make the family cater to her every whim. If Beatrice's talent could be bottled and sold, Charlotte mused, she'd make a fortune.

"Charlotte! Are you listening to me?"

Aunt Beatrice's grating voice jolted Charlotte out of her reverie.

"Of course, Aunt Beatrice. I'm sorry, what were you saying?"

Aunt Beatrice sniffed in an offended manner, a difficult task but so frequently undertaken that she'd become an expert.

"I was inquiring as to whether you planned on gracing us with your presence in the breakfast room. We've been waiting for you for over five minutes now. You realize this is simply unacceptable behavior, especially at your age."

That makes two age references, thought Charlotte, with morbid satisfaction, and she seriously doubted that anyone had been waiting for her at all. If her relatives had suddenly decided to treat her in a civil manner, she would likely have died outright from the shock. Aunt Beatrice was simply acting according to pattern. Of course, that didn't ease Charlotte's hurt or stop her anger from rising.

"Of course, Aunt. I do apologize."

These were the words that came out of Charlotte's mouth, her tone and posture the model of deference. Her mind, much more dexterous than her family ever dreamed, was flinging verbal darts with alarming rapidity. She was forced to step lightly around her aunt and head to the breakfast room lest she finally let loose with all the pent-up sarcastic retorts her wit had concocted over the years. Such an event, though thoroughly satisfying, would have spelled disaster, for Charlotte could not afford to offend the family.

She kept this thought uppermost as she walked down the corridor towards the breakfast room and Aunt Beatrice's husband and daughter. At least the food would be good, she thought, trying to shake her dark mood. Mrs. Brown, the cook, was quite fond of her, and Charlotte felt the same about the older woman. It was with this in mind that she crossed the threshold and turned to face something more horrifying than any haunted castle or desolate moor she had ever written: the breakfast room.

Chapter

3

*C*harlotte often thought it a blessing that others were not privy to the thoughts that flitted through her head as she sat across from them while they ate. For people who espoused such devotion to propriety, the Smythe-Pooles somehow remained unable to conduct themselves with any kind of refinement. Though they saw themselves as paragons of elegance, in reality, the Smythe-Pooles were, at best, barely endurable in even the lowest circles of society. Only her uncle's position as a banker and his resultant access to people's financial information kept the family on the invitation list to most balls and parties—that and their tenuous connection to nobility through Charlotte's father, Lord Charles Edwards, despite his untimely demise.

It always amused Charlotte to count the number of times that particles of food remained on the face of her cousin, Louisa, after a forkful had been thrust in the general direction of the mouth. She was constantly reminded that Louisa was everything she was not: outgoing, sociable, pretty, with her golden hair and big blue eyes, and, most important, a legitimate part of the family. Charlotte often wished others could see past the pretence that was so obvious to her. Louisa, though in possession of all the qualities previously mentioned, was mean-spirited and petty, often making sly remarks on Charlotte's appearance and status when only close family were present. In public, she fawned over her cousin, carefully crafting the illusion of philanthropy sparked by devoted familial affection. Charlotte knew she was socially awkward, due mostly to her fear of speaking her mind. She knew quite well that if she ever dared to insult her relatives, she would soon find herself cast out of the only home she had, condemned to make her living in whatever way she could. Unfortunately, her silence led others to believe that she was jealous of her cousin, who was, without question, the darling of the family.

As Charlotte entered the breakfast room, she couldn't help grinning when she saw her adored cousin busily shoving eggs into her mouth. Though she seldom, if ever, ate in the presence of men, Louisa loved to eat and seldom slowed down long enough to notice the smears of yolk running down her chin and crumbs of toast tumbling into her décolletage until after she was satisfied. It reminded Charlotte, when she felt most lonely, that she probably didn't want to be an accepted part of the Smythe-Poole family anyway. They were all flattery and façade to her need for the genuine. The only thing real about any of them was their greed.

"Lottie! Why do you continue to vex me by staring at me that way? You know I don't like it! Stop grinning at me like that! Honestly, Mother, can't you make her stop?"

Louisa's tones were anything but dulcet when addressing her cousin. She had inherited her mother's shrill voice, and she took special pleasure in using the nickname she knew Charlotte despised. Louisa saved what she thought of as a charmingly breathy tone for young men, though she sounded more asthmatic than attractive, and employed her naturally high-pitched whine the rest of the time. She also assumed that everyone found her delightfully playful and tried to cultivate this image by twirling her hair around her finger and affecting what she thought was an adorable pout while tilting her head. Charlotte thought the result looked suspiciously like a cross between a disobedient toddler and the neighboring household's little pug. She was, as usual, quite accurate in her assessment.

"Charlotte! Honestly, girl, why can't you simply sit and eat like a normal person?!" said her Uncle Roland.

Unlikely, thought Charlotte, as she lowered her head and kept her gaze on her plate, trying to hide the smirk that still lingered on her face, for she was fairly certain that Uncle Roland's definition of "normal people" bore little resemblance to her own.

Charlotte had always thought that there was no one else on earth that could possibly be a better match for Aunt Beatrice than Roland Poole. He was physically Aunt Beatrice's opposite in every way, short and round in contrast to Aunt Beatrice's tall, spindly figure. His hair was white and bushy, and though he looked like a type of St. Nicholas, his disposition was anything but jolly. Uncle Roland was a banker by trade, which made him moderately acceptable in society, but he desired much more recognition and power than he had attained. Thus, he thrust his daughter in the general direction of every wealthy or titled young man he could find and spent the rest of his time grousing about society's inability to recognize his importance.

Aunt Beatrice and Louisa wholeheartedly agreed and seemed to have concluded that Charlotte's primary function was to bear the brunt of all their disappointments, which they inflicted by snubbing and insulting her anytime the mood struck. Charlotte had never been able to understand their obvious dislike of her, though she had come to accept it. She had read the tales of the Brothers Grimm as a little girl and had decided that while "Cinderella" was just a fairy story, she had somehow been placed into an evil stepfamily of her own. Even more depressing was the fact that it was unlikely that a Prince Charming of any sort was going to come to her rescue. That hope had died a long time ago.

"I'm sorry, Uncle Roland. I'm afraid I was thinking of something and became distracted," said Charlotte, without looking up.

"Thinking? What business do you have thinking? For heaven's sake … you had better take a lesson from your cousin Louisa. She doesn't go around thinking all the time, and see how many beaux she has? You haven't even managed one!"

She remained silent, not quite managing to squelch a smirk at Uncle Roland's unwittingly derogatory remark, and concentrated on finishing her breakfast without further incident. Her silence allowed her to escape any more attention from her family. After all, she had to save up her stamina for the guests who would be arriving later that morning to offer token birthday salutations. In reality, they were only coming by for the tea and cakes Mrs. Brown would set out and to catch up on the latest gossip and scandal, as both Louisa and Aunt Beatrice were unparalleled gossips.

Charlotte comforted herself with the reminder that, even though she faced another day filled with dread, she could pretend that she was just gathering more experience to draw upon for her latest novel. This one featured an impoverished young woman in yet unseen danger who would end up having great improvement in love and fortune. Well, thought Charlotte sadly, at least one of them would.

Chapter 4

A gathering of the entire Smythe clan was always an occasion. Charlotte dreaded it. If she could have asked for one birthday gift from her family, it would have been a day of complete solitude and undisturbed writing. However, they had never and likely would never give her any sort of gift, and solitude was a concept with which none of the Smythes were familiar. To their thinking, if one was alone, who was there to impress? Charlotte sighed. At least she had managed to sneak off to the kitchen shortly after finishing her breakfast to visit Mrs. Brown, Graves, and the two upstairs maids, Betsy and Eliza.

Her longtime friendships with Mrs. Brown and Graves, who were more family to her than the residents whose blood she shared, were what had kept her sane since her parents died. It was one of her secret amusements that she had been clever enough to keep her friendships with the servants hidden from her family for years. Of course, it wasn't terribly difficult to hide things from people who seldom acknowledged the existence of their niece, let alone their servants.

Charlotte clearly remembered the day, when she was seven years old, that she had snuck away from her cousins during a game of hide-and-seek, when she was supposed to be the seeker, and had spent three glorious hours making the acquaintance of Mrs. Brown, Graves, and Betsy and Eliza. She smiled as she recalled the expressions on her cousins' faces when she had strolled into the sitting room long after they had given up the game. When pressed for an explanation as to her whereabouts, she had merely stated that she had not been able to find their hiding places. She figured that if they assumed she had been looking for them the whole time, that was their prerogative. This event, naturally, went down in the family annals as yet another indicator of Charlotte's stupidity, though this, at least, did not bother Charlotte, since it reminded her that there were some people in her life that cared for her—and others who had no idea who she really was.

When the doorbell rang to announce the arrival of the guests, Charlotte briefly considered locking herself in her room. Dismissing the thought since the defense would be unlikely to succeed; she mentally girded her loins and walked slowly into the parlor. Her aunt, uncle, and cousin were already there, impatiently waiting for their company. Three sets of eyes glared at her as she entered the room and sat down.

"Where have you been, you ungrateful girl?" cried Aunt Beatrice. "The least you could have done was help set up for tea, even if it is your birthday. Honestly, I don't know what to do with you. It's not as though we chose to take you in, so I would think that you would be a little more inclined to lend a hand around here."

Charlotte had to bite her tongue to refrain from commenting that she could see how straining it had been for her aunt to stand around issuing orders while the servants set up the trays. Fixing her eyes on the floor to give her time to school her features, she took a breath and then lifted an impassive face to her aunt.

"I apologize, Aunt," she said evenly, "and beg your pardon." Beatrice merely sniffed and turned away. Charlotte moved to the sofa and sat down, her mind wandering back to the plot of the latest novel she was reading, a gothic romance obtained on the sly by Betsy and secretly placed under her pillow by Eliza, so that her aunt would not find it. She could hear Aunt Beatrice muttering under her breath and thanked heaven that these comments were inaudible, as the content was bound to be the same as always.

At the sound of a throat clearing, Charlotte looked up to see Graves, the butler, standing in the doorway.

"Mr. and Mrs. Gerald Smythe, Miss Mariah Smythe, Miss Elsa Smythe, Mr. Horace Smythe," he announced in proper, formal tones.

Gerald Smythe, her mother's elder brother, along with his family, was a main source of inspiration for Charlotte's writing. He was the only member of the family to have gone into manufacturing. According to the rest of the family, this made him a black mark on a formerly spotless legacy of aristocracy.

Charlotte smiled inwardly as she thought of the Smythe family claim to nobility. It seemed her great-great grandfather had married the youngest stepdaughter of an earl. Since he was a groom and worked in the stables on the earl's land, the marriage was not looked upon favorably by his young bride's family, and she was promptly disinherited. Though her descendents could, and did, claim a hint of aristocratic blood, family money was not a reality. No wonder Gerald had found it necessary to go into trade to provide for his family, not that he would admit to such a thing. He told anyone who would listen that he was too intelligent to while away his days when he could advance modern man into the twentieth century, never mind that they were only just midway through the nineteenth one. Charlotte did not consider the wigs he manufactured to be of assistance in thrusting anyone into any century. She rather thought that if the men wearing them were thrust anywhere, the precariously balanced wigs would be left behind anyway. She smiled at the mental picture.

"Papa, how long must we stay here?" whined Horace. "I have plans with Johnson and Moore to play some cricket today. I don't see why I had to come at all anyway."

Horace took no pains to lower his voice in his address to his father.

"Yes, Papa, we also have plans today." said Mariah. "Elsa and I want to go shopping for new gloves. Please, Papa, can we?"

"Gerald, you know that our darlings must have their freedom. Yes, girls, Horace, we will not stay long. Simply long enough to pay our compliments to your cousin on her birthday. You know we do this *every* year." Frances Smythe's emphasis seemed to imply that Charlotte had a good deal of nerve having a birthday that often.

"Of course, my dears, of course," said Uncle Gerald, acquiescent as usual. "Just as soon as we finish tea, you can go."

Charlotte watched this exchange with little interest, a replay of what happened every year. Her aunt Frances, Gerald's wife, glanced over at her with an expression of distaste on her wide face. Charlotte wondered, as she often did, whatever had possessed her uncle to court and marry Aunt Beatrice's longtime best friend, the perpetually irritable Frances Wilson. Of course, she thought, Uncle Gerald was no great catch either. With his mild nature, it was a wonder he had managed to propose at all, though it wouldn't surprise her a bit it Frances had orchestrated the whole thing.

Whenever she was around her aunt, Charlotte inevitably found herself more clumsy and awkward than usual. When she was alone, her natural grace and refinement were clearly apparent even to her critical eyes, but something about the way Aunt Frances looked at her made her feel that if she died of some wasting disease in order to considerately remove herself from their midst, it would be the greatest gift she could give her family. Perhaps Charlotte's ingrained sense of melodrama encouraged these thoughts, but her family did little to encourage a more rational outlook.

Glancing around the room, Charlotte noted that Aunt Beatrice and Cousin Louisa were engaged in a scintillating conversation about the latest trends in bonnets, while Uncle Roland entertained himself by marching from the fireplace to the window and back again. Give him a bayonet, she thought, grinning, and he would be quite the little foot soldier. The rest of the guests invited, including the vicar and his wife, to whom she had never actually spoken, were due any minute. Sighing at the thought, she settled back on the sofa and gave herself over to the business of plotting the next section of her serial. She thought a highwayman, a murder and a damsel in distress would be rather thrilling and threw herself into her imaginings with enthusiasm.

Chapter
5

By the time the rest of her extended family and guests had arrived, eaten all the cakes, and had their tea, Charlotte was exhausted. Hearing disparaging remarks about her appearance, her spinsterhood, and her existence in general always tended to wear her out. She was counting the minutes until she could go up to her room to change for dinner, simply because she would finally have a few minutes to herself. She looked down at the plain, washed-out purple of her muslin gown. Sitting amid the silks and satins of her aunts and cousins, Charlotte was sure she could not look more the part of the poor, unwanted relation.

The late morning tea was only endurable because of the entertainment of watching her aunts and uncles blatantly flatter the vicar and his wife, pretending a piety that was, in her opinion, completely unnecessary given the vicar's obvious fondness for sherry and his wife's obvious fondness for Charlotte's twenty-year old cousin Horace. Though she was saddened, Charlotte couldn't help being a bit amused at the irony as she watched the vicar stumble toward the door, oblivious to the small note and lustful glances that passed between his wife and Horace. She suspected that as long as his wife was discreet about it, the vicar didn't care who she gave her favors to. Discretion meant everything when it came to moving in Society, where the word *sin* was as antiquated and ignored as last year's fashions.

In the early afternoon, when the rest of the family was attempting to sleep off too much cake, sherry, or both, she had managed to slip away, up to her room, grab her manuscript, and, mustering all her courage, make the journey to London's second most prominent publisher. She had chosen Brooke, Chapman and Jones because they were the editors of some of her favorite novels, and she suspected they would be more open to a female writer than some of London's other houses. Though smaller than most, they were well respected for the more popular "horrid" novels that Charlotte favored as well as a wide variety of other types of literature.

It had not been easy to gain entry into the editor's office without an appointment. Charlotte had waited in the quietly elegant outer office for almost two hours before she was called in to see the editor, Mr. Anderson. She grew pensive remembering her surprise at the editor's appearance. Charlotte had expected a middle-aged or elderly man, but Thomas Anderson couldn't have been more than thirty. He had also been very polite, a welcome change from those people usually inhabiting her world.

He had not, however, been overly interested in her novel. Charlotte knew, as she pressed her case, that there was small hope he would ever read it, to say nothing of publishing it, but she hoped that she had managed to interest him in it enough to at least take a look. Sighing, she allowed herself a moment to recall how handsome he had been, tall and slim with auburn hair and such warm, kind brown eyes, and then kicked herself for it. She had no business thinking about him that way, she reminded herself. She was long past the age at which young men would consider her worth looking at, and they obviously never had when she was younger anyway. He'd had a lovely smile, though, she thought a little sadly.

It had just been nice to be treated as a lady, if only for a short time. Of course, there had been quite a row when she returned home after a three-hour absence. The family had woken up sooner than she hoped, but she simply said she had run an errand and refused to discuss it further. It was the first time that she stood up to her family in any fashion, and she found the experience exhilarating. She could not afford to anger them, but she knew that they would never understand her need to write and her desire for publication. In fact, they would deem it scandalous, an irony given their own lax morality, and forbid her to continue to write. That prospect, Charlotte knew, would kill what little hope she had left.

In her room, Charlotte briskly washed her face and redressed her hair, and then opened the tiny wardrobe to pull out her dinner dress. It was, as always, one of her cousins' cast-offs, but she loved the way the silk felt when she put it on, and she thought that the cream color did suit her rather better than most of the dresses she had. She felt almost pretty when she had occasion to don this particular gown.

To her surprise, however, Charlotte discovered not only the cream gown hanging in the wardrobe, but another dress beside it. The new one was a lovely shade of moss green that would accent her eyes and the pale delicacy of her skin. A note was attached to the front, reading, "Charlotte, this dress is for you to wear to dinner this evening. We have a special guest coming, so please do try your best to look as attractive as you can. Aunt Beatrice."

Charlotte held the dress out in front of her. It was very lovely indeed. In fact, she had never in her life owned anything so beautiful. Confused, she slowly turned from the wardrobe and moved to put it on. The silk shone softly in the muted light of the candles on her bureau. Once dressed, she put on the matching slippers she had found on the floor under the gown and looked at herself in the mirror.

"I wonder," she said aloud to the stranger in the glass, "who this mystery guest is?"

Perhaps a new suitor for Cousin Louisa, she thought, or one of Uncle Roland's business associates. But then why would she need a new dress? If it were one of her novels, there would be something devious afoot, but she was more aware than most young ladies that life was nothing like a novel. She shook her head and gave up trying to figure it out and let her thoughts wander back to her latest plot. A murder was essential, she decided, maybe even two.

Since she had never had a new dress before, Charlotte took a moment longer to study herself in the mirror, once she was ready to go down to supper, and a small smile crept across her face at her reflection. The smile made all the difference in the world to her appearance. Little dimples winked in her cheeks, and her eyes sparkled. Charlotte was so seldom treated to the sight of herself looking happy that she was pleasantly surprised to see a pretty woman looking back at her. She turned from the mirror and headed for the door, a lightness in her step that hadn't been there the moment before.

Downstairs in the parlor, Uncle Roland and Louisa simply nodded their acknowledgment of Charlotte's entrance. Aunt Beatrice looked at her critically, announcing, "I suppose you'll do. Do try to make some conversation at the dinner table. We don't want Mr. Warren to think you're dimwitted."

"Who is Mr. Warren?" asked Charlotte, though she had little interest in the answer. Her mind was consumed with her new story. Yes, she thought, a highwayman will be most thrilling, and a duel—perhaps with the heroine's guardian?

"Charlotte! Did you hear me? I said that Mr. Warren is a friend of your uncle's."

"Of course, Aunt Beatrice. I heard you." She had spoken the words so often that they were an automatic response. *As if I could not hear you*, she thought, *when your voice is shrill enough to break glass.*

Silence reigned as they sat and waited. Eventually the door opened, and Graves appeared.

"Mr. Warren, sir."

"Thank you, Graves. Please inform Mrs. Brown that we are ready to dine. That will be all."

Graves turned and left the room, giving Charlotte a quick wink just before he left. The simple gesture warmed her heart, not caring whether friendships with the servants were proper or not. As Graves left, Mr. Warren stepped into the room. Or rather, he waddled in. Charlotte would not have believed it was possible for one's stomach to precede their advance by so great a degree had she not seen it herself.

Mr. Warren was of medium height, with a face that spoke as much of overindulgence as his body did. His nose was quite red, and the veins in his face that were not broken bulged in a most unattractive manner. His eyes were bloodshot, but sharp in a way that made Charlotte most uncomfortable when he turned to her and let his eyes roam leisurely over her form, starting at her feet and working his way up. By the time Mr. Warren's gaze met hers, Charlotte was ready to turn and run upstairs to her room. She had never felt so exposed in her life.

"Well, Poole, it's a fine specimen of a woman you've got here in your niece! A fine specimen indeed! I'm most pleased."

Charlotte's uncle preened under this praise, while she grew increasingly discomfited. If he wanted to look at her teeth next, she really would run upstairs, she decided. She waited for him to turn his attention to Louisa, hoping that her obvious charms would soon eclipse her meager ones in Mr. Warren's obviously filthy mind.

Uncle Roland cleared his throat. "We're quite pleased with her appearance this evening ourselves. Mind you, she's not always so well turned out, but that can be managed, given time and a little effort."

The backhanded compliment caught Charlotte by surprise. It was the closest thing to something nice that Uncle Roland had ever said to her. She looked at her uncle curiously, noticing that he appeared almost nervous, fidgeting and walking around in circles. Now that she looked, her aunt also appeared a little nervous, and Cousin Louisa looked suspiciously happy. The sense of apprehension that had begun the moment Mr. Warren walked into the parlor grew as Charlotte studied her family.

"Dinner is served," announced Graves from the doorway.

"Warren, why don't you escort Miss Charlotte here?" said her Uncle Roland.

"I'd be delighted, sir. Thank you."

Mr. Warren held out his arm for Charlotte, and as she could find no plausible escape within the bounds of propriety, she laid her hand on his elbow and allowed him to escort her in to dinner, slowing her step to keep pace with his. By the time they reached the dining room, a short walk down the hall, he was sweating and breathing heavily. Her aunt had specified that Charlotte be seated directly across from Mr. Warren, and so she had a most regrettable view of his dinner as it moved from his plate to his mouth and occasionally to the front of his shirt. It was quite possibly the most disgusting dinner she had ever had the dubious privilege of attending.

"So, Miss Charlotte, I hear it's your birthday today. Your aunt tells me that you have a new dress on this evening. Very lovely. Fits you like a glove, which I must say, is most fetching. You have a very nice figure, my girl, very nice indeed. Never did have much use for overly meaty women myself. Like 'em slim, but nicely rounded, I do!" Mr. Warren's common accent only emphasized the crudity of his language.

Charlotte stared at Mr. Warren and then at her aunt and uncle, who pretended not to hear Mr. Warren's increasingly inappropriate comments. Cousin Louisa was smirking into her napkin. Charlotte turned back to Mr. Warren and gave him what she hoped was a quelling look of disgust while her stomach roiled.

"What do you think, Poole? A summer wedding? I quite like what I see, and she knows when to keep her tongue as well. Yes, I'm altogether very pleased indeed. A good bargain, right, my girl? You get a husband, no small feat at your age, and I get a good-looking woman to care for me and my young ones. Wife passed away last year, you know, and what a shrew she was, God rest her soul. I can't thank you and Sanders enough for coming up with the idea."

Mr. Warren kept on speaking, but Charlotte did not hear anything further. A wedding, she thought slowly, with Mr. Warren as the groom. Nausea filled her stomach as reality set in. The new dress, the note insisting she look her best, her aunt and uncle's awkward behavior, and Mr. Warren's presence at dinner. They planned to marry her off to Mr. Warren, she thought, anger rising. This pompous, fat pig of a man, with squalling children, expected her to become his wife. Impossible!

Something within her broke at the realization that her family saw her as so burdensome that they would marry her off to a man that was clearly a lecher and a drunkard rather than pay the small amount it took to keep her. Charlotte raised her head slowly, allowing her face to mirror her thoughts for the first time she could recollect.

White with fear and barely composed, she looked at Mr. Warren and said exactly what she was thinking. "I could never marry a man such as you, sir. If your behavior had not been inappropriate enough, your filthy, disgusting comments would have been enough to convince me that I could never marry you. In fact, I would be most obliged if you would cease speaking and would remove your leering, gluttonous self from my presence, you obscene swine."

"Charlotte Edwards! How dare you speak to our guest in such a manner! Your uncle and I have taken you in and provided for you all these years, and this is how you repay us? Here we have gone to the trouble of arranging a match for you; a confirmed spinster! You ungrateful wretch of a girl!" Aunt Beatrice's eyes bugged out of her head, emphasizing the chin that receded into the folds of her neck.

Charlotte turned to look at her aunt with an icy stare. "Yes, Aunt, you took me in, fed me and clothed me, barely, but I owe you nothing. If I have been, as you so frequently remind me, nothing but a burden, you will find yourself most pleased to hear this: I am leaving. You need not concern yourself with me anymore, and I will not concern myself with you. Since you have never shown me an ounce of consideration, it should be no hardship for you. Please, do not say a word. I do not wish to destroy the illusion you hold of your own importance, and I fear, if you try to dissuade me, I may say exactly what I've been thinking these past twenty-five years. Excuse me."

With that, Charlotte rose and walked away from the table. While her aunt, uncle and cousin sat in stunned silence, she walked unsteadily down the hall to the kitchen. Mrs. Brown was standing over a pot of soup, stirring it idly while chatting with Betsy and Eliza.

"I've done it, Mrs. Brown. I've finally done it," said Charlotte, numbly. "I told them I wanted nothing to do with them and that I'm leaving. What can I do, and where will I go? I've submitted my novel, but we all know it is unlikely anything will come of that. I don't have enough money saved to live on yet!"

Hysteria rose, the growing panic clawing at her throat. "I couldn't marry him, though! Filthy, vile man! I would rather die!

"Oh, what will I do?" she cried, laying her head on Mrs. Brown's shoulder. Emotion taking over, Charlotte wept until she had no tears left, dry shudders racking her slight frame. Betsy and Eliza moved beside her, occasionally patting her shoulder or stroking her back. Finally Charlotte raised her head, her features drawn with despair.

Mrs. Brown reached up and wiped a tear from Charlotte's cheek. "You are not alone, Charlotte," she said, softly, cupping the girl's chin, "even if you feel as though you are."

At Charlotte's questioning look, she elaborated.

"For weeks now, the staff have heard rumors of your uncle's plans. Graves overheard much, and once he determined the information was accurate, he began to set his own plan in motion. He, Betsy, Eliza, and I are leaving this house, and you're coming with us. Graves has secured lodging for us in the little village where I was born. We'll be fine until your book gets published, which, I daresay, will be sooner than you think.

"Charlotte, you have always been the daughter that I and my late husband never had, and you will always have a home with me. You are like a daughter to Graves as well. Come, it will all work out, you'll see."

She stared at the cook. Straightening, she looked Mrs. Brown in the eyes. Soft blue eyes looked back at her with an affection far deeper than she'd ever been allowed to see. She looked over to Betsy and Eliza, seeing, for the first time, the depth of their affection as well. The thought struck her that while she had prayed for years for someone to love who would love her, God had answered her prayers abundantly already. She simply hadn't seen it. Mrs. Brown, Betsy, Eliza, and Graves were the family she'd always longed for, and though she was no longer a child, there was a part of her that ached for her mother and father. She could never get them back—but it seemed that perhaps God had heard the lonely cries of the little girl from so many years ago after all and had answered in His own way and time.

Dragging her mind back to the present, Charlotte replied, "I accept your offer, Mrs. Brown, provided you allow me to contribute the money I have saved as well. Do you think we'll be able to make it? All four of you are planning to come? But ... I don't understand how you can all simply walk away from your positions. It is just not done! You will have no references, no hope of employment in another situation, especially in town."

"We are most certain, Miss Charlotte," said Eliza. "Betsy and I have talked it over, Mrs. Brown having informed us of your aunt and uncle's plans, and we do not wish to stay on in a house owned by such people. This will be an adventure, just like in your stories!"

Charlotte grinned suddenly. "Oh, just picture the looks on their faces when they discover we've run away! You're right, Eliza, it's just like something out of a novel!"

The four women burst into laughter. From the doorway, Graves cleared his throat. Charlotte was again struck by how blind she had been. Graves had been a father to her ever since his arrival in the house in Berkeley Square, twenty-five years ago.

"Oh, Graves, how can I thank you enough?" she cried, rushing over to him and throwing her arms around his neck. "After all, it's you and Mrs. Brown who planned our escape. Can you retrieve my money from the bank?"

Though he looked uncomfortable with her arms around his neck, propriety warring with affection, Graves tentatively patted her back as she hugged him.

"Yes, Miss Charlotte. I will send a message to the bank once we reach Kennington, should we need to use your savings. However, for the moment, I have found lodgings at a most reasonable rate."

This said, Graves pulled out a chair for Charlotte, then for each of the other three, and the five of them sat down at the kitchen table to plan their escape, careful to lock the door against invasion by her family. However, if the sounds of shrieking, bellowing, and breaking dishes coming from the dining room were any indication, the Smythe-Pooles would be occupied blaming one another for some time. Perhaps, Charlotte mused, looking around the table, finally, her life could really begin.

Chapter

6

*C*harlotte fully expected that there would be an uproar from the Smythes and Smythe-Pooles over her leaving. She would not put anything past them, especially now that they had already promised her to Mr. Warren. Therefore she and the soon-to-be former staff decided to leave early in the morning after her birthday, not allowing her aunt and uncle any chance to foil their plan.

With Betsy and Eliza doing reconnaissance, Mrs. Brown and Charlotte managed to slip upstairs to Charlotte's and carefully pack her few belongings into the trunk that used to belong to her mother. It didn't take long, as most of her writing was already hidden under the false bottom, and three dresses, undergarments, nightgown and toiletries were easily laid in and arranged to their satisfaction. After a quiet knock from Betsy to give the all-clear, Mrs. Brown slipped out and left Charlotte to spend her last night alone in the Smythe-Poole home.

She readied for bed quickly and then knelt beside her bed for her evening prayers, her father's worn Bible clasped near the locket she wore next to her heart. Slipping under her covers, Charlotte smiled sleepily at the silence in the corridor. Graves had assured her that he would see to it that her family didn't bother her that night, and he always kept his word. Though she couldn't imagine how he had managed to keep her aunt and uncle at bay, Graves seemed to have a gift for accomplishing extraordinary things without ever being noticed, which, she supposed as she drifted off to sleep, was what made him such a fine butler.

After only a few hours of sleep, Charlotte rose to finish packing. A quiet knock sounded on her door at a quarter past four, and Betsy slipped inside the second-story room.

"Are you sad to leave at all, Miss Charlotte?" she asked.

"I suppose there are always some regrets, Betsy, but no, I'm not sad to leave. My only regret is that I have nothing to miss from this life." *What a sad thing to say,* she thought, *and even sadder that it's the truth.* "To tell the truth, I'm rather excited at the prospect of leaving. And remember, you can call me just plain Charlotte."

"I'll try, Miss Charlotte, er … I mean Charlotte, but it will take some getting used to. Are you done packing then?"

"Yes, I've just finished. I didn't have much to pack, and Mrs. Brown and I did most of it last night. Is everyone else ready to leave?"

"Graves has arranged for a carriage to come at five o'clock sharp, and everyone else is packed, yes. I believe Mrs. Brown has written a note for the Smythe-Pooles, giving our resignations, without mentioning where we are going."

"I suppose that's everything then, isn't it?" said Charlotte, looking around her room one last time. Her trunk was packed and sitting near the door. Other than that, there was nothing of hers left in the room. As she walked out the door, Charlotte felt an unfamiliar sensation settling in her heart. It wasn't until she and Betsy reached the stairs that she identified what it was. Freedom.

Once downstairs, the five prospective travelers waited in the front parlor for the carriage Graves had hired. When a soft knock sounded at the door at precisely five o'clock, Charlotte felt butterflies in her stomach. This was it. She was taking a step, and there was no going back. As her anxiety grew, she forced herself to remember the look on Mr. Warren's face as he had inspected her the night before. He was what awaited her should she decide to stay.

Glancing up, she caught sight of Graves watching her. The look of concern in his eyes confirmed that she was making the right decision. Even though the future was uncertain, they would stand together and support each other, something she had never fully experienced before. Smiling, she moved to stand next to the butler.

"Are we ready to leave, Graves?" she asked.

"I believe so, Miss Charlotte. Mrs. Brown has left a note for your aunt and uncle informing them of our departure, and I've sent a note round to Brooke, Chapman and Jones with your change of address."

"Why Graves, thank you! I hadn't thought of that ... but where did you tell them I was going? I know we are heading to Mrs. Brown's hometown, but I'd forgotten we actually had a place to go." Not that the editors would care, she thought wryly, but it was kind of Graves to believe they would.

"I've found us lodging in a small house, miss. It's called Violet Hill Manor, I'm told."

"How lovely! Oh, Graves, God is so good to us, isn't He?" exclaimed Charlotte.

"Indeed He is, miss. Indeed He is."

Conversation about God came easily to Charlotte's lips. Though her parents had died before she could really remember them, the staff had worked for them before they were inherited, along with the house and Charlotte, by the Smythe-Pooles. Graves and Mrs. Brown had told her, ever since she had wandered into the kitchen some twenty years earlier, of the way Charles and Amelia had met at a revival meeting in a field, both new believers in Jesus and newly baptized. Their whirlwind courtship had surprised London, given Charles's aristocratic background, but the two young people had only had eyes for each other. Charlotte heard much of their beliefs from Graves and Mrs. Brown. All she had from her own mind were soft remembrances of evening prayers and gentle kisses on her forehead before sleep claimed her.

By the time she was eight years old, Charlotte's already grown-up heart had recognized her need for a Savior, and she had come to the same beliefs that had brought her mother and father together. Her father's Book of Common Prayer and Bible and her mother's locket were the only tangible reminders she had of them, and their spiritual significance only made them more precious.

Graves had been her source of steadiness and guidance, and Mrs. Brown's affection was a salve to Charlotte's wounded heart. It was with Betsy and Eliza that she had first experienced the simple wonder of playing with girls who liked her and, as they grew up, sharing confidences and dreams alike. Now, Charlotte realized, there were more dreams and more futures at stake than hers alone.

The carriage loaded and all five passengers inside, Charlotte took one last look at the house that contained her former life. In the early morning mist, it looked like any other house on the street, but Charlotte knew it would always hold the bittersweet memories of her childhood and the faded hopes she still hung on to. With a renewed sense of determination and purpose she turned away from her past and, with no small amount of trepidation, breathed deep and looked wholeheartedly toward what lay ahead.

Chapter

7

homas Anderson found himself in a less than amiable mood on this particular morning. He had broken his own ironclad rule of never retiring later than midnight, and now he was paying the price. It was all that Miss Edwards's fault, he thought. If only she hadn't looked so vulnerable and nervous when she sat in his office yesterday, he wouldn't have felt obligated to take her manuscript and read it. He was getting soft already, and he was not yet thirty.

His few years in Society had enabled him to develop strong indifference to the appearance of vulnerable young ladies, for, as his friend Jonathan never failed to point out, it was inevitably part of an act designed to catch a man of good fortune. Thomas had quickly tired of the façades and had removed himself from Society in general, preferring solitude or the company of a few close friends and family. Thus, he was not altogether pleased to find himself unable to rid his mind of plaintive, luminous green eyes and ink-stained fingers.

Shaking his head, Thomas turned his thoughts back to Miss Edwards's manuscript. He did not regret reading it, despite the sleep it had cost him. The very first paragraph had drawn him in, and he found himself journeying with her characters through the gothic romance and danger with ease. Miss Edwards was a most gifted writer, he had soon discovered, and before he was halfway through, Thomas decided to approve the publication of her novel. It would not be terribly difficult to proceed, given her previous publication in the newspaper serials, as well as his own considerable influence in the firm.

The inconspicuous editor known to most as Mr. Anderson, was, in fact, Thomas Brooke, youngest son of the Earl of Shrewsbury and nephew of the Brooke in Brooke, Chapman and Jones. His pseudonym kept fortune-hunting ladies and their mothers at bay when in Society and allowed him a degree of freedom in his work. His plan worked very well, and, as a young businessman, he found himself able to move through town in relative obscurity.

Thomas laughed now, remembering that a number of mothers and fathers had thrown their unattached daughters at him in his youth, a seemingly endless parade of vapid, silly girls who were only interested in gowns and gossip. His own sisters had spoiled him, both being intelligent, well-spoken ladies who were comfortable with their femininity and their brains. They had each married men who appreciated this fact and were contentedly providing grandchildren for his parents. His elder brother was also long married and had four children, for whom Thomas had great affection. His parents, happily married for the last thirty-five years, had given Thomas such a grand example of the kind of marriage he desired, one of equality and mutual affection, that he refused to settle for anything less.

Miss Edwards had, unwittingly it seemed, unsettled the life Thomas enjoyed. He found himself so intrigued by the woman herself, as well as her novel, that he was going to have to use his influence to pursue a deeper acquaintance with Miss Edwards. He had never found himself so drawn to a young woman, but something told him that he was going to have to tread carefully with her. Since Mr. Anderson already made her nervous, perhaps, he thought, it would be wise to refrain from revealing his true circumstances just yet.

Thomas recalled, with perfect clarity, the look of determination on her delicate face, which contrasted so adorably with the air of shyness that she exuded. He gathered, from her evasiveness regarding her background, that whatever family she had was less than enthusiastic about her desire to be an author. He could well understand such hesitations, as female authors were rare and not always well respected. However, after no more than five minutes in her presence, Thomas had known that he was going to have to at least read the manuscript that Miss Edwards gripped so tightly. The intelligence that shone in her eyes and the quick wit evidenced in her response to his questions captured his attention far more thoroughly than any practiced wiles had ever done.

It was unusual for him to receive potential writers in his office without appointments, but after Miss Edwards had waited for over an hour, he had decided to take pity on her and give her a brief audience. He was glad now that he had. Although he had not appreciated this nearly as much when he was unable to put her manuscript down in the wee hours of the morning, now that he had breakfasted and was more fully awake, Thomas found himself in an unfamiliar state of anticipation as he entered his office.

"Mr. Anderson, a note for you," said his assistant.

"Thank you, Travers," he said, accepting the piece of paper.

Mr. Anderson, it read, this is to notify you of a change of address for Miss Charlotte Edwards. She may now be reached at Violet Hill Manor, Kennington, Shropshire County, England. I should be much obliged if you would keep this address confidential.

Sincerely,

Mr. Graves

Thomas read the note again. Miss Edwards had made no comment yesterday indicating plans to relocate. He wondered what had caused the sudden change. As he allowed himself another moment to recall her face, the protective instinct he had tried to squelch the day before began to rise again. His curiosity had been piqued, and the note had only served to fan the flame. His mind made up, Thomas sat down to compose a letter to the quiet woman who so completely consumed his thoughts.

Chapter

8

Violet Hill Manor was everything Charlotte had ever dreamt a home could be. From the moment she saw the weathered stone and climbing ivy, Charlotte was in love.

The weary travelers had arrived in the evening, after a long day in the close confines of the carriage, so upon arrival they accomplished no more than assigning rooms and taking a quick meal of bread and cheese before retiring for the night. Charlotte spent her first night lying awake, waiting impatiently for the dawn so that she could explore her new surroundings. She finally drifted off to sleep just as the stars began to wink out and did not waken again until Eliza knocked on the door to call her down to breakfast.

In the next week after their arrival in Kennington, Charlotte found great enjoyment wandering down narrow country lanes, reveling in the solitude and silence. Her pen flew faster than it ever had before, and already she had three installments ready to send off for her newspaper serial in London. She, Betsy, and Eliza explored the village itself, greeting the friendly villagers who introduced themselves. She tried not to think about what she had left behind and, for the most part, succeeded quite well. So well, in fact, that her life in London was beginning to seem more like a dream than reality.

Mrs. Brown, Graves, and the girls insisted that she not take part in the running of the household but instead devote herself to writing, to which Charlotte, after a halfhearted protest, agreed. In a few short days, the small company had done an admirable job of making Violet Hill Manor their home. They decided to invite the vicar and his wife for dinner on Sunday after the worship service at the nearby chapel. Mrs. Robinson, the vicar's wife, was a childhood friend of Mrs. Brown, and the two women had already briefly discussed Charlotte's situation. As a result, Mrs. Robinson and her husband had discreetly dropped hints about the woman writer who had taken up residence in the manor and her penchant for using people she met as fodder for her stories. They figured the rumor would either keep the vultures far away—or else bring them close enough to control the morsels they fed on.

&

"Miss Charlotte!" called Eliza. "Are you walking to the village to pick up the post?"

"That's what I was planning, Eliza. Do you want to come along?" asked Charlotte.

"No, thank you, miss. I just forgot to tell you that Mr. Cobb, the proprietor of the village shop, was asking to speak with you when last I was in town, and I forgot to mention it. Would you give him my apologies when you arrive?"

"Certainly, Eliza. I'll be home in a couple of hours."

Charlotte hurried down the lane that led from the manor into the village. The fresh, brisk wind carried just a hint of rain in its scent. Charlotte half hoped to complete her errands without getting wet, but part of her loved the thought of walking home to the soft rhythm of a gentle spring shower.

Mr. Cobb's shop was located in the center of the village. Charlotte loved examining the different items he sold without feeling the pressure to hurry that had always accompanied her on errand run with Aunt Beatrice. She wondered briefly how her family was doing in her absence and realized that the letter she had allowed Graves to post to them, informing them she was alive and well, should have reached them by now. She had been careful not to reveal her whereabouts, and Graves had told her he would send it to a friend in London who would then send her letter through the general post there. Charlotte hated that she still felt a responsibility to let them know that she was safe and sound, especially after the way she had been so cruelly used, but she couldn't lose the concern she felt for her family's well-being—and deep down, did not want to.

A little bell tinkled over the doorway as she entered the store.

"Good day, Mr. Cobb," she said, nodding to the proprietor.

Mr. Cobb was a portly, pleasant-looking man. His thinning blond hair was always carefully arranged, and his blue eyes were kind. He had a knack for making each customer feel important and welcomed and therefore did a great deal of business not only with the villagers of Kennington but with people from nearby areas. His wife was just as personable as he was, and between the two of them, they had already discovered that Charlotte was an aspiring authoress.

Mr. Cobb had a soft spot for her already, and Mrs. Cobb, thrilled with the romance of Charlotte's profession, was already secretly plotting to introduce Charlotte to as many worthy bachelors as she could. Sadly for her, and for Charlotte, these consisted of the vicar's eldest son, who had just reached the tender age of seventeen, and a certain Mr. Tribbley, the town's one and only barrister, who had just celebrated his seventieth year. However, Mrs. Cobb possessed a stout and determined nature and intended to write to her sister in the very near future to inquire of single young men in her village. Charlotte did not yet understand the genial manipulations of village life, or she might have suspected what was lurking in the mind of the placid-faced, hospitable Mrs. Cobb.

Mr. Cobb looked up as she entered. "Good day to you, Miss Edwards. And how is our fine village treating you today?"

"The villagers are very welcoming, Mr. Cobb, particularly yourself and your wife," replied Charlotte, setting her basket on the counter. "Eliza mentioned that you wanted to speak with me?"

"I did, indeed, Miss Edwards. You see, I find myself in a quandary, and I was hoping you would be able to provide me with a solution."

"I'll do my best, Mr. Cobb, if I can, but I don't see what I can do."

"Well, you see, we have our own school here in Kennington, but alas, two years ago, we lost our teacher, Miss Havers, when she retired and went to live with her sister in Brighton. Since then, we've been unable to find anyone to teach our children. I was hoping that perhaps you would be interested in considering the position."

"Why, Mr. Cobb ... I don't know what to say," said Charlotte. She was not immediately averse to the thought of teaching, but neither was she at once thrilled with it. Children were a strange and wonderful mystery to her, and she wasn't sure she wanted to change that just yet.

"Take a few days to think it over, Miss Edwards. School doesn't start until September, so we still have time to look for a teacher if you refuse the position."

"I do thank you, Mr. Cobb, and I promise to let you know as soon as I've come to a decision. I must tell you, though, that my education comes only from various tutors over the years."

"That's not a problem, miss. To be quite frank with you, it's unlikely that you'll have to deal with anything more than the basics. We're mostly farmers here, and parents need their children to help out at home. We just want them to have enough schooling so that they can read, write, and do a little arithmetic. Now, I suppose you came for the post, did you?" he said, reaching under the counter. "You have a couple of letters waiting for you and a parcel."

"Thank you, Mr. Cobb. I appreciate it. Mrs. Brown has also sent a list of goods she needs."

Mr. Cobb busied himself filling the list while Charlotte stayed at the counter, flipping through the letters and turning Mr. Cobb's unexpected offer over in her mind. Returning to the counter, he set the requested items in the basket for Charlotte. "I'll just put that on your account then, miss," he said, briskly.

"Thank you, sir," replied Charlotte, "and a good day to you."

"And to you, as well," he responded, returning her smile.

With that, Charlotte picked up the letters and the small wrapped package that was addressed to Graves and headed out the door. With a spring in her step, she started down the narrow lane that led back to the manor just as the first gentle drops of rain began to fall. Laughing, she lifted her face to the sky and breathed in the fresh, clean scent, only vaguely if at all aware that she was the object of conjecture among the villagers and of talk among the idle.

Chapter
9

Charlotte's name was also on the lips of one whose interest in her was keen and a great deal more specific. Thomas stood outside the fashionable house in Berkeley Square, wondering if he had completely taken leave of his senses. Despite his best efforts, he had been unable to remove Miss Charlotte Edwards's lovely face from his mind, and so, as a result, he found himself about to embark on an endeavor to discover as much about her as he could. He admitted to himself that his interest was much more personal than that of editor to author, and that admission rankled. He had never found himself smitten with any woman before, and he didn't quite know what to do with himself. He recalled the advice his uncle, Ernest Brooke, had given him the night before, when Thomas had gone to him to discuss the situation. Thomas had been close to his uncle since he was a child, and though he had never married, he trusted his uncle's opinion as much as he did anyone's.

"Thomas," said his uncle, "your parents and I have been praying for the right woman for you since you were born. Now, I haven't met this Miss Edwards, but if she's everything you say, then I think that you should go ahead and pursue the matter. She certainly sounds a good deal more interesting than those bits of fluff that were after you when you moved in Society. God has just the right young lady for you, and if Miss Edwards is that woman, then He will make it plain. However, there's no harm in you doing a little digging into her past while you're seeking His answer.

You know your friend Jonathan always says one cannot be too careful in such matters.

"In fact, that name rings a bell … an accident of sorts, twenty-some years ago. Oh, yes, I remember! Saddest thing, really. Must have been her parents, then, Thomas. Footpads attacked their carriage on the way to a ball, stabbed them both to death, and made off with the jewelry. Never caught, as far as I remember. Very sad, indeed. Just goes to show you that you can never be too careful."

With this conversation fresh in his mind, Thomas made his way to the Smythe-Pooles' front door and knocked. He waited. After some moments, he knocked again, quite a bit more insistently this time. After a few minutes, he heard steps coming toward the door, and in short order, it was opened by a quarrelsome-looking woman of about fifty.

"Yes? What do you want?" she said impatiently.

"I understand Miss Charlotte Edwards lives here," he said. He thought that perhaps if he appeared to be in the dark as to her whereabouts, he might be able to find out more than if he admitted who he was and why he was there.

"Not anymore she doesn't," said the woman crossly, "and I must say, I'm not sorry about that. She was a most troublesome creature, always moping about and staring at people with the strangest look on her face. We're not sorry at all to have her gone, but it was most inconsiderate of her to take most of the staff with her. I can't imagine how she's managing to keep them, but that's her own affair now, selfish creature that she is. And who are you to inquire, might I ask?"

Then, as if she had just realized the improper amount of personal information she had disclosed, the woman went silent and stared at Thomas.

"My name is Anderson. I have some business with Miss Edwards," he said smoothly, "but if she no longer resides here, I will take my search elsewhere."

"What possible business could you have with my niece?" asked the woman, giving him a narrow look.

"Your niece, madam? I hadn't realized. And you are …?" asked Thomas.

"Mrs. Beatrice Smythe-Poole. My husband, daughter, and I live here, and until a week ago, so did my niece. We took her in after her parents had the audacity to die together in a carriage accident when she was just two years old, and we have looked after her ever since, though I tell you, it was not an easy task. Sly, the girl was, very sly. Always creeping around and refusing to talk. Very queer."

Thomas found himself forming an interesting picture from Mrs. Smythe-Poole's descriptions. The Miss Edwards he had met was very unlike the one her aunt described now. Given his impression of Mrs. Smythe-Poole, he was fairly certain that the Miss Edwards he had met was closer to reality. Besides, already, he could well understand not desiring to talk to Mrs. Smythe-Poole. He was already wearied by their conversation, and it had only been a matter of minutes.

"I see," he said, nodding as though he understood and agreed with her, "Well, I'll keep that in mind. Thank you so much for your time, Mrs. Smythe-Poole. I bid you good day."

He turned and briskly strode down the front walk, hoping to avoid further conversation. Quarrelsome women, or women in general, he thought dryly, were not his forte. He had gotten most of the information he had come for, and a bit of a picture of what life must have been like for Miss Edwards. He wondered what it was that had finally made her decide to go. His initial inquiries had uncovered that she had endured such treatment for many years before finally leaving. With most of the staff, he recalled, the fact giving him brief pause. How strange. No matter; he would find out soon enough, if Miss Edwards answered his letter. If not, perhaps a trip to the village of Kennington would further illuminate the situation and her character.

Remembering the nervous way she had sat and fidgeted in his office, Thomas found himself smiling. There was an inner resolve in Charlotte Edwards that he suspected most people missed. He was convinced that she was not the sly, ungrateful creature her aunt described, but he did not yet have enough information to make out her true character. She had appeared so fragile when she entered his office, and yet within minutes he knew that she was in possession of great strength and a keen mind. He had found her completely without artifice, which was a welcome change.

Walking down the street toward the carriage he had waiting, Thomas's lips curved as he thought over his recent behavior. His pursuit of Charlotte was more akin to the actions of a fictional hero than of a reserved, bookish editor. Miss Edwards's shining eyes had a strangely emboldening effect on him. And perhaps, he allowed, it was the protectiveness she sparked in him that caused his instant dislike of her aunt. If Mrs. Smythe-Poole were any indication, he trembled to discover what her uncle and cousin were like, and there was another entire family apart from them. He would need time to prepare for that meeting, he thought as he reached his carriage.

Climbing in, Thomas knocked on the roof and directed the coachman to take him back to his office. He had work to do and maybe, just maybe, there would be a letter from the lady herself waiting for him when he got back. He tried to ignore the warmth and eagerness that suffused him at the thought. At the very least, he would have a chance to go through the preliminary report from his friend Jonathan, head of the finest private investigation firm in London. Thomas did not consider himself an impulsive, foolish man, and, shining eyes or not, he was not about to do anything to change that. Perhaps his behavior had been a bit out of character, but the woman intrigued him. That was all. Smiling slightly, he closed his eyes, leaned back and settled in for the ride, his mind full with the schemes of a man well on his way to being quite in love, whether he knew it or not.

Chapter

10

On the other side of the door that led into the fashionable house in Berkeley Square, Beatrice Smythe-Poole stood trying to figure out what had just taken place. *Since when did Charlotte know anyone outside the family*, she thought, *and what does that young man want with her? He surely isn't interested in her for personal reasons.* The thought of Charlotte attracting any romantic attention made her giggle, it was so ridiculous, and the sound echoed in the empty foyer.

"Mama? What are you laughing at? Who was that at the door?" Louisa's penetrating voice sounded from the front parlor.

"No one important, my darling," said Beatrice, "no one at all."

"Well then, can you help me sort out my bonnet strings? I've gotten them all in a tangle, and I simply must call on Lady Julia North this afternoon!"

"Coming, my dear, but I thought you found Lady Julia a complete bore," replied her mother as she turned toward the parlor.

"I do, Mama, but her elder brother, Reginald, is just recently returned from Oxford, and he is most assuredly not a bore." Though her mother did not see them, Louisa's cheeks were flushed and her eyes bright with the remembrance of a brief, ardent embrace she had experienced at the latter's hands two nights earlier.

Mrs. Smythe-Poole was almost to the parlor when she stopped short. Memories from twenty-five years ago rose and poured into her thoughts. She hated her niece and had wanted her gone, but Mr. Anderson's unexplained inquiries touched too close to events better left buried. She knew he was too young to know about the whispers that had followed the tragic deaths of Charlotte's parents.

That horrible night was etched into her memory with perfect clarity. The sheen of Amelia's satin dress and the snowy perfection of Charles's impeccably tied cravat. Then the knock at the door, the police and the questions. And she had known, oh she had known, even then. *No*, she thought, *I can't think about that. He couldn't have done it. Not even for the money that followed. Blood money*, she thought, and shuddered. Every time Charlotte had looked at her with Amelia's eyes, she'd remembered, and she'd hated her for it, for the noble blood of her father that flowed in her veins instead of Louisa's and for the inheritance her stupid niece had not even known was hers.

Turning, she walked quickly through the foyer and into the parlor where her impatient daughter waited. She forced the memories from her mind, locking them securely away in the dark part of her that had been their home for the past twenty-five years.

"Here I am, my darling," she said, brightly, as she approached her daughter, "Let me help you."

∽

Charlotte read the letter through a third time, scarcely able to believe her eyes. She was still not convinced that the words would not shift when she laid the paper down, and so she gripped it tightly and hurried down the stairs.

"Mrs. Brown!" she shouted, running down the hallway toward the kitchen. "Eliza, Betsy, Graves! Come quickly!"

"Charlotte! What is it, child?" fretted Mrs. Brown. "Is there some sort of trouble? Is that a letter from your family? Pray, tell me!"

In the weeks since leaving London, there had been no word from the Smythe-Pooles and no news of them, but none of the refugees was ready to relax their guard.

"No, Mrs. Brown, it's from Mr. Anderson at the publishing house! They've agreed to publish my manuscript!"

Charlotte danced excitedly around the kitchen while Eliza, Betsy, and Graves came running in. They stared in astonishment at Charlotte, having never seen her so visibly excited. Even as a child, she had been somber and quiet, a pale little ghost hiding in corners and corridors to escape the notice of her family. This bright-eyed, rosy cheeked woman spinning circles around the kitchen was almost a stranger to them.

"Whatever is wrong with Miss Charlotte?" asked Eliza. "She's acting so strange. Is she running a fever, ma'am?"

"No, Eliza, she's just excited. They're publishing her book!" said Mrs. Brown, pride radiating from her.

"Oh, Miss Charlotte, that's wonderful," cried Betsy. "We always knew you could do it, and now you have!"

"Indeed, miss. I'm most proud of you," said Graves formally, though he couldn't quite hide the fondness in his eyes. His years as a butler had given him unparalleled control over his emotions, but his affection for Charlotte was so strong that it broke through in a smile that meant more to her than the applause of thousands.

"Thank you, everyone. I can scarcely believe it. Oh, I must write my response to Mr. Anderson! What do I say? Oh, I don't deserve such happiness!" Charlotte had stopped twirling, but, unable to keep still, she began pacing in front of the big iron stove.

"You've worked extremely hard for this," said Graves. "Of course you deserve it. Simply accept his offer."

"Graves is right, as usual," said Mrs. Brown, casting a glance at the man. "That's exactly what you should do."

"Well, then," said Charlotte, "I suppose that I had better start writing an acceptance. Oh! When I was at the store today, Mr. Cobb made me an offer. What do you think of my teaching at the village school? Mr. Cobb has kindly offered me the post, but—" She paused, unsure how to continue.

"You needn't work if you don't want to, miss," said Mrs. Brown. "Graves and I have discussed the situation, and we are quite satisfactorily taken care of for the time being. The girls and I are planning to take in sewing, and Graves will manage the household. It's up to you."

"I hate to refuse such a kind gesture," said Charlotte, uncertainly. "I want to contribute too, and it will be a while yet until my manuscript is published, and who knows if it will sell?"

Betsy stepped forward, a little timidly. "If you wouldn't mind, Miss Charlotte, I'd enjoy trying my hand at teaching the young ones. I do not know if what you've taught me over the past few years would be enough, but if so … do you think Mr. Cobb would be willing to give me a chance? Really, there's only enough housework here in the manor for one, and I could still sew in the evenings."

"I think that's a wonderful idea," said Eliza with a decisive nod. "Betsy's right about the housework, and I enjoy doing it. Mrs. Brown and I can handle the sewing between the two of us."

"It's perfect, Betsy!" exclaimed Charlotte, the relief on her face obvious to everyone. "Now I don't have to feel guilty about refusing!" A sheepish grin appeared as she realized how self-centered she sounded. "I mean, you'll get the chance to try something I'm sure you'll love."

Betsy smiled at Charlotte, a twinkle glinting in her eye, as the others snickered. Charlotte groaned. "I'll never hear the end of that, will I?"

"Not likely, no, miss," said Betsy, smartly, as she slid one arm around Charlotte's shoulders and the other around Eliza's.

"Well then, that settles it," said Graves. "Should I let Mr. Cobb know while I'm in town today, seeing to some errands?"

"Yes, please do, Graves. I'll send a note along with you, vouching for Betsy's qualifications."

All the necessary arrangements in place, Graves set off to town, with Betsy and Eliza in tow. Mrs. Brown started pulling out pots and pans to start dinner, so Charlotte left her in the kitchen, went to her room, and sat down at her desk which overlooked the narrow lane that led to the manor. She smiled every time she compared the view from the manor to the dismal one in her room in London. The cruel treatment and easy dismissal from her family still sent an occasional pang through her heart, but she found herself healing slowly.

Of course, the memory of warm brown eyes and a kind smile still invaded her thoughts, and when not her thoughts, her dreams. Charlotte was increasingly glad that her communication with her editor was of the long-distance variety. She pulled a fresh sheet of paper from her desk drawer and took up her pen. She would write her response to Mr. Anderson directly, but first there was a story tugging at her that needed to be set free.

Matilda was not the most common of heroines, she wrote, for most heroines had never committed murder. But Matilda had, and it haunted her.

Smiling contentedly, Charlotte dipped her pen again and immersed herself in the dark and dangerous world she was creating.

Chapter

11

Roland Poole walked into the office of his brother-in-law, Gerald, and shut the door behind him.

Gerald looked up from his desk, annoyance creasing his brow. "Roland! What do you think you're doing? I have work to do here. I don't mind a visit, but you could have made an appointment with my secretary instead of barging in."

"We need to talk, Gerald. Charlotte's gone."

Roland sat down heavily in the chair across from Gerald's desk.

"She's been gone for over three months," he said, "and I've been unable to trace her whereabouts. She's also taken four members of the staff with her."

"Four members of the staff? Whatever for? Besides, you never liked the girl. Why search for her? And why didn't you inform me of this sooner? Three months?"

"Don't you recall that as long as she lives with us, I control her inheritance? If I'm unable to locate her and she discovers that she was supposed to come into money when she turned twenty-one, there's no telling what she'll do. She may even go to the police, and they may decide to look closer at her parents' untimely demise … and we both know where that could lead. Blasted girl! She could ruin everything for us!"

Gerald stared at Roland as the blood drained from his face. "I told you never to mention that to me again," he whispered furiously. "We both know that what happened to them was unavoidable."

"And I told you that this would come back to haunt us. We never should have trusted that the loan came without strings. However, what's done is done, and we must deal with the consequences now!"

"Well, how do you suppose we go about finding her?" asked Gerald, reluctantly acknowledging the reality of their situation. "Is there someone to hire?"

"We're going to have to ask him for help again," said Roland, his face set and his jaw clenched tight.

"No! I refuse to allow you to drag me into another mess like the last one! We will not involve Mr. Sanders in this. You, of all people, are well aware of what happened last time! Do you really want a repeat of that night twenty-five years ago? You know that carriage was meant for you, don't you?"

"I know that, but what other choice do we have?" he asked miserably. Roland had thought that the whole mess was finally behind them, but now it appeared that he would never be free of it. It was all he could see every time he looked at Charlotte and saw her staring at him with Amelia's eyes, or, rarer, smiling the same, dreamy smile Charles had smiled when he was painting. Roland had thoroughly hated Charles and Amelia for everything they stood for and for having money when he did not, and he hated their daughter even more.

Gerald sat back in his chair. "What exactly have you promised this Mr. Warren you told me about before Charlotte's birthday? Are you able to free yourself from that obligation, at least?"

"I'm afraid," said Roland, slowly, "that Mr. Warren is to collect the final payment on what we owe Mr. Sanders. That was the arrangement. He is well aware that, while we've been living off of the interest on Charlotte's inheritance, I'm unable to touch the full amount. Only her husband has that authority, a role he intends to fill. I have no way out. There's no way for me to raise enough money to finally pay off our debt. You know that as well as I do. I'm mortgaged to the hilt already, and so are you. It's hopeless. Charlotte must marry Mr. Warren, or we're all doomed. Mr. Warren and Sanders have an agreement, one that requires an influx of money, and Charlotte's inheritance was to provide it while finally making good on our loan."

"Well, then, we must find her. But I refuse to go to Sanders with this. We cannot afford to be any more indebted to him. We must find her ourselves. I will begin an investigation myself. I have a few connections, so perhaps we will be able to find her yet."

"All right. I will leave the matter in your hands ... but if word of this leaks out to Sanders, we're done for." Roland rose and picked up the hat he had set on the desk. He plodded toward the door.

"Then we must not allow word to leak out," Gerald said. "If anyone asks, we've sent her to the country for her health, before her impending marriage. Wait a minute! What have you been telling Mr. Warren all this time?"

Turning at the last moment, Roland directed a hard glance at his brother-in-law. "Just what you said, that she has been sent to the country for her health and to prepare her dowry. We can't afford to lose on this proposition, Gerald. We have to find her. We both know that what happened twenty-five years ago will be a pleasant memory if Sanders doesn't get his money."

With that, he walked out the door, leaving it open behind him. Gerald sat at his desk, staring thoughtfully out the window. No, they couldn't afford to fail, or have any gossip circulate. Grabbing the pen from the inkstand in front of him, he began to write a short, succinct note. He knew just the man for the job. Though he did not enjoy revisiting the past, and some of the unsavory characters he had been forced to rely on to build his business, particularly now that he had become a respectable businessman, occasionally proved useful in situations similar to his present difficulties. Standing, he went to the door and called for Mr. Johnson, his secretary.

"Mr. Johnson, please deliver this note to the address on the outside as quickly as possible. Notify me immediately of any response."

"Yes, sir."

Staring at Mr. Johnson's departing figure, Gerald Smythe wondered what the odds were that he would manage to come out alive, should his plan fail. Somewhere, he thought, between vanishingly small and none at all.

With a sigh, he walked back to his office and sat down at his desk to oversee the operation of his plant. Twenty-five years ago, it had only been a vision likely to fail without the capital to get it off the ground. If only he had known then what he knew now of Mr. Sanders's true nature and business, he would never have gotten involved with him. Had he not, he would not now have two deaths on his conscience. He could never be free from the heaviness of that guilt.

It was too late now. Twenty-five years too late. Gerald stared bleakly at the wall in front of him. Trapped, he thought, miserably. He was trapped.

Chapter

12

*C*harlotte was certain she was ill. No matter how many times she told herself that it was not she but Betsy would have to face the students in the village school, she was still filled with anxiety.

Charlotte was very confident in Betsy's knowledge, having taught her and Eliza to read, write, and cipher. Still, children were a great mystery to her, and the thought of a sea of little faces staring at her terrified her. Her respect for Betsy grew by the minute, but her worry grew in the same increments, and centered on all the childish pranks and tricks her cousins had pulled over the years, and the likelihood that one or two of Betsy's students would share her cousins' inherent meanness.

Mrs. Brown smiled as she saw Charlotte creeping down the stairs. The poor girl looked absolutely terrified, she thought, pale-faced and shaking. It was Charlotte's nature to take on the burdens of those she loved, but Mrs. Brown did wish she had not gotten into the habit of making herself sick over it.

"Come here and have your breakfast, my dear," she said. "I've made your favorite breakfast, porridge with brown sugar and milk. I thought you might look a little peaked this morning from worry about Betsy, and I see I was right. It's certainly a good thing you didn't agree to do the teaching yourself, or we might have had to carry you out of the house, down the lane and to the school." She laughed aloud at the aggrieved look on Charlotte's face. "I've packed Betsy a lunch, which you and Eliza can drop off at noon, to give her a little adult company."

"I don't think I can eat a thing, Mrs. Brown," said Charlotte, her voice shaky. "I think I'm terribly ill."

"Charlotte, you are just fine. Sit down and eat your porridge. You always make yourself ill when you're worrying about something or someone. Betsy's excited about teaching, you know. She'll do just fine."

&

Charlotte glowered into her porridge. She should have expected Mrs. Brown to be an unlikely source of sympathy. Graves had already gone to town on some business of his own, and Eliza was already tidying upstairs. If Betsy was still in the manor, she had yet to make her presence known. Charlotte sighed and then dug into her porridge. By the third spoonful, she had to admit that her stomach was settling, and Betsy's fate did not seem quite so dreadful.

As she finished her breakfast, the sound of footsteps echoed in the corridor. Betsy sailed into the kitchen, rosy-cheeked and radiating excitement. Charlotte felt her tension begin to ease at the sight of her. She heaved a sigh and drank the last of her of her tea before rising from the table.

She thanked Mrs. Brown, and then went to where Betsy was hurriedly grabbing an apple from a bowl over on the counter. Charlotte held out the piece of buttered toast that Mrs. Brown had slipped her.

"Would you like some company on your walk to school?" she asked, eager for a reason to wander the lanes, now that her stomach had stopped its antics. She loved the little village, with its crooked lanes, charming shops and friendly people.

"I'd love it, Miss Charlotte," responded Betsy. "To tell you the truth, I'm starting to get butterflies in my stomach." She rubbed her hand lightly over her abdomen.

"Why, Betsy, there's not a thing to worry about!" cried Charlotte, ignoring the snort of laughter from Mrs. Brown's general direction, "I have complete faith in you, and you're going to be wonderful!"

She hooked her arm through Betsy's and led her out of the kitchen toward the front door. If Betsy heard the sound of Mrs. Brown's laughter, she did an excellent job of pretending that she didn't. Grabbing their cloaks and bonnets from the hall rack, the two women headed outside, into the fresh morning air.

By the time they reached the schoolhouse, Betsy's excitement outweighed her apprehension, and Charlotte left her happily ensconced behind the desk at the front of the schoolhouse. There were a few children playing in the yard as she walked past, and she watched them curiously as she walked past. Running had been forbidden in the Smythe-Poole home, as well as outside it.

The sound of the school bell rang out, announcing the beginning of the school day. Two little girls flew past Charlotte, giggling as they went. They looked so free and happy that Charlotte couldn't take her eyes off them until they came to a stop, whispering to each other with their heads bent together conspiratorially. She smiled softly, even as she rubbed her heart with the heel of her hand to ease the ache there. Charlotte knew she had never looked so innocent and carefree as those two had as they'd run past her, and the thought stung.

Shaking her head, she turned away from the schoolhouse and headed back down the lane in the direction of the manor. Stopping, she glanced over her shoulder; the children had filed inside for their morning classes. She could not resist a mischievous impulse as she took in the empty green that stretched for miles beyond the village. Laughing, she picked up her skirts and took off across the soft grass, reveling in the slap of wind on her cheeks as she ran.

Charlotte made it back to the manor eventually. Her foray into the joys of childhood had taken her through the woods that flanked the village, and she arrived home at the manor grass-stained, slightly muddy, and wearing a sheepish smile on her flushed face. Mrs. Brown clucked her tongue at the state of Charlotte's dress, but smiled as she turned back to the stove. Charlotte's rosy cheeks and bright eyes were worth any amount of laundry, to her mind. After slipping upstairs to change, Charlotte came down to find Eliza standing by the door, the lunch basket already hooked over her arm.

"Ready, Miss Charlotte?" she asked, raising her eyebrows at Charlotte's fresh gown and bonnet.

"Yes, I am, Eliza. Let's hurry; Betsy must be anxious for her lunch." Charlotte linked her arm with Eliza's, and the two women hastened down the lane, heads bent together conspiratorially as Charlotte regaled her friend with the plot of her latest story.

Chapter

13

efore Charlotte knew it, months had flown by. She could hardly believe that the process of publication was almost complete. Though she eagerly awaited the time when she would hold a printed, bound copy of her very own words, she dreaded that it would bring about, at the very least, a decrease in correspondence between herself and Mr. Anderson—*Thomas*, she thought, still blushing at the use of his Christian name, even in her thoughts, though he'd requested she use it soon after they began corresponding about the necessary business arrangements.

Unfamiliar as she was with young men in general, and more sheltered than she liked to admit, Charlotte had no frame of reference for her relations with Thomas. Her only experience in matters between men and women had been gleaned through extensive novel reading, particularly the gothic horror romances she had always preferred. Now she found herself utterly at a loss, with no mysteries, dungeons, or ghosts to expose Thomas's true intentions, and here she was, rather hopelessly in love with him.

Their letters had become more and more personal with each exchange, but she stoutly refused to allow herself to read anything more into them than correspondence between a writer and her editor. At least, that was the thought she continued to use to castigate herself on the frequent occasions she caught herself imagining a certain set of kind eyes and handsome features. She gave herself a mental slap, berating herself for allowing her romantic nature to gain a foothold in anything other than her writing.

She propped her chin on her hands, staring out the window that framed her writing desk. It was a grey, drizzly day—just the sort she liked best. Often, her best ideas came to her on such days, but today, she was brooding. She didn't brood often, but when she did, she did it well. She had fallen in love with a man she had only met once, and whose interest in her was purely business.

She sank deeper into her morbid humor, groaning inwardly over her own foolishness. She had no thought that Thomas loved her in return. Plain, quiet spinster women were not the sort that men of any sort fell in love with. Especially plain, quiet spinster women whose livelihood was dependent on their own efforts rather than family money. No, she thought, the sooner she could convince her heart to give up its imprudent attachment, the better for all involved.

Sighing, she rose from her desk and headed toward the door. A long, solitary walk in the woods would do much to ease the ache in her chest and bring her peace of mind. At least, she hoped it would.

⌇

At dinner that night, Charlotte listened with half an ear as Betsy chattered on about the many and varied antics of her students. A long walk had done a great deal to restore her spirits, but she still had no idea what to do about her feelings for Thomas. Unrequited love was all very well in the pages of a book, but she found her experience with it to be less than pleasing. It irked her that all the logic in the world did not seem sufficient to convince one small organ, her heart, that it had bestowed its affection on an unrealistic prospect, and the pain of rejection, even unspoken, unwitting rejection, was still acute.

Spying a concerned look from Mrs. Brown, Charlotte realized she had sighed out loud. Working up a smile, she picked up her fork and turned her attention back to Betsy in time to catch the end of her depiction of the failed attempts of one of her young charges to win the heart of his lady fair by presenting her with his most prized possession. Apparently the poor little girl was not nearly so fond of frogs as her young suitor was, particularly when they were placed anonymously in her desk during the noon hour.

Betsy had quickly fallen in love with the bright young faces before her that morning, and it appeared the feeling was mutual. Her students were very fond of bringing her gifts, and just that afternoon, she had received three wildflowers, one shiny, red apple and one well-intentioned, lint-covered peppermint. If things continued as they were, she would have no trouble keeping her position as schoolteacher, and the rest of the household were thrilled for her. Charlotte was simply happy that she was free to write and that she had a second manuscript pages away from completion.

⌇

Though he laughed at Betsy's anecdotes with the rest, Graves's smile didn't quite reach his eyes. He looked at Charlotte, remembering the quiet, sad little girl who had so easily captured his heart so many years before. Months away from London and her family had done much to erase the pallor and strain that had been etched onto her face since childhood, but her eyes still carried the wounded look that tore at his heart. Glancing at her again, Graves sighed to himself. Catching the worried look on Mrs. Brown's face, he made a mental note to speak to her after the meal to see if she had any idea what was bothering Charlotte. He didn't have any children of his own, though, as he turned to glance at Mrs. Brown, he did occasionally think about what it would be like to have a family of his own. However, Charlotte was as dear to him as if she had been his daughter instead of his late master's child. He would do anything to protect her.

Graves had been monitoring the actions of Charlotte's family since she had left London. Shortly after arriving in Kennington, he posted a letter to a friend of his in London who had been a Bow Street Runner before the police force was established. Matthew Hayes had written him every week with progress reports, and everything had seemed to be calming down.

Graves had almost been ready to relax his guard when he opened the letter that had arrived that morning from London. The first line had leapt out at him. *I fear, Graves, that Mr. Poole and Mr. Smythe are about to do something very foolish. They met late last night with Mr. Sanders in the Black Heart, his most profitable tavern, brothel, and gaming hall. I know you are well aware of Sanders's character, as per a conversation we had last fall that I am sure you recall, and so you also know that Miss Edwards is now in greater danger than ever before.*

Graves dreaded what the news would do to Charlotte, but unless she was told of the danger that loomed over her, she wouldn't be able to stand against it. He made up his mind. He hoped that Charlotte's love of a good mystery would soften the knowledge that she was tangled up in the middle of a very dangerous one. *Twenty-five years of silence*, he thought, *twenty-five years.* He had made the decision to keep certain information from Charlotte, matters that he had worried would jeopardize her safety if they were made known, but now … there was no choice. They must come to light, and he must be the unwilling bearer of painful, sordid news to a woman he had sworn he would protect at all costs.

Sighing again, he steeled himself and rose abruptly from the table. "Excuse me. I have something I need to discuss with Miss Charlotte privately. Miss, shall we adjourn to the parlor?" he asked, his tone betraying his urgency.

The women stared at him. Graves did not often speak, especially when in a group, and it was quite a shock to hear him utter two full sentences. Only Mrs. Brown did not look surprised. Graves had long ago taken her into his confidence when he realized that he could not protect Charlotte alone. Glancing her way, he felt his anxiety ease slightly under her warm, calm gaze and slight nod of approval.

∾

"Certainly, Graves," said Charlotte. "Shall we go now?" Slightly confused, but not concerned, she rose from her chair. Likely he needed to discuss some financial matter with her. Then dread congealed in her stomach as she wondered whether there was news from her family. Pushing aside the unpleasant thought, she followed the butler through the doorway as Eliza, Betsy, and Mrs. Brown began to gather the dishes for washing up.

They walked from the dining room to the small parlor in silence. Charlotte grew increasingly uneasy as she noted that Graves's shoulders were set even more firmly than usual, if such a thing were possible. Preceding her, Graves preceded her, leaned down to stoke the fire, and, keeping his back to her, spoke at last.

"Miss Charlotte, you may want to sit down. I have some rather disagreeable news for you, which is likely to upset you greatly."

Charlotte sat down on the settee, the knot in her stomach growing larger with each second, and looked at Graves expectantly.

"You know, miss, that I've been with the Smythe-Pooles for twenty-five years now, ever since your parents passed away. The house in Berkeley Square was once your father's, and I was his valet before taking on the role of butler. When he died, your aunt and uncle moved in to raise you, and simply retained the staff that was already there. As butler, I oversaw the running of the household and so became privy to certain facts that the servants overheard or I myself heard by accident.

"Your aunt and uncle," he said, visibly searching for a delicate turn of phrase, "are less than discreet when out of temper with each other and tend to forget that servants have ears." He smiled, ruefully, catching the amused look in Charlotte's eyes. "I know you are well aware of their tendencies, Charlotte. Unfortunately, their mistreatment of you goes much deeper than you know. There is danger, Charlotte, and I fear I cannot protect you from it."

Charlotte stared at Graves. His face was pale, yet firm. She saw, for the first time, a fear lurking deep in his eyes, and a chill passed through her. If Graves was afraid, she knew that whatever secrets he held were far darker than he was letting on.

"Go on, Graves, please," she said, trying not to betray her own anxiety.

"Twenty-five years ago, Roland Poole and Gerald Smythe borrowed a large sum of money from a man by the name of Sanders. If you knew anything about the London underworld and the criminal enterprises there, his name would surely strike fear into your heart. As it was, they were foolishly confident of their ability to pay it back. They wanted to appear in Society, you see, and your Uncle Gerald's manufacturing plant, for which the money was borrowed, coupled with your Uncle Roland's banking income, were to provide them with the monies needed to keep up appearances. They simply needed capital to establish the plant, but neither of your uncles had access to such large amounts of money. They asked your father, but he refused to back them. They both despised him for his refusal."

Graves cleared his throat nervously. "Your father, Charlotte, was an extremely wealthy man. He was the last of his line and so inherited everything after his own father's death, shortly before his own. He and your mother planned to give away the majority of the inheritance, keeping only enough to live on. They hoped that if they did not have wealth, your family would cease asking for money and would be content to enjoy their company."

Charlotte raised her eyebrows skeptically. "They would never have done that, Graves. You and I both know that. Were not my parents aware of the selfish natures of my mother's siblings and their spouses?"

"They were, miss," replied Graves, slowly, "but they hoped. They had such hope that God would yet touch the hearts of your mother's family. Sadly, they never saw that hope realized.

"I don't know how they stumbled across Mr. Sanders, but it would not surprise me if your uncles were already testing the boundaries of the law. Sanders saw fit to lend them ten thousand pounds, for what reason I know not, with the assurance that they would pay it back in regular installments. The plant had some difficulties at first, however, and did not immediately turn a profit. As a result, they were unable to make two of the payments Mr. Sanders required."

Graves stopped for breath and wiped his brow. Charlotte simply sat silently on the settee, bewilderment etched on her features. Her mind whirled with questions. Before she could say anything, Graves went on.

"The night your parents died, they were traveling to a ball in a carriage that belonged to your Uncle Roland, as he and your aunt had come to stay with them for a time. While they were en route, two footpads stopped the carriage, conceivably to rob them. However, the footpads had another mission. They were hired to kill, but they killed the wrong couple. It was your Uncle Roland and Aunt Beatrice that were meant to be taking that carriage. Their deaths would have served as a severe warning to your Uncle Gerald."

What little color had remained in Charlotte's face drained away as unwanted images of the attack on her parents filled her thoughts. Hesitating only a moment, Graves reached out and grabbed her hand. She gripped his fingers so tightly that the tips went white, but he didn't flinch. After a few minutes, when the color had filtered back into her cheeks and she could meet his gaze steadily, Graves squeezed her hand. He hated that the worst was not yet revealed, but he had to finish his tale, for her sake.

"Please, Graves," she said, smiling weakly, but determinedly, "I must know everything. I can bear it, I swear."

"Of course, miss." The purposely formal tone brought a small quirk of the lips from Charlotte, and she began to breathe freely again. "As it was, the deaths of your parents allowed your Uncle Roland, as your legal guardian, access to the interest off your inheritance."

He stopped again as Charlotte held up her hand. "My inheritance? What inheritance, Graves? The only income I have is from my writing! All I heard for years from my family was how grateful I should be that they were supporting their 'poor, destitute, orphan niece.'" She shook her head in frustration.

"They lied to you, Charlotte," responded Graves bluntly. "Your father left you everything, and his estate and assets were quite substantial. I thought it would only cause you greater pain to know of it, since, because you're a woman, you are not legally able to claim it. Only your guardian or your husband has access to it, and only your husband has access to the entire fortune. Your uncles used the interest to pay their debt off, bit by bit, until the plant began to turn a profit, but they never forgot Mr. Sanders's brutal warning."

"I shouldn't have forgotten it either, if I were in their place," muttered Charlotte, darkly. She wanted someone to blame for her parents' deaths, but she could not figure out where to focus her anger—her uncles' foolishness or Sanders's cruelty. Expressing her anger was a new experience for Charlotte, and she found it immensely frustrating not knowing where to aim it. Unfortunately for Graves, the more he told her, the better he looked as a target. Charlotte swallowed back the fury rising inside her as he continued.

"Everything went as planned for twenty-five years, as you grew up in your uncle's home, unaware of your title and inheritance."

"My title?" asked Charlotte, her attention diverted. "What title?"

"Your father was an earl, miss," replied Graves, "and as his daughter, you are nobility. In Society, you should be addressed as Lady Charlotte Edwards, but if your family had done that, you would have discovered the truth about your past and the money that your father left in trust for you."

"Why did you never tell me, Graves?" she asked, quietly, the anger simmering in her eyes. "I know, you thought it was easier for me if I didn't know, right? Didn't you ever think that if I had known, I could have left sooner?! I could have lived my life, Graves!"

She glared at him as tears spilled down her face. Charlotte swiped at her cheeks, furious with herself for yelling at him. She stared at her lap, crying harder when a clean, white handerkerchief was placed in her hand. Refusing to look at him, Charlotte used the square of linen to wipe her cheeks, then offered it back to Graves.

"Keep it, miss," he said, calmly, regret in his eyes. "It's likely you'll need it again before we're through with this mess."

She choked out at laugh, and raised her gaze to his face. "I'm sorry, Graves," she said. "I didn't mean that … it's just that I'm so angry. It feels as though I've lost everything all over again."

His look of understanding almost sent her into a fresh spate of tears, but she held them off. His eyes regretful, Graves leaned closer and spoke again.

"It wouldn't have made a difference, Charlotte," he said. "The money would have remained with your uncle and aunt, as your guardians, until you married, so you would still have been without the funds you needed to be on your own. I'm sorry, miss."

Charlotte sighed and looked down again. "Keep going, Graves, please," she whispered, resignedly.

"According to the information I've received from London, Sanders has agreed to forgive the rest of the loan if you marry Mr. Warren, giving him direct access to your inheritance, just over twenty thousand pounds, per annum. I've been following their movements through a friend of mine in London. Until three days ago, it appeared that you would be safe and left alone. I wanted to protect you, and it was working, but now I fear I am unable to do so. As we speak, Sanders and your uncles have men looking for you. They still intend to see you married to Mr. Warren. You must be on your guard."

Graves sat back, utterly drained. Twenty years of secrets exposed in a single hour. The relief he felt was short-lived, for his heart was heavy for the pain he had caused Charlotte, regardless of the fact that he had done nothing but keep the cruelty and manipulations of her family from her.

"So," asked Charlotte in a low voice, "there is no way I could have left, with money of my own, no way for me to be free of their greed?"

"No, miss. Your uncles will never allow it now. You know the courts do not favor young women. It appears we are at an impasse—for I will never let them take you back, and they are unlikely to relinquish their objective."

His face was set in stern lines, mouth grim, as he finished speaking.

"I need to think, Graves," murmured Charlotte, her gaze far away and sad. "I need to think."

With that, Charlotte rose and walked unsteadily from the room. Graves sat a moment longer, staring out the window. Such a peaceful view, he thought, with its crooked, narrow lane banked with wildflowers. He wondered how he could protect her, the beginnings of desperation creeping in. He had to keep her safe; nothing else mattered.

The soft sound of a throat clearing pulled him out of his musings. Mrs. Brown stood in the doorway, her white cap askew over her blond corkscrew curls. He could read the question in her soft, blue eyes.

"I told her, Mary. I told her everything," he sighed, shaking his head. He could still see the pain on Charlotte's face.

"You had to, Timothy. She needs to know." Mrs. Brown walked over and put her hand on his shoulder, squeezing it gently. "But then you know that, don't you?" She gave him a soft smile. "Are you all right then?"

"Yes and no," he replied, with a wry smile of his own.

"I understand completely," she responded, rubbing his shoulder lightly. Looking up into her plain, kind face, Graves felt his heart pulse in his chest. He had loved Mary Brown for over ten years, unable to resist the contrast between her calm, practical nature and the fierce, passionate way she loved those around her. He'd never known her husband, but he envied the man every day for the time he'd had with Mary Brown as his wife. He wanted the same privilege, if only he could figure out how to tell her. Of course, if ten years hadn't given him any ideas, or the nerve, he admitted to himself angrily, he wasn't sure anything would. He sighed again, reveling in the feel of her soft, capable hand on his shoulder. It was possible, he thought, that the coming weeks could be the death of him.

Chapter 14

C harlotte stared at the piece of paper before her. Thomas's latest letter lay next to it, his bold, clear writing running in even lines down the page. She had so much she wished to tell him, but none of it was appropriate for their business relationship. Charlotte had escaped from the parlor to her room immediately after her meeting with Graves. She had already broken down once, and she would far rather be alone if she did it a second time.

She fought back a fresh spate of tears, unwillingly remembering her uncles' betrayal and the terrible circumstances of her parents' deaths. Annoyed with herself for dwelling on things beyond her control, she dipped her pen violently into the inkwell and barely kept from splashing ink on her desk and herself. Breathing deeply, she tried to calm herself before she ended up throwing a tantrum.

She reminded herself, turning her thoughts back to the task of writing to Thomas, that a business relationship was all they had. She wished, rather desperately, that there was something more between them, but she knew it was pure foolishness on her part. Sometimes she thought she sensed something deeper in his writing, but it was only wishful thinking. Such a man would never consider her a suitable match, and she certainly was not the type of woman whose beauty and charm could strike a man senseless.

Thomas had written only four days before, full of interesting tidbits about his life, but always including matters relating to her novel. Charlotte had no experience with men, and she found herself quite perplexed every time she sat down to write a response. She was inclined to think that most letters of business did not include so much of the personal, but she knew she would never be able to give up the communication, nor did she want to. She simply tried to echo the pattern of his letters, describing the various details of country life and answering any questions he posed.

At the moment, however, she was unsure how much to say. Should she tell him of the danger that lurked over her shoulder? How could she? She had to tell someone, and she had always been better at communicating in writing than in person. She couldn't bear the thought of seeing pity on his face, but if she wrote, then she wouldn't actually have to see his reaction. The last thing she wanted was his pity, and she was sure that this strange story, with herself so vastly inferior in every respect to any heroine she'd every read, she thought sadly, would garner nothing but sympathy, at best. It was just that she needed to tell someone that she trusted, and Thomas was the one person who knew her as she was now, and not as who she used to be.

Charlotte made up her mind. She would write to him and relay what she had learned and the danger in which she found herself, but she could never share what was in her heart. Rejection would be more than she could bear. How was it, she wondered, that she found herself so attached to a man she had only met once, to the degree that, at the moment she felt as though her life had fallen in on her, he was the one person whose presence would bring her the comfort she so greatly needed? Groaning in self-reproach, she picked up her pen once more and, after a brief hesitation, began to compose her letter to him.

Dear Sir, she began, I have argued with myself for some time as to whether or not I should share some personal information with you, of which I myself have recently been apprised. I do hope that you will not perceive the following account to be the melodramatic ravings of an author, but will see the truth in what I am about to write. I am in grave danger, Thomas, and I do not know where to turn. I only hope that, somehow, you will be able to advise me as to what I should do. She paused to think, then hurried on. It began twenty-five years ago, with the sudden death of my parents …

By the time Charlotte finished writing her letter, she was exhausted. She knew that what she had done was unconventional at best. She had poured out her heart to a man who wasn't even a suitor, in the hopes that his connections as a businessman in London might help shed some light on the situation and maybe even unearth more information on her uncles' actions. She had even briefly considered telling Thomas that she had fallen in love with him, before reason prevailed, and the page she'd begun to write had joined the fire burning in the hearth. For all the stories she had written, she had lived very little of the danger and romance she wished for herself. Now, she thought miserably, she had all the danger and none of the romance. Life was dreadfully unfair.

Realizing that she had been writing and daydreaming for over an hour, Charlotte rose and stretched. Picking up the candle she had brought to her room when she left the parlor, she crossed to the bureau to prepare for bed. Unsure she would sleep, she picked up the novel that Mrs. Brown, Betsy, and Eliza had given her for her birthday and settled in under the bedclothes. A soft knock sounded at the door.

"Charlotte? Are you awake?" asked Mrs. Brown.

"Yes, Mrs. Brown. You may come in."

Charlotte rose and was putting on her wrapper when Mrs. Brown opened the door and entered.

"I just wanted to make sure you were all right," said Mrs. Brown. "I'm sure the news that Graves shared with you was quite a shock."

"So you knew too, and it never occurred to you to tell me anything?"

Mrs. Brown didn't flinch, her eyes honest and open. "Would it have done any good for you to know, Charlotte? I believe it only would have added to your misery to know of your uncle's perfidy while you still lived under his roof. I understand if you are angry, but Graves and I believed it was for the best. We hoped that between the two of us, we could deflect some of the pain your family caused while remaining anchors for you to cling to as you grew up. Though neither of us is connected to you by blood, I assure you, the love he and I both have for you runs just as deep as if we were truly family."

Charlotte knew that Mrs. Brown was right, but being kept in the dark still rankled. She supposed it was just something she'd have to live with. A thought struck her, and she watched Mrs. Brown's face carefully as she spoke.

"Mrs. Brown, are you and Graves in love with each other?"

Mrs. Brown started, and a flush spread up from her neck, suffusing her cheeks with color. "What kind of question is that, Charlotte?!" she retorted, sharply, averting her eyes.

Charlotte laughed, relaxing for the first time since she and Graves had talked.

"I think you just answered my question," she said, smiling broadly, fully aware of her own impertinence, as Mrs. Brown sputtered incoherently. "Do you plan to marry, then?"

"Charlotte Edwards! That is none of your business!" Though obviously embarrassed, Mrs. Brown strove to regain her dignity. "I will say that he is a fine man, and, should he choose to marry, his wife will be a very fortunate woman, but that is all."

"So," asked Charlotte, slyly, "if he asked you, you would say yes?"

"I will not answer such an impudent question," replied Mrs. Brown and then paused. With a small smile, she muttered, "Besides, the blessed old fool hasn't asked me yet."

"Well, then," said Charlotte, with a conspiratorial smile, "we shall have to convince him that he should."

"That, I fear, shall have to wait for morning," retorted Mrs. Brown, "as will any further discussion about how to deal with your family— and don't even think about breathing a word of this to Betsy and Eliza."

"I would never!" exclaimed Charlotte with what she hoped was an angelic smile, wondering the while what she could tell Betsy and Eliza without actually speaking.

"Charlotte ..." Mrs. Brown's tone brought back vivid memories of rare occasions that she had incurred the wrath of the cook.

"You have my word, Mrs. Brown," she said, her manner submissive, though a sparkle lurked in her eyes, matching the one that Mrs. Brown was trying vainly to suppress. Charlotte grew serious again.

"I admit, I am very much afraid of what my uncles might do. Is there any hope that Graves will be able to protect me from this Mr. Sanders and from my family as well?"

"We must trust that God sees what is happening, my dear, and that ultimately it is He who will protect you. However, Graves is indeed taking steps to secure your safety here."

"Perhaps tomorrow then, I should ask Graves if he has any ideas as to how I can protect myself?" Charlotte looked at Mrs. Brown intently.

"I believe that is a wise decision, Charlotte. I will let you go to sleep now. You need your rest, as do I. I will continue to pray over us all. God is protecting you, and He is the first One we need to ask for help."

"You're right, as always, Mrs. Brown. I'll do the same."

After wishing her a good night, Mrs. Brown kissed Charlotte's cheek and then left the room. Crawling into bed, Charlotte settled in again and picked up the novel she had set down at the knock on her door. It lay unopened on her lap as the events of the evening flashed through her mind. She was still afraid, she thought, but Mrs. Brown was right. God was on her side, which meant that somehow He would protect her. Perhaps, she thought, He would also expose the truth of what had happened to her parents so long ago. She needed to know; the violent manner of their passing had kept her from being able to be at peace with their deaths.

And perhaps there would be some resolution to her tender feelings for Thomas. The thought filled her with as much fear as her uncles' plot did. Sighing, she set the book down and blew out her candle. Lying in the darkness, she began to pray.

Chapter
15

*T*here are occasions in every life where imagination and longing become reality. They do not happen often, and thus, when such things do occur, they inevitably take one by surprise. So Charlotte was suitably amazed when, three days after her discussion with Graves, she looked up as she sat on the steps of the schoolhouse, sharing lunch with Betsy and Eliza, to see Thomas Anderson walking up the crooked lane toward her.

Her heart began to pound, and her suddenly shaking hands dropped the sandwich she was holding, making her grateful for the napkin she'd laid across her lap. She nervously clasped and unclasped her hands, quickly patting her hair before returning her hands to her lap. She was utterly unaware that the flush in her cheeks and the uncertainty in her expressive eyes made her a very becoming picture to the man who now stood before her.

Stepping forward, Thomas took off his hat. "Good day, Miss Edwards," he said, smiling.

"Good day, Mr. Anderson. Forgive me, I wasn't expecting you. Betsy, Eliza, and I were just finishing our lunch." She gestured to the two women who had just risen and were gathering the leftover food into the basket. They nodded at Thomas, their eyes twinkling as they hurried inside the schoolhouse, leaving Charlotte alone on the steps.

Charlotte kept staring at her hands, flustered. Her fingers were ink stained, as usual, from her early morning writing. She felt completely unprepared to see Thomas in person and was having great difficulty thinking rationally when all she wanted to do was throw herself into his arms. That, she thought wryly, was what she got for all the novel reading—and writing—she did. Gathering her courage, she met his gaze and, to her chagrin, immediately felt herself blushing.

"It's a pleasure to see you again, sir," she managed to say, congratulating herself on not stuttering.

Thomas grinned, amused by her jumpiness as he came over and sat on the step beside her. Sitting face to face with her, Thomas found himself fighting the urge to brush a stray lock of hair back from her finely featured face. The wide-set green eyes that had occupied his thoughts for months stared at him as though he was a figment of their owner's imagination. He hoped that meant that she had grown as attached to him as he had to her—but he brought his focus back to his reason for coming. There were things he needed to talk to Charlotte about that had little to do with matters of the heart. His smile faded and his eyes grew serious.

"I received your letter yesterday. As soon as I read it, I left the office to make some arrangements, then packed and hired a coach to bring me here. I stopped at your home first, but your butler told me that you were here at the schoolhouse with your friends and that he was to come to escort you back soon. He mentioned that he has been accompanying you wherever you go. I asked if I might have the pleasure of walking you home, and he agreed. I … ah, I wanted to see you with my own eyes and make sure that you were safe," he finished in a hurry, his own nerves suddenly making an appearance. Color bloomed on his cheeks as well, matching the crimson stain still present on Charlotte's cheekbones.

"Thank you kindly, sir," she replied, still feeling shy in his presence, though the flush on his face amused her as well as settling her nerves a bit. "I am quite well … as well as I can be, I suppose, until this mess is sorted out. You must think me quite presumptuous for dragging you into this. I would apologize for doing so, but I'm afraid I wouldn't mean it. I wanted your help—and I want somebody to talk to who hasn't been hiding things from me."

Charlotte could not meet his gaze as she spoke, but looking up after she finished, her eyes daring him to disapprove, she was relieved that there was no censure in them, but rather, deep concern. She breathed deeply, realizing she had been holding her breath until she saw his reaction.

Thomas felt warmth spreading inside him while she spoke, though he flinched when he thought of the secret he'd been keeping from her. That was different, he decided, and he would tell her—as soon as the opportune moment presented itself.

"No, indeed, I am glad that you trusted me enough to write and tell me you were in danger. I only hope I can help. As soon as I received your letter, I dispatched a note to a good friend of mine, a Mr. Hayes, who makes his living as a private investigator. He discreetly looks into matters brought to him by those who, for one reason or another, do not wish to involve the police. He agreed to come with me, instructing his associates to discover what they could about your uncles' movements. I left him with Graves and the rest of your staff at Violet Hill Manor." He half-smiled. "Jonathan's probably interrogating them as we speak. We had arranged to stay at the Lion's Crest Inn, but Mrs. Brown invited us to stay at the manor. I hope that's acceptable?"

"Oh, how wonderful! How can I ever thank you?" cried Charlotte, forgetting her shyness in her excitement. Her eyes shining, she stood up, with the first full smile Thomas had ever seen on her face. Either his heart had just stopped and he was about to die, or it was time to admit, to himself at least, that he was completely smitten. However great the temptation to do otherwise, he rebuked himself sharply, he had to see her safe and settled before he could think of romance—as his primary goal, at any rate. He was well aware that he could not be in Charlotte's presence without experiencing the full intensity of the attraction between them.

"You may thank me, perhaps, by allowing me to call you by your given name," he said quietly, "and by using mine in turn."

"I would be pleased to do so … Thomas." Charlotte blushed even brighter as she said this.

Thomas enjoyed the sight of her rosy face, allowing himself the pleasure of hoping that, perhaps, he affected her heart the way she affected his. *Business first*, he thought again. Remembering this might be more difficult than he had anticipated.

"We should likely make our way back to your home," he suggested. "I would imagine that Graves will be getting anxious, and Mr. Hayes will have some questions for you."

Thomas offered his arm to her. Charlotte looked at it, noting the great contrast between the slim, well-formed limb he presented and the short, fat one Mr. Warren had possessed.

With a secret thrill in her heart, Charlotte placed her hand in the crook of Thomas's arm, and they started down the steps toward Violet Hill Manor.

❧

Betsy and Eliza watched them from the small, front window of the schoolhouse, giggling with pleasure at the picture the couple made as they walked past the children playing on the green, oblivious to everything but each other.

"Aren't you going with them, Eliza?" asked Betsy with a lilt, smiling as she reached for the bell to call the children in for the afternoon.

"I'll let them do their courting in peace, thank you very much, Miss Johnson," replied Eliza with a superior air. "However," she said, mischief flashing in her dark brown eyes, "I may have to return to chaperone you when little Andy Wilson's widowed father comes for his son this afternoon."

"Oh, hush, you!" cried Betsy, swatting at her friend while trying not to smile. "If my students hear you, I'll never hear the end of it."

Eliza laughed as she ran down the schoolhouse steps, lunch basket on her arm. "I'll call for you at three o'clock, Betsy," she said, with a wink over her shoulder, "just in case."

✍

Back at the manor, Jonathan Hayes was already hard at work. Unlike his friend, he did not have the look of a nobleman; no aristocratic tilt of the head, slim jaw or easy manner. Instead, his jaw was strong and square, and he carried himself with the confidence won by experience, not the innate arrogance of those born to station and wealth. His unruly black hair gave him a rakish look, accented by a quick, dangerous smile. His surprisingly light blue eyes held kindness, though their intensity often hid it. There was experience there, and the knowing, almost world-weary gaze of one who has seen more of the dark side of life than the light.

His long strides took him across the parlor in five steps as he paced back and forth, thinking. He was tall and well-muscled, which came in handy in his line of work, particularly when he was required to engage in the retrieval of information or items from private homes. These ventures sometimes resulted in a gentle brush with the local gendarmerie but seldom caused him real concern, as he had many friends in the newly established London Metropolitan Police Force. To Jonathan Hayes, justice, true justice, that is, was everything. Even if Thomas were not his best friend, Jonathan would have found Charlotte's predicament worthy of investigation, but the double incentive made the case very intriguing indeed.

It was his recent interview with Graves that occupied Mr. Hayes's mind, at the moment. Though he had dealt with a number of convoluted mysteries in his career as a private investigator, he had seldom come across such a complex puzzle. After hearing Graves's testimony, he had no doubt that Miss Edwards's parents had been murdered, but there were a number of loose ends that nagged at him. Hearing the sound of voices in the hall, he turned to meet the young lady who was both the source of his friend's concern and the recipient of his affection. Thomas had not expressly told Jonathan of his feelings for Charlotte, but it was easy to see that Thomas was thoroughly attached to her already.

Charlotte and Thomas entered the room together, looking infinitely at ease with each other after the walk to the manor, her hand still nestled in the crook of his arm. Jonathan wondered, with a small smile, if Thomas had any idea how utterly besotted he looked. They were followed directly by Graves and Mrs. Brown, between whom his instincts had already detected a fascinating mixture of familiarity and purposeful secrecy. It never failed to astonish him, the lengths people went to conceal what could never be truly hidden. It only took one unguarded glance or smile, and the mysteries of the heart were laid bare to any who cared to see. Though he was only eight and twenty, Jonathan's keen powers of perception had the unfortunate effect of making him extremely doubtful of the lasting nature of most romantic unions. The older couple moved quietly over to the hearth and took seats in the chairs positioned on either side of it.

"May I introduce my good friend, Mr. Jonathan Hayes?" began Thomas, drawing Charlotte further into the parlor.

"It is a pleasure to make your acquaintance, Miss Edwards." Jonathan bent low over the hand she offered and then straightened.

Charlotte, surprised by the display of formality, dropped into a slight curtsey as she replied, "And yours, Mr. Hayes. Thomas has spoken very highly of you."

Charlotte stood at Thomas' side, taking stock of his friend. Having lived the majority of her life with liars, she had a finely tuned ability to spot them. Mr. Hayes, she decided, though he looked as though he could be a dangerous man, was absolutely trustworthy, his direct, frank gaze meeting hers without a hint of artifice. She glanced at Thomas, comforted by his presence at her side. The unquenchable writer in her was already weaving an intricate plot containing elements of both men. She was not interested in Mr. Hayes romantically, but she was already patterning her next hero after him. His roguish look and dangerous air would make him most fascinating to the feisty, independent heroine she had already begun to pen. Her writing, Charlotte mused, was certainly benefiting from her personal peril.

"Thomas has spoken very highly of you as well, Miss Edwards," replied Jonathan, an inscrutable look on his face. It seemed to Charlotte that he was perhaps skeptical as to the accuracy of Thomas's opinion. She couldn't decide whether to take offence and decided to withhold judgment for the time being. There were, Charlotte considered, sagely, enough people in her life to be angry with already.

"I appreciate your interest in my present situation, sir," said Charlotte. Then she looked to Thomas for direction, unsure of the next step. "Perhaps, Thomas, you could decide where to begin? I'm afraid I'm at a loss."

"I've informed Miss Edwards of your line of work, Jonathan," said Thomas. "I feel we can proceed to sort through the information straightaway." He gave his friend a hard look as if to remind him to confine his questions to Charlotte's safety, leaving aside her affections. Thomas knew Jonathan would be tempted to try to ferret out Charlotte's feelings for him if even the slightest provocation presented itself. He smirked a little, realizing that Jonathan had very likely never met anyone with Charlotte's ability to stonewall when she felt threatened. As much as he would enjoy watching two of his favorite people spar with each other, he wanted to make sure Charlotte was as attached to him as he was to her before letting Jonathan begin the personal inquisition.

"Of course, Thomas," said Jonathan with a glint of amusement in his eyes. He quite enjoyed seeing his normally staid and composed friend so flustered. "We'll begin at once, then. Now, I've met with Graves already, and I believe I have the general outline of events. Miss Edwards, is there anything further that you can add? Impressions of your family, bits of conversation you may have overheard at any point? Even the smallest, seemingly insignificant details can be important." His keen eyes were intently focused on Charlotte as he drew a small notepad and pencil from his pocket and flipped through it to a fresh page.

"Why don't you all sit down first?" said Mrs. Brown, gesturing to the other chairs spaced around the hearth. "I've asked Eliza to bring tea and some sandwiches and then to join us. I assumed you would want to speak to all of us, Mr. Hayes. Eliza will have to leave and fetch Betsy shortly before three o'clock, but you can interview both of them after they're home again."

"Yes, of course, Mrs. Brown. Your foresight is admirable." Jonathan couldn't help smiling at the short, slightly rounded cook. He sensed that behind her placid smile lay a will of iron which, coupled with her protective nature, made her a force to be reckoned with.

Footsteps in the hallway announced the arrival of Eliza. She swept into the room with the tea tray and set it down on a table pressed against the wall. As Mrs. Brown began to pour the tea, Eliza darted out for a moment and reappeared with a second tray containing an array of sandwiches and cakes. Once everyone had been served, Jonathan set down his tea and shifted his eyes to Charlotte.

"Can you tell me more about your family, Miss Edwards?" he asked, "Thoughts, impressions, incidents?"

He took an occasional bite of his sandwich while jotting down notes, now and again letting his gaze take in the whole room to gauge the reactions of the others as Charlotte spoke. Charlotte began as far back as she could recall, describing her childhood, or what there was of it with the neglect and distinct dislike shown by her family. Jonathan periodically stopped her with a question or two before nodding to proceed. She told him of every conversation she could remember, particularly the one regarding her schooling.

Without her realizing it, Thomas had reached out and taken her hand, and by the time Charlotte was done, she was holding his so tightly that the tips of his fingers had gone white. Thomas was so caught up in her story, and in imagining what it must have been like for her to grow up as she did, that he didn't even notice.

When Charlotte finally fell silent, the entire room was still. The only movement was the slight start she gave when she realized she was clinging to Thomas's hand. Reflexively releasing her grasp, she started to slide her hand away but stopped when his fingers curled more tightly around hers. Charlotte hoped the others hadn't noticed her quickened breathing, though, judging by the knowing gleam in Mrs. Brown's eyes, she would be hearing about this later. At the moment, however, she was simply thankful for someone to hold onto in the face of what looked to be an increasingly long and painful afternoon.

"Mrs. Brown," said Jonathan, flipping to a fresh page in his notebook, "I wonder if you would be willing to recount your experiences with the Smythe-Pooles. I believe I'm getting a good idea of their characters and their plans, but is there anything else you can tell me?"

"Well, Charlotte has already told you most of what I know," replied Mrs. Brown with a little shrug. "My interaction with the Smythe-Pooles basically amounted to consulting Mrs. Smythe-Poole about the meals. Graves is the only one who really heard anything important." She glanced over at the butler with a small smile as the man in question shifted uncomfortably at the attention.

"All the same, Mrs. Brown, anything you can remember could be important." Jonathan's eyes were sharp, never leaving her face as she sought to recall details from the past.

By the time they finished, it was past time for the evening meal. Mrs. Brown had left after Jonathan had finished interviewing her to attend to the food, and, when he was finished asking questions of Betsy and Eliza, she announced that dinner was served.

"Graves, perhaps you and I could meet here after the meal to go over everything," suggested Jonathan, raising a brow. "I could use another pair of eyes with all these notes, especially someone who knows Miss Edwards's family.

"I would be pleased to assist you, Mr. Hayes," replied Graves, inclining his head formally toward the young man. Charlotte bit back a grin at the return of his proper manner. She was still torn up from reliving the worst of her past, but it was comforting to see that some things, like Graves's adherence to the constraints of propriety, were constant. The insight briefly lightened her heart, but only briefly. Glancing down, she sighed. Her hands lay loosely clasped in her lap, where they'd lain ever since Thomas had released the one he was holding so he could help Mrs. Brown carry the tea things from the parlor to the kitchen. Ever since, Charlotte had found herself sinking deeper into a melancholia that sapped the happy color from her cheeks and stole the sparkle from her eyes. Thomas had returned within minutes, but the loss of his touch was like stepping from a warm, well-lit entrance into the frigid air and flying snow of a dark winter's night.

After everyone had left the parlor, Charlotte continued to sit on the settee, staring blindly out the window. Her already pale skin had taken on the kind of pallor only caused by illness or grief. Her entire life had been a lie, she thought. There was no love to be had from her family; just an all-consuming hunger for the money she hadn't even known existed. All those years of craving the attention and affection of her aunts and uncles, only to be rejected and ridiculed time and time again, and now … to find out, without doubt, that they would have liked her better dead. She couldn't decide whether she should be angry, relieved, or something else entirely. All she felt was cold.

"Charlotte? Are you all right?"

She started at the sound of Thomas's voice. She had been so immersed in her own thoughts that she had lost track of the time. Thomas had not gone in to dinner with the rest but had waited for her, watching the play of emotions across her tired face. He stood in front of her, holding out his hand to help her up from the settee.

"I was just thinking, Thomas. Forgive me."

She reached to take his hand, foolishly feeling tears well up at the contact as she rose.

"There is nothing to forgive, Charlotte. You have just had to hear some extremely unpleasant things about what should have been a happy time in your life. It is completely appropriate to be upset. You may cry if you need to, you know. I have sisters and a mother and thus have some experience with the tears of a woman." He gave her a soft smile.

Charlotte looked at him, trying to understand why he was being so kind to her. Suddenly, it didn't matter in the least. Without warning her face crumpled, and she began to weep, wrenching, heartbreaking sobs that shook her entire body. Thomas reached out, drew her into his arms, and held her close as she cried until she was utterly drained.

When Charlotte's sobs finally ceased to wrack her slight frame and she was able to raise her tear-streaked face from his chest, he simply reached into his breast pocket for his handkerchief and offered it to her. As she mopped her face, he continued to hold her close, savoring the feel of her in his arms.

Charlotte looked up at him with red-rimmed eyes, unaccountably comforted and surprisingly unembarrassed.

"Thank you, Thomas. I'm so sorry, but I do believe I've completely soaked the front of your coat." She gave him a weak, watery smile.

He smiled at her. "You're welcome, Charlotte. It was my pleasure. My coat is of no consequence and will dry soon enough at any rate."

They stared at one another for a long moment. Then their smiles faded as an emotion, something deeper and more intimate than either had ever known, passed between them. Try as she might, Charlotte could not keep her eyes from revealing the feelings in her heart, and she was terrified that he would see how deeply in love with him she was.

Thomas maintained a calm and gentle expression as he examined her face but found himself needing every bit of self-control to keep from kissing the woman he held, kissing her with such passion and single-minded purpose that she would never again fear she was not loved. Only two thoughts stopped him. First, as bound to Charlotte as he already felt, he had not yet ascertained her feelings for him. Second, if either Mrs. Brown or Graves were to catch him kissing their charge, he doubted that his life would be of any more value than the pine box it took to bury him. Still, he could not help lightly brushing his thumb over her cheek to wipe away a last, solitary tear.

"Shall we go in to dinner?" he inquired softly.

"Yes, that would be lovely," said Charlotte, breathing a sigh of relief that he had apparently only seen the blotchy, tear-stained face of a distraught woman and not the vulnerability of her heart. His touch was meant to soothe her, she was certain, but instead, it made her long to be held in his arms once more.

Thomas smiled and offered his arm to her. Taking it, Charlotte walked with him out of the parlor to join the others in the kitchen, neither noticing the face that had been pressed close to the window, silently observing the entire exchange.

Chapter

16

*I*f there was one thing William Sanders took pride in more than anything else, it was the fact that his name was feared, not only throughout London but throughout England in her entirety. He may have looked like a gentleman with his fine clothes and practiced manner, but though he craved standing in Society, Sanders had nothing of the true nobleman in him. Growing up in the slum, Billy Sanders, accomplished pickpocket and son of a drunk, had dreamt of the day he would escape the poverty he was born into and achieve the wealth and power he deserved. He had been successful in his quest for both.

As a boy, he had realized that he had two great assets: his sharp mind and his almost complete lack of conscience. Naturally, there had been sacrifices along the way, people who knew too much or those who felt the need to involve the police in his business. Both kinds of people did not last much longer than the breath it took to whisper their information. A disappearance every now and again, and he was unchallenged in his position as head of the underworld of London. It amused him to no end when he heard the police were out in boats dragging the Thames or saw them loading a black-shrouded corpse into a wagon as he passed the riverfront in his carriage. He preferred to keep his hands clean, but the knowledge that it was his authority, a single spoken word, that brought death to anyone who opposed him was almost as thrilling as personally stealing the life-light from the eyes of his enemy.

Of course, the lending of money to impoverished nobility and those who had lost everything in the gaming halls was his second favorite occupation. It was just so easy to apply a little pressure here or there and then sit back and enjoy watching them squirm, trying to repay what they had borrowed without letting their circumstances be known to Society. Half the time, they had lost their money in his establishments in the first place. Like rats in a maze, he thought idly, stupid creatures.

He occasionally cancelled a debt in exchange for either information or power, but it was rare that a situation like that of Gerald Smythe and Roland Poole crossed his desk. The men had foolishly tried to hide their niece's disappearance. He might have to punish them for that, he mused.

He had not seen the girl in question, but it seemed that Mr. Warren was quite taken with her. Of course, Warren was a filthy lecher who fancied anything in skirts, but that was of no consequence in their business relationship. Mr. Warren offered new opportunities for investment and expansion, and Sanders was not about to see them disappear simply because some chit of a girl had run off while her inept uncles had their backs turned. The girl's fortune would enable him to rise to new heights. It was for this reason that he had employed one of his best men to hunt her down.

He looked with disgust at the two men sitting across from him. "When were you planning to tell me that the girl had disappeared?" he asked icily.

"Well, Mr. Sanders," said Gerald, nervously, "you see, we thought that we could find her, and there would be no need to involve you in such a trivial matter. It was only when we realized that she had disappeared so completely that we felt you should know." He was well aware that, should he so choose, Sanders could easily have his and his brother-in-law's throats cut immediately.

"It is highly fortunate for you both that I am in good spirits today, or your wives would soon be occupied in planning your funerals. However, I have taken the liberty of dispatching my own man to find your niece, and he has just this morning informed me of her whereabouts."

"Where is she?" cried Gerald, forgetting himself in his excitement. "Were you able to convince her to return and do her duty?"

"Her whereabouts, Mr. Smythe, are no longer any of your concern. I shall have her brought here myself and will inform you as to when the nuptials between your niece and Mr. Warren will take place only because Mr. Poole here is her guardian. It may be beneficial to have you here in that role to help persuade Miss Edwards that this marriage will indeed take place, whether she desires it or not. As agreed upon, Mr. Warren's acquisition of her inheritance will void your debt to me."

"Thank you, sir, thank you."

Both men were almost unintelligible in their relief.

"I will send for you when the time comes. Until then, you will speak of this to no one. And gentlemen," he said coldly, his eyes flat, "it would be wise for you to consider how close you came to forfeiting your lives today before conspiring to keep anything else from me."

Mr. Sanders remained seated at his ornate desk while the two men exited his office. Once they had left, he leaned back and folded his hands together. His hands were strangely graceful in all their movements, the result of years of perfecting the art of lifting the valuables of others without their knowledge. His appearance had been an asset to him as a young boy, his golden blond hair and angelic looking features masking the devilish nature underneath. Glancing around at the expensive furnishings, he allowed himself a moment of enjoyment. His pride in the fact that he had begun to achieve his goal in his youth, and nothing stood in his way even now, at the age of forty-five, was fully credited. Among the brothels and gaming halls that first turned a profit for him, he had more recently invested in legitimate enterprises. This deal with Mr. Warren would be the pinnacle of his achievements. He stood to make a fortune off the investment, and it wasn't just about the money, he thought, it was about creating a name for himself in the Polite World. He'd already conquered one London. Society was just waiting for him to take advantage of its poor, bored ladies and irresponsible, discontented men. He laughed to himself, the mocking sound erupting from his lips as he tried to stifle it. It would almost be too easy, he reflected, still chuckling.

"Mr. Sanders, sir. You sent for me?" The gruff voice belonged to his most trusted employee, Mr. Clark. The slums had birthed them both, the poverty of their surroundings and the crudity of their neighbors fanning the flames of ambition to escape. The two youths had been responsible for several lucrative burglaries that provided the capital for Sanders's first enterprises. Well, he amended, he had been responsible; Clark had simply been the muscle. The man was loyal as a dog, and useful, but his intelligence was certainly not his strongest point. A quick, cold smile crossed Sanders's face as he recalled the complete ineptitude of the investigators of his youth. He and Clark had quite enjoyed watching as the Bow Street Runners fumble around for information while his illegal activities thrived.

Clark's appearance matched his voice, coarse and rough, his broad face and large frame belying the quickness and grace of his movements. His gift for stealth had been invaluable to Sanders. Indeed, it was this ability that had allowed him to observe Charlotte and the others for some time without their knowledge. Clark had never been the sort of man to hurry a thing before its time. His patience was practically boundless, and he was often employed with the task of watching and waiting. It had taken him only two days of searching to find Charlotte in the little village of Kennington, but his orders were only to locate her, not to take her ... yet. For all his patience, when the time came to act, Clark was swift, sure, and often deadly.

"Yes, Clark. I have another commission for you. This time, it may involve a little more danger than my last request."

"Not a worry, sir. I can handle myself."

Clark's eyes were as flat and cold as his employer's. The bond between the two men, forged in the darkest, filthiest slums of London, was the closest thing to true friendship that either man knew. Above all else, Sanders demanded loyalty, and Clark was loyal to no one and nothing else but Sanders and his wallet. After all, he'd been the reminder to many who hadn't realized, or had forgotten, that disloyalty to Sanders brought a painful, merciless death. The thought made him smile. Clark considered it essential that a man enjoy his work. He certainly did his.

"You are to take the girl and bring her back here, to my private offices. Let nothing stand in your way. You have my permission to use whatever force is necessary, but the girl herself must not be harmed. We need her alive and well in order to obtain her inheritance for Warren. Of course, what happens to her after the marriage is Warren's affair. Given what I've heard of his first wife, the girl may not have to suffer a long life with him anyway."

"Consider it done. I'll report in when I have her."

Turning, Clark walked smoothly toward the door. "Oh, and Clark ..."

"Yes, sir?"

"After the ceremony ... you may have opportunity to exercise your considerable skills on Mr. Smythe and Mr. Poole. I shall let you know when you return."

"With pleasure, sir."

Stepping lighter in anticipation of his favorite activity, Mr. Clark left the room. Sanders again cast an eye around. *All mine,* he thought, *and soon, even more shall belong to me.* Sitting up, he searched on his desk for a sheet of paper and then picked up his pen. There was business to be attended to.

Chapter
17

harlotte knew the happiest moments of her life in the days that followed the arrival of Thomas and Mr. Hayes. Every day, Thomas accompanied her on her rambles through the lanes in and around the village. His presence and ideas helped her create her stories even faster than usual, and when they weren't occupied with the horrors of misty moors and haunted castles, quiet conversation in softly scented woods did much to ease her anger and her fears.

She found herself believing, for the first time, that God had perhaps not made a mistake in making her the way He had. Charlotte had always known she was not like other ladies, especially in mind, but for the first time, she was surrounded by people who enjoyed her quirks. It was a novelty she intended to enjoy for however long it lasted.

At the end of every day, when all its occupants returned home, the manor was full of life and laughter. The dark cloud that hung over them still felt unreal. Though she had moments of fear and anger when something reminded her of her family or her situation, she spent most of her evenings soaking in the joy of friends and a home, for however long it lasted.

She reflected wryly that most of her turmoil over Thomas seemed to have been for nothing. Aside from the occasional awkward moment when hands brushed or eyes met, he seemed determined to set her at ease. Of course, she admitted to herself that she might very well have preferred the tension of unspoken or unrequited feelings to being treated as his sister. If she'd had any faith at all in her charms, Charlotte rather thought she might have tried to exert them, just to see what the man would do. She was, however, well aware that whatever charms she might possess, and she doubted they were many, were useless in her inexperienced hands.

☙

Mr. Hayes had hastened to call in an associate from London to guard Charlotte and to watch the house at night, but his arrival had been delayed. Mr. Hayes felt, privately, that he had a good idea of what was being planned for Charlotte, but, not wanting to frighten her unnecessarily, he hadn't yet shared any of the evidence his employees had compiled. The more he learned, the more questions he had, and the more he sensed there was something bigger than Charlotte's problem afoot. He was certain of one thing, though, that the household, and Charlotte in particular, were in need of protection.

The rest of the household were aware of the active search for Charlotte, but Jonathan had noticed, on the night of his arrival with Thomas, that the house was being watched by a large man that he immediately recognized as Sanders's right-hand man, Mr. Clark. Jonathan was quite familiar with Sanders, as well as with his minions. His line of work required him to delve into some of the seediest areas of London and the more disreputable establishments located there. He was well acquainted with not only the name of Sanders but with his reputation.

Jonathan's hand clenched into a fist under the dining table. He could not risk the life of Thomas, his best friend, or the lives of the people he had come to care for in the manor. He was silent, turning the matter over in his mind, while the rest of the household conversed during the meal.

After dinner, Thomas pulled his friend aside. There were times when Jonathan found his friend's uncanny ability to read people extremely irritating.

"You were unusually quiet at dinner tonight, Jonathan. Is something wrong? Is there some new development I should know about?"

Jonathan debated how much to share with Thomas. They had been friends for more than ten years, ever since they met at Oxford, Thomas a nobleman's son and Jonathan working his way through. Thomas had been the only man of aristocratic birth who had refused to mock the young man, and had actually gone out of his way to offer friendship. When he and Thomas discovered their common faith in God, their friendship had become unshakable. The other nobility had been affronted by a working

86

man in their midst, particularly an intelligent, driven one. Thomas had simply ignored his peers and their derision and had never treated Jonathan with anything less than complete respect, as though the circumstances of his birth did not matter. Jonathan had never forgotten that, and it was out of the loyalty born so long before that he decided let Thomas in on the truth.

"It's Sanders, Thomas. He's not only looking for Charlotte, he's found her. I noticed on our first night here that the house was being watched. It was Clark, Sanders's best man, if he can be called such a thing. He doesn't know I saw him, but he does know she's here. He will come for her, Thomas, make no mistake. I've sent for assistance from an associate, and he should arrive in time. If he doesn't, however …"

Jonathan grew silent once more. Thomas felt the blow keenly. He had allowed himself to be lulled into the illusion of security, simply having Charlotte within his sight. The two had spent hours together every evening, discussing their interests and beliefs and enjoying each other's company. He knew that she was unaware of his growing affection for her, and it only made her more attractive to him. It made him sick, the thought of harm coming to the woman he … loved?

"Thomas, are you all right?" asked Jonathan, studying his friend. "You've gone completely white."

Thomas shook his head, tucking his feelings away for later perusal. It appeared he had some decisions to make.

"What can we do?" he asked quietly. The manor was not a large house, and there was no guarantee that they wouldn't be overheard. He didn't want to spread any more fear around than was already there.

"Be on your guard, my friend," replied Jonathan. "Anything out of the ordinary, you report to me. We must be careful. If he does manage to take her, we have to have a plan." He hesitated. "I'll be honest, Thomas, the odds are against us."

"We have God on our side," said Thomas, with a confidence he did not feel. "We must cling to that. But you are correct. We need a plan."

The two men looked at each other, understanding that it would fall to them to keep Charlotte safe or, failing that, to rescue her from a fate worse than death.

"Excuse me, sirs," said a voice from the doorway, "but I believe that I'd like to be a part of whatever you're plotting."

Graves entered the parlor, walked to the chair by the fire, and sat down. He stared at the two men. They glanced at each other, and then each moved toward a seat.

"If you're trying to decide what to tell me," said Graves, mildly, "I've heard enough to have a general idea that Charlotte is in more danger than we thought." He glanced at the doorway. "The corridors really are terribly conducive to carrying sound."

Attempting to hide their smiles at his euphemistic explanation for his eavesdropping, Thomas and Jonathan both settled into their chairs.

"We're going to have to be creative," said Jonathan. "Sanders is a formidable enemy, and his resources are extensive."

"After all, recall his actions toward Charlotte's parents," said Graves.

"Yes, that is something ...," replied Jonathan, his voice trailing off. There was something about their deaths that bothered him. The two of them, found as they were, stabbed through the heart. Such a personal method—

"Well, then, let us plot," said Thomas, rubbing his hands together. In spite of the danger, or perhaps because of it, he found himself looking forward to the coming trouble as much as fearing it. He needed resolution as much as Charlotte did, for their lives were on hiatus until someone acted in the game they unwillingly played.

"Yes," Jonathan agreed, putting aside his questions for the moment, "let us plan."

The three men moved their chairs closer to the fire as they began to converse in hushed tones. Standing quietly in the hallway, shrouded in the shadows, Mrs. Brown listened intently. *Men*, she thought, with a fond smile, *always trying to protect the women from the dark side of life—as if we were not already quite aware of it*. She turned silently and moved toward the kitchen, making some plans of her own. It couldn't hurt to be on the safe side, she thought, just in case. Ten years with the Smythe-Pooles had shown her just how vicious and selfish they could be. *If this Mr. Sanders is worse than they, God help us all*.

Chapter

18

M r. Clark had a plan. Lurking outside Violet Hill Manor, well hidden by the plentiful shrubbery, he had noted Miss Edwards's habit of rising early to write. This could certainly be turned to his advantage. Every other hour of the day, she was in the company of either the older man—the butler, he assumed—or one of the two young men staying with them.

Clark knew how soon news of a stranger got around small towns. Not wanting to alert anyone to his presence, he had been camping outside the village. He spent his nights watching the manor, piecing together the habits of those inside, matching residents to bedchambers. He spent his days sleeping, rising in midafternoon to perfect his strategy for kidnapping the woman. He knew quite well that he would not receive his wages until he delivered her to Sanders, friends or not.

As the hours of the night passed, Clark sat silent, cloaked in darkness. He was skilled and experienced in the art of stalking, and the long hours of waiting and watching gave him a sense of power. The stars were just beginning to fade when he saw the light of a candle in the window of Charlotte's bedchamber. He had spent a number of hours examining the manor house and had discovered that the crumbling stone walls had enough cracks and crevices for him to scale the wall to Charlotte's window. From there, he would simply need to break the glass and force the woman out of the house with his pistol. The mere sight of the weapon made people jump to do his bidding. It was the devil to aim, he admitted, patting the gun in his pocket fondly, but since most of his victims had no idea it held only one shot, aiming it had not presented a problem.

Besides, Clark reflected as he reached for his first handhold, the knife tucked inside his boot, a relic from his youth, had helped stain more than one cobblestone street with the blood of an adversary. His movements quickened at the thought that he might have a chance to use it. Yes, he thought happily, there was nothing like the smell of freshly spilled blood drying in the morning sun.

❧

Inside her room, Charlotte sat at her desk, fully dressed, pen in hand, staring at the blank sheet of paper in front of her.

"You cannot think of anything to write, Miss Edwards?" inquired Mr. Worthing in a low voice, from where he sat just inside the door. She had been introduced to him yesterday as an associate of Mr. Hayes. She'd found herself immediately comfortable with the plump, balding man, especially since he couldn't manage to keep from bragging about his wife and children at any break in the conversation. However, he'd become all seriousness when Jonathan had explained his assignment, and Charlotte had glimpsed the keen investigator Mr. Worthing kept hidden under the affable bluster she suspected was as useful in his business as pen and ink were in hers.

"I'm afraid not, Mr. Worthing. I've written so often about such situations, yet I find myself simply wanting to enjoy the thrill of living one out."

Charlotte smiled slightly. *How odd.* She had been living afraid the past two weeks and was well aware that by rights she should be terrified at the prospect of abduction by force, arranged marriage, and everything therein, but against all odds, the writer in her was fascinated by the danger and the romance. *Imagine, pale, dull little Charlotte Edwards a heroine in the midst of mystery and danger.* She found herself enjoying the entire experience immensely, particularly the male attention. Thomas and Graves practically doted on her, and she and Jonathan—for they'd soon dispensed with formalities—shared the sort of repartee she'd always imagined siblings enjoyed. With an entire household of protectors, she felt certain that Sanders would never be able to touch her.

Of course, the wicked looking-pistol that Mr. Worthing was pointing toward the window was a little intimidating. She wished that Thomas had been able to stay with her while they waited for Sanders's man to show up, but he must be either asleep or else huddled with Graves. Jonathan had expressly forbidden him, and the rest of the household, from involving themselves in the potential capture of whoever Sanders sent for Charlotte. She figured Graves and the rest of the household were in their rooms, waiting silently in the dark for a sign that all was well. Jonathan expected that her kidnapper would probably make his attempt in the early hours of the morning, but he'd had Mr. Worthing guarding her as she slept, just in case. Even when she'd risen to wash and dress, Mr. Worthing had stepped out and sent Mrs. Brown in so that she was never alone.

As she stared down at the blank sheet in front of her, she heard a faint scrape outside, followed by another. The sense of expectation that she had been feeling all night as she tried to sleep became almost unbearable. The soft clatter of pebbles hitting the ground sounded in time with her heartbeats, steady and unstoppable. She began to move her pen across the page, writing frantically, whatever crossed her mind, the image of a feverishly inspired writer in the early morning hours. There were three more scrapes, louder this time, and then, suddenly, the piercing sound of glass shattering as a fist crashed through the window. Charlotte shrieked automatically, as the large figure quickly hauled himself through the opening and landed lightly on the floor.

"You're coming with me, Miss Edwards," said the man, in a low, gruff tone, "and don't even think of screaming again, or your friends will pay for it."

He moved toward Charlotte, as if to grab hold of her and drag her away by force.

"I suggest you step away from the young lady," said the quiet voice of Mr. Worthing, "or you may find yourself sporting an extra hole in your head."

"What?! Who are you? What are you doing here?" cried Clark, his face displaying amazement at the unexpected threat. He would have taken hold of Charlotte, but his eyes caught the gleam of the pistol in the candlelight.

"We've been watching you these past few days, Mr. Clark—at least I presume that's who you are—believing that you would try to snatch Miss Edwards. Once we saw that you had discovered a way up the wall, it was simply a matter of taking turns watching over the young lady until you made your attempt. We'll be turning you over to the police straightaway, and I imagine that Sanders will not be overly happy with your failure.

However, if you work with us to apprehend your employer, I will do my best to see that you get a reduced sentence. I have some friends in Scotland Yard."

"I won't say anything, sir," spat Clark, glaring malevolently at the man. He turned his furious gaze on Charlotte. "It's most unfortunate that you chose to be difficult, miss. Sanders hates to be crossed. You'll pay for this, you will."

With that, he folded his arms across his chest, and stood, waiting.

Mr. Worthing gave her a sidelong glance. "If you would be good enough to alert Mr. Hayes to the capture of Mr. Clark, we'll get him ready to be delivered to the London police. I would imagine you'll probably also want to send word to Mr. Anderson and let him know that the danger is ended, for now."

"Thank you, Mr. Worthing. I'll do that," said Charlotte, stepping around Mr. Clark toward the door. As she did, his arm shot out, wrapping tightly around her neck and dragging her back against him. He smiled grimly, eyes glittering fiercely as he stared at the shocked man.

"Thought you could trap me, did you—Mr. Worthing, is it? Well, the tables have turned now, haven't they? You'll be stepping aside to let me pass with the lady here. One wrong move, and I'll snap her neck, you see if I won't." He held her tightly as he reached down and slid the knife from his boot, holding it in his free hand.

Charlotte stood still, terrified. Why had she ever thought that this was entertaining? If she ever, somehow, made her way out of this mess, she was going to confine her love of the dramatic to the pen and page, and that was that. The increasing pressure on her throat from Clark's immovable arm was making breathing, let alone thinking, more and more difficult.

Mr. Worthing nodded and stepped aside. Clark pushed her forward, prodding her with the tip of his boot. They passed the other man, and Charlotte could see that he was struggling between attacking and letting them go. She looked at him steadily, silently pleading with him to do nothing. She could not live with his death on her conscience, and she was certain that, should he try anything, one of them would die. While the thought of her own death did not fill her with any great anticipation, she would rather face that than have someone else's life snuffed out in exchange for her own.

Clark slid the knife up her arm slowly and then pressed the tip ever so slightly into her neck. A drop of blood welled up and ran down her collarbone, staining the neckline of her gown. Charlotte's eyes widened at the prick of pain, then narrowed. She had spent her entire life as a pawn for greedy, selfish people, and if that wasn't enough, the great lummox dragging her around like a feed sack had just made her bleed on her favorite gown.

"Nobody make a move," shouted Clark, dragging her toward the stairs. "You do anything, and I kill her here and now, Anyone follows us and she's dead, I swear it! You'll never get to me fast enough to stop me from killing her!"

Jonathan had been guarding the stairwell, and she could see the strain on his face as she was pushed past him. If there had been any way to get her away from Clark, he would have done it, but the risk was just too high. She racked her brain, thinking through every novel she had ever read, trying to come up with some way to free herself. She could try a swoon, but, knowing her, she thought wryly, she'd swoon right into the tip of the knife. With her luck, she'd likely skewer herself right through on the way down.

At the base of the stairs, she sent a pleading glance to Graves and Thomas, begging them silently to do nothing. The pain on their faces betrayed how much it cost them, but the sight of her held at knifepoint was enough to deter them from any foolish interference, no matter how greatly they desired to save her. Perhaps, she wondered, it was the fire of indignation she felt in her eyes that helped them believe she would not give up. She prayed she would have the courage not to disappoint them—or herself.

Once outside, Charlotte could see a wagon waiting some distance down the road, past the village green and schoolhouse. It was partially hidden in the shadows, and she could just make out a vague figure sitting in it. She hoped against hope that somehow, Thomas had disobeyed his friend's orders and come after her. Charlotte found herself slightly peeved with the man. If this was a novel, she thought, he would be striding toward her right now, cloak flapping in the breeze, pistol gleaming in the moonlight. If ever Charlotte was aware that life was most certainly not like a book, this was the moment.

She shivered in the cool air, wishing for her cloak. The walk from the manor to the wagon they now approached had seemed to take forever, her back aching from the pressure of the pistol pressed there. As soon as they had been out view of the manor, Clark had released his hold on her neck and had prompted her acquiescence with his gun instead. She looked closely at the driver of the wagon as she and Clark approached it. Fear struck hard as she noted the brutish cast of the driver's face, his nearly toothless grin more malevolent than anything. Beside him sat a woman. Even in the soft light of dawn, Charlotte could see the hardness in her face, and the coarseness of her features. She was similar in size to Charlotte, but that was where the resemblance ended. Turning to look at her, the woman's lips curved upward, but her smile held no warmth. Charlotte sent her a pleading glance, but the woman simply stared at her for a moment, then looked away again.

"You have her, I see," the man said to Clark. "Are you ready to go? We'd better hurry. They'll be after us directly."

"Not if they want to keep the girl here alive, they won't, but all the same, we'll follow the plan. You take Miss Edwards directly to Mr. Sanders, without delay. Rosie and I will keep her friends occupied for a time."

"Please," said Charlotte, speaking for the first time, "don't do this, I'm begging you." Her tone was quiet, earnest but not desperate.

Clark ignored her and turned to the woman who was tying on a bonnet to hide the color of her hair.

"Come along, then, Rosie, we've got a job to do. Get yourself down here!"

The woman climbed off the wagon and came to stand beside Clark and Charlotte. Though the knife was no longer digging into Charlotte's neck, the neckline of her gown was thoroughly stained with her blood.

"Get in the wagon, Miss Edwards," said Clark calmly.

"No," said Charlotte stoutly, "you'll have to kill me here." She figured that since there was no sympathy to be had, she had rather die now than face what lay ahead with Sanders and Mr. Warren. Now that she'd tasted freedom, she thought fiercely, she refused to be sent back into slavery.

Clark sighed and turned to Rosie. "You have it?" he asked.

"Of course," she replied, her voice crackly and hoarse, matching the well-used, worn cast of her features.

She drew out a small bottle and cloth. Opening the bottle, she wet the cloth with the contents thoroughly, and then passed the cloth to Clark. Charlotte's stomach turned at the sickly sweet smell, and she whirled to run. Clark's heavy hand grabbed her arm, jerking her back against him. The last thing Charlotte heard, as the cloth covered her nose and mouth and blackness closed in on her, was the eerie, unsettling sound of Rosie's laugh.

Chapter

19

The sound of voices and the glare of light on her face called Charlotte from her deep, drugged sleep. Turning away from the light that burned her eyes even through her tightly shut eyelids, she struggled to recall what had happened. The last thing she remembered was Clark and Rosie, and that awful, sweet-smelling cloth over her nose and mouth. It must have been chloroform, she thought sluggishly. Certainly an effective method of rendering her unconscious and easy to transport, and one she had often inflicted on her hapless characters. Her dark sense of humor returning as her mind cleared, she couldn't help laughing inwardly at the joy she had taken in inflicting dire circumstances on her heroines. She might have a little more sympathy for the poor women, should she ever have the chance to put pen to paper again.

"I see you're awake, Miss Edwards," said a smooth voice. "You caused me a good deal of trouble, you know. You should be very grateful that you are more valuable to me alive than dead."

Charlotte pushed her eyelids up over gritty eyes and turned to view the man whose voice she heard. He was handsome, she could not deny that, but there was a coldness, a cruelty to his features that marred the almost angelic beauty of his face. His eyes were a deep, dark blue and utterly devoid of emotion.

"I suppose you are Mr. Sanders," she said, striving for a matter-of-fact tone. If she could not escape her fate by force or flight, she might try to talk her way out of it. It was the only chance she had.

"I am indeed," said the man. "I take it, then, that you are acquainted with the reason I require your presence here this evening."

Charlotte sat up slowly, the effort momentarily stealing her breath. She gripped the edge of the sofa under her, struggling to regain her equilibrium. She pushed back the hair that had escaped its confines and leveled her gaze at him.

"If you are asking if I am aware that I have been bartered by my uncles as payment for their debt, then, yes, I am perfectly informed as to why you were so insistent on bringing me back to London. I assume that we are indeed in London?"

"Yes. You are currently occupying space in my office, above the very first gaming hall I established. You should feel privileged. I do not often allow visitors in this particular location."

"Forgive me if I do not feel flattered, Mr. Sanders. I was rather imposed upon by your employees and am not in the most amiable of moods."

Charlotte felt that her bravado was less than convincing, but she had to keep him talking. Unfortunately, the very fact that he wanted to talk made her extremely uneasy. In her novels, that was a sure sign that death was not far away.

"I do apologize for their rough treatment of you, Miss Edwards, but you must own that you did bring it on yourself. If you had simply agreed to come with them, they would not have been forced to render you unconscious. Speaking of which," he said in the tones of the jovial host, "I imagine that you are likely more than a little thirsty at the moment. May I offer you some refreshment?"

She felt oddly detached from the situation at hand. Sanders's polite manner was almost laughable, given the circumstances that lay ahead of her at his bidding. She only hoped that whatever time she could buy herself would allow Mr. Hayes and Thomas the time they needed to find her. She had to hang on to that hope. After all, would God allow such misfortune into her life, after all she had already suffered? Charlotte believed that God was truly good, she honestly did, but all the same, she was terrified of answering the question she had just posed. Somehow, the knowledge of God's goodness did little to comfort her soul as the prospect of being sold into marriage to the odious Mr. Warren loomed. Well, she thought, she would have to have things out with her Maker later. Right now, she just wanted Him to help her get out of this mess.

"I would very much appreciate a glass of water, sir," she said, presenting, with great effort, a calm and composed face to her abductor.

"Certainly, Miss Edwards. In fact, I will ring and have Mr. Bailey, my man of affairs, show you to your room so you can dress for your upcoming nuptials. I do hope you will come to see your union with Mr. Warren in a more favorable light than I assume you currently do. It's just business, you see. Simply business."

Mr. Sanders smiled then, a smile so icy it stole the breath from her lungs. She knew then, without doubt, that nothing would get in the way of Sanders and what he wanted. She thanked God that he only wanted her money and not her virtue as well. She could not have borne that, for he surely would have achieved his goal, and she would have found herself not only ruined in the eyes of Society but shamed in spite of her defiance. Her inevitable marriage to Mr. Warren sparked the same revulsion and would bring the same result; ruined, perhaps not in the eyes of others but certainly in her own. The thought of those fleshy lips and puffy hands touching her made her gorge rise. *Please, God,* she prayed frantically, *please send someone to rescue me!*

A knock sounded at the door, and at a word from Sanders, it opened to reveal the man of affairs, Mr. Bailey. Charlotte found no cause for hope in his appearance, as his eyes displayed the same wintry cast as his employer's, and though his features were carefully schooled into a near-perfect mask of expressionless submission, the smirking leer he casually directed at her did nothing to offer any hope that he could be convinced to help her. In fact, she was certain he would do nothing to upset his employer until he was assured that he could either walk away undetected and unscathed or else slit the man's throat and take charge of his criminal empire. She shivered at the thought. No, her only hope for salvation lay in the efforts of the two men and family she had left behind in Kennington, and she had little faith that they would be able to do anything in time to avert the upcoming disaster.

"Mr. Bailey, please escort Miss Edwards here to the red room so she can freshen up. Make sure she doesn't leave until I send word for you to bring her back here."

Mr. Bailey turned to her and mockingly offered his arm as though he was simply escorting her to dinner. The polite farce being played out made her sick with fury, yet there was nothing to do but play along. She laid her hand on his arm and, as regally as she could, let him lead her from the office and down the corridor to a staircase. They climbed until he turned her along a landing to halt in front of an ornately worked door. He unlocked it with a flourish, then gestured for her to enter. Awed by the opulent furnishings, Charlotte unconsciously moved further into the room, only to whirl when she heard the door bang shut and the lock click into place.

Mr. Bailey's voice sounded through the heavy wood. "I'll soon be back to collect you, Miss Edwards," he called, "and don't try anything, if you please. A guard is posted outside your door, and you'll soon find that there's no other way out. Have a pleasant time preparing yourself for your wedding, Miss Edwards."

Charlotte glared at the door as his footsteps receded. Looking around, she saw that Mr. Bailey was correct. Though quite spacious, the locked door was indeed the only way in or out. Her skin crawled as she realized this was possibly the last time she would be alone in a bedchamber without the stain of Mr. Warren's filthy touch on her soul. Walking slowly toward the enormous bed, Charlotte saw that a stunning gown in rich ivory satin, overlaid with lace, had been laid out for her, along with fresh undergarments and accessories. Frustration filled her as she stared at it all. Honestly, she thought, why was it that the only time she received a beautiful dress was when that pig of a Mr. Warren was involved? She tilted her head, straining to hear what sounded like approaching footsteps. There was a quick knock, then Mr. Bailey unlocked the door and stepped just inside.

"I neglected to inform you that the apparel laid out is from Mr. Warren, for your wedding. You may change your clothing at your discretion, Miss Edwards," he said, with a malevolent smirk on his face, "but I will return to collect you for the ceremony in precisely one hour.

"Will you need help dressing?" he added, with a lascivious look. "I'm sure one of Madam Covington's girls would be more than happy to help you ready yourself. They're quite experienced in preparing themselves for men, you know. This used to be the madam's room, before she moved her girls over into the Black Garter. Or perhaps I might be of some assistance?" His smirk grew more pronounced as he finished.

"No, thank you, sir," she said, as calmly as she could. "I am fully capable of preparing myself."

"I leave you to it, then," he said. With a final look around the room, Mr. Bailey stepped out and closed the door behind him. Charlotte heard the telltale snick of the lock turning, the sound echoing in her mind as her eyes slid shut in despair.

⌒

Back in the village manor, Charlotte's abduction had caused quite an uproar. As soon as Mr. Clark had walked through the door with Charlotte at knifepoint, Mr. Hayes and Mr. Worthing had gone into action. Graves was sent to rouse the sleeping Mr. Cobb in order to try to procure transportation to London for himself, Mr. Hayes and Mr. Worthing. Betsy, Eliza, and Mrs. Brown would stay at Violet Hill Manor in the vain hope that Charlotte might escape and return there.

As soon as Clark had departed with Charlotte, Jonathan and Mr. Worthing, taking care to remain unobserved, began to follow them at a distance. So careful were they, in fact, that they arrived at the village green only in time to see the wagon pull away. They were not fooled, as Clark had assumed they would be, however, by the substitution of Rosie for Charlotte. The wagon itself suggested to Jonathan that it was meant to convey Charlotte to London, and Mr. Clark's attempt at misdirection as he propelled Rosie along in front of him only convinced Jonathan that he was trying to buy time for the wagon to travel without being overtaken by a speedier horseman. Though he hated to leave the woman who had become a good friend in the hands of villains, he knew that until they dealt directly with Sanders, the attempts on Charlotte would not cease. Because he knew this to be true, Jonathan had instructed the others to stay at the manor until he and Mr. Worthing returned.

However, Thomas was not, as directed, lying low at the manor with the others. He had been concerned that Jonathan would not be able to stop the planned abduction of the woman he loved and had taken measures of his own to protect her, though no one knew it. While he knew in his head that Jonathan was right to force Sanders's hand, Thomas's heart refused to allow him to stand still while Charlotte was in trouble. Realizing that, as the son of an earl, he had certain advantages at his disposal, he was determined to do everything in his and his family's power to rescue her.

And so it was that as the unconscious, unwitting heroine was being transported to London in the back of a wagon, and Mr. Hayes and his associate were led by Mr. Clark and his woman accomplice, Thomas was riding in all haste toward the city himself. He knew that Jonathan and Mr. Worthing would soon discover his absence, and he, having anticipated their concern, had left a note informing them that he was on his way to meet with Sanders himself.

Though he was terrified that he would not reach Charlotte in time, Thomas had to smile briefly as he imagined first the shock and then the anger on the face of his longtime friend. Not that he enjoyed giving his friend grief, but it was heartening to feel that he had, in a sense, come out ahead on this one. His smile disappeared quickly, however, when he thought of Charlotte. He, too, had watched from the shadows of the woods as she was rendered unconscious and placed unceremoniously, with all the care allotted a feed sack, into the back of the wagon.

Thomas continued to ride for all he was worth toward London. He had only a vague idea of where to find Mr. Sanders, never having frequented any of the gaming halls and brothels for which the man was well known, but he was quite capable of making the necessary inquiries once he arrived. He was well aware that he was now all that stood between Charlotte and a future no one deserved. He could not bear the thought of losing her, the only woman he had ever loved or ever would. Thomas crouched lower in the saddle, praying with all his strength that he would arrive in time. Heeling his horse again, he flew through the early dawn, a dark, shadowy figure shrouded in the early morning mist. The hero Charlotte had long dreamt of was finally on his way.

Chapter
20

Charlotte stared at the stranger in the mirror. The slim, pale figure dressed in ivory satin, trimmed with what she was sure must be Belgian lace, was elegant in both face and figure. She blinked back tears, and the wide green eyes in the mirror did the same.

Turning away, she began once again to pace the room. After her first fit of despair, which lasted all of fifteen minutes before her practical nature won out, she had given in to the temptation to exchange her bloody, soiled gown for the dress laid out for her, the shimmering material making her skin luminescent, its creamy sheen accenting the delicate cast of her features.

She had then gone on to thoroughly examine her prison. There were no windows, only one door which was locked, and the large, ornate bed which she found increasingly disconcerting. She was, after all, a writer of gothic novels and was not entirely naïve as to the seedier side of life. She found herself sincerely hoping that the room that held her captive had always been intended to be a guest room and had not been previously used for business purposes. Not, she thought firmly, the direction she wanted her mind heading at this point. Whether or not the madam of a brothel had been the former tenant had no bearing on Charlotte's plight.

Getting married in a brothel had never crossed Charlotte's mind, which was astonishing, given the many and varied story lines she had created over the years. In the moments since she had been unceremoniously delivered to her prison room, she had in the moments since she had been unceremoniously delivered to her prison room, allowed her emotions to run the gamut from disgust and terror at the thought of being united in what she had to term "unholy" matrimony to Mr. Warren, all the way to a morbid amusement at the strange events of the last six months. She would not admit to herself that she had given up hope of rescue, even if she had allowed herself a wild fit of tears as she mourned her lost future. She planned to refuse, regardless of threat or consequence, to marry Mr. Warren. She knew quite well that her acquiescence was not required in the proceedings, so she steeled her will. She would use everything at her disposal to escape her current fate … or die in the process.

A sharp knock sounded at the door, and Charlotte heard the sound of the key turning in the lock. She quickly picked up the empty water pitcher beside the basin and ran over to hide behind the door. It swung open slowly, and footsteps sounded as her captor moved into the room.

"Miss Edwards? I've come to collect you for the ceremony," said Mr. Bailey. "Come now, cease this silly game, and reveal yourself. I have no time for this."

He moved further into the room, scanning left to right. Charlotte seized her opportunity and swung the pitcher at his head with all her might. For a moment, she thought her plan was working. The pitcher sped toward Mr. Bailey just as she had intended. Unfortunately, just before it could connect with his head, Mr. Bailey ducked, and with the momentum of her swing, the weapon slipped from her fingers. It sailed across the room, landing unharmed on the bed while she struggled to maintain her balance. Mr. Bailey quickly grabbed her arm and steadied her as he began to urge her out of the room.

"You are very fortunate that your attempt misfired, Miss Edwards," he said softly. "I do not take kindly to people wishing to harm me. In fact, I have a nasty habit of returning the favor."

The stare he gave her as they made their way down the hallway chilled her to the bone. "You will receive no apology from me, Mr. Bailey," she said, with a bravado she most certainly did not feel. "I also find attempts to harm me most offensive. I had no choice, as I imagine you understand."

The man said nothing, just quickened his pace so that she was forced to trot to keep up with him. After a number of hallways, stairwells, and doors, Charlotte and her guard found themselves at the door to Sanders's office. It was at this final barrier that the cruel, unavoidable reality of her situation overwhelmed what little courage she had left. In a completely uncharacteristic move, she went into her first ever swoon. The last thing she saw before everything went black was the irritated look on the face of Mr. Bailey as he reached out to catch her.

When she woke, Charlotte was surprised to find herself comfortably ensconced on the same settee in Sanders's office upon which she had woken earlier. She shook her head slightly, trying to clear it, as she looked around the room. There was, thankfully, she thought, no sign of her prospective husband. Sanders and Mr. Bailey seemed to be involved in an intense discussion.

"Surely you don't intend to go along with it, do you?" asked Mr. Bailey, with a note of disdain in his voice.

"I have my money. Quite frankly, that is my only concern. Besides, I find myself enjoying the prospect of causing more trouble for those two fools."

"But after all the lengths you've gone to, it simply doesn't make sense!"

Sanders eyed Mr. Bailey frigidly. The man visibly quailed at the look.

"You forget your place, Bailey. It is my decision, and mine alone."

Before Charlotte's mind could comprehend what she had heard, there was a knock at the door. Knowing that it was quite likely Mr. Warren and whatever foul-minded mockery of a clergyman they had found to perform the ceremony, she shut her eyes tightly and prayed with all her might that somehow, some way, she would be saved. A voice spoke.

"Is everything ready, Mr. Sanders? If you don't mind, I'd like to have my future wife in my possession as soon as possible."

At this, Charlotte's eyes flew open, and she sat up abruptly. The voice, that dear voice, belonged to none other than the man she loved.

"Thomas!? How? What? I ..." Charlotte's voice trailed off as she stared at him. His thick hair was windblown and tousled, and his brown eyes were tired and strained, but underneath the fatigue was a fire of passion that caused her heart to pulse wildly as her breath caught.

"Charlotte! Are you all right? Unharmed?" He looked at her keenly. Turning to Sanders with a questioning glance, he asked, "She has been well treated?"

The cool authority of his tone startled Charlotte, but Sanders simply nodded. "She has not been harmed."

Thomas turned to the men who had entered with him. Charlotte felt herself growing faint again, allowing herself the brief acknowledgement that she might be growing a little too like her heroines. The younger of the two strangers, still middle-aged, smiled slightly at her, his kind brown eyes too like Thomas's to be coincidental. The elder, a small, frail man with a full head of white hair and clear blue eyes, was, if his collar was any indication, the vicar needed to perform the marriage ceremony. Charlotte's thoughts were in a whirl. Apparently the marriage was still to take place! How could Thomas and Mr. Hayes allow her to be virtually sold to the filthy, lecherous Mr. Warren in payment of her uncles' debts? It was not possible!

"Of course, Thomas," said the brown eyed stranger, "likely the sooner, the better. Though, judging by the expression on Miss Edwards's face, you may want to discuss the matter briefly with her."

Thomas, whose eyes had constantly strayed back to Charlotte, flushed at his companion's words.

"If I might have a word, Charlotte?" he asked quietly. He drew her to her feet and led her into the corner of the room.

"Of course, Thomas," she replied, and stood expectantly as he cleared his throat and adjusted the cravat that had apparently suddenly grown too tight. The men began to converse with each other in low tones, allowing the two a degree of privacy, with the exception of Mr. Bailey's obvious attempts to listen in. She was too happy to feel Thomas's hand on her arm to give Mr. Bailey more than a disdainful glance.

"I'm afraid I've been rather presumptuous, Charlotte, but it was really quite necessary." He paused, as if unsure what to say next.

"Go on, Thomas," she urged. "I'm sure whatever you've done was needed. I'm just so pleased to see you. I prayed and prayed that God would save me, and here you are! You could do nothing to upset me now, I assure you." She smiled brilliantly at him, or hoped she did, beginning to feel that, if it caused this man to notice her, becoming a damsel in distress was once again a thrilling and wonderful experience.

"You see, Charlotte, Sanders was truly set to marry you off to Mr. Warren to settle your uncles' debts, which you knew, I assume?" At her nod, he continued, "I was not at the manor as I was ordered to be when you were taken. Instead, I assumed that you would be taken to London, to Sanders himself, and so I came myself as well, on horseback. I thought, if your abduction was averted, no harm would be done, but I wanted to be prepared. As it was, having ridden hard, I arrived quite some time before the wagon transporting you did. Upon my arrival, I came straight to Sanders with a proposition."

He paused, taking a deep breath. The flush in his cheeks deepened to crimson before he spoke again. She waited while he searched for the right words, finding the newly reddened tips of his ears utterly adorable.

"Before I go any further, Charlotte, I must tell you something. I believe I have loved you from the first day I met you, when you came to my office with your novel, so shy and determined. Even if it had been terrible, I would have sought some reason to meet you again, so I was most pleased to have the excuse to write to you when I found the manuscript was truly exceptional. I admit, I was even thankful for the danger in which you found yourself because it allowed me to be near you again. As I have written to you and been with you these past months, my heart has become more and more firmly attached.

"I love everything about you, Charlotte. The very sight of you steals my breath away. You have become my dearest friend, and I want nothing more than to spend my life with you by my side. Will you ... could you consider marrying me?"

Charlotte's breath had caught the instant Thomas had begun to speak, and she seemed unable to fill her lungs. Gazing up into the face of her dear friend and seeing in his eyes the confirmation of his words mingling with nervous hesitation, she feared her racing heart might leap out of her chest at any moment.

"I would be honored to be your wife, Thomas. My heart has been yours since I met you, and the letters that we exchanged only showed me how safe it was with you. I love you and want nothing more than to marry you immediately!"

As she spoke, the light in Thomas's eyes grew brighter, and his face was transformed with a smile so infectious that Charlotte could not help mirroring it with one of her own. When she declared that she would indeed marry him, Thomas stepped forward, and, grasping her hands tightly in his, began to lower his face toward hers. Charlotte enthusiastically raised her face, breathlessly anticipating her first kiss. His lips were but a breath away from hers when a voice spoke.

"I take it that you have settled the matter then, Thomas," said his friend, wryly. "I hate to interrupt, but I'm afraid we must get on with things, before Miss Edwards's family learns of our plan."

"Of course," said Thomas, the flush in his cheeks still a flaming signal for all to see. Charlotte also felt her cheeks warming, seeing that the smiles of those who had come with Thomas were filled with a general amusement at her and Thomas. Sanders and Mr. Bailey were stoic and flat-eyed, as always. Despite her embarrassment, Charlotte had never felt as light and free as she did at that moment.

"If the two young people would step over here," declared the vicar, in a strong, clear voice that belied his frail appearance.

Thomas, never releasing Charlotte's hand, led her over to the vicar while the rest of the men simply watched. As they passed Mr. Sanders, Charlotte looked up and saw what she could only term a look of satisfaction on his face. She puzzled for a moment over his acquiescence to in the change in plans but, upon reaching the vicar, promptly forgot everything but Thomas. She turned to face him, and despite the brief shadow that flitted across her face at a thought, her appearance was utterly radiant with happiness.

"Dearly beloved," began the vicar, "we are gathered here today to join this man and this woman in holy matrimony ..."

Chapter
21

The arrival of an invitation of any sort created unbearable expectation in the Smythe-Poole home. When the morning post arrived, there lay, among the usual letters of business and pleasure, a heavy, embossed invitation bearing the crest of nobility. Louisa shrieked long and loud at the sight of it.

"Mother! Mother! Come quickly!" she cried.

Mrs. Smythe-Poole rushed into the front hall, her footsteps hurried as she made her way from the dining room.

"What is it, Louisa? I was in the middle of trying to talk some sense into our new cook. That woman has absolutely no concept of proper meals. Stew, indeed. How could stew possibly be construed as the food of gentry?"

"Oh, Mother, hush! Finally! We are included on the guest list of the Earl of Shrewsbury! It must have been that lovely interlude I had with their daughter, Catherine, at the Harrisons' ball last month. I fancied I made quite an impression."

Louisa fanned herself with the envelope, recalling the lovely interlude that had actually consisted of her curtsy and offer of a simpering greeting and inquiry as to the whereabouts of the young lady's eligible brother. This improper advance was sidestepped with such grace and dignity that Louisa failed to recognize the evasive maneuver, even after Lady Catherine excused herself to rejoin her husband.

With her daughter hovering close behind her, Mrs. Smythe-Poole carefully opened the seal on the envelope and unfolded the missive.

The elegant script was clear and to the point.

Mr. Poole, Mrs. Smythe-Poole and Miss Louisa Smythe-Poole,

It would give me great pleasure if you were to attend an afternoon tea I am giving in honor of my youngest son's recent return from the country. It will take place a week from Tuesday, on the 12th, at three o'clock in the afternoon. If you are amenable, I will send my carriage around for you at half past two. Please RSVP by the 10th of September.

Sincerely,

Lady Elizabeth Brooke

"I don't believe it," said Aunt Beatrice, "you're right, Louisa! Finally, we have gained the attention we deserve. Well, we must respond directly. —Graves! Oh, wait … confound it! What is the name of the latest one, Louisa? Rivers? —Rivers! Come here at once!"

Almost immediately, the sound of a heavy tread in the hallway announced the impending arrival of the Smythe-Pooles' recently acquired replacement for Graves. Though dressed formally and moving with the bearing of a trained butler, Elliot Rivers seemed more suited to the life of a soldier than a gentleman's servant. His large, muscular build and dark features seemed out of place for a man whose job practically demanded at least the illusion of refinement. There was also an awareness in his eyes and hard cast to his features that suggested his life had not been an easy one. In the month he had been with the Smythe-Pooles, however, his abilities had proven exemplary, but the dichotomy between his appearance and his position had not gone unnoticed by the young lady of the house.

Her mother would have been horrified if she knew exactly how much information Louisa had garnered regarding their newest employee. Despite growing up in a household that was obsessed with class and propriety, or perhaps because of it, Louisa had early on developed an unhealthy fascination with those men who epitomized everything her parents despised. Before the arrival of Rivers, she had pursued the stable lad, footman, and coachman, with little success. It appeared her quarry valued their positions more than the shallow attentions of a bored young lady of the manor, especially once it became clear that while she enjoyed flirting and occasional risqué embraces, she was not willing to compromise herself completely. Smiling idly to herself, Louisa reflected that her mother and father would certainly be horrified at the thought of their precious daughter with a servant, of all things. Something drew her inexorably to Rivers, sparking her interest to a far greater degree than her previous liaisons ever had.

Looking up, she saw that her mother had finished writing her reply, and was handing it to the butler. Turning away from Mrs. Smythe-Poole to proceed down the hallways, Rivers's eyes met Louisa's hungry gaze for a moment before he left the room. A gleam of interest lingered there, and his lips quirked. As quickly as it had appeared, the gleam was gone, and the impassive face of the servant was once again in place. Louisa watched his retreating back, turning plans over in her mind as to how she could surreptitiously come upon him alone. Her mother's strident voice pierced her thoughts.

"Now, Louisa, we must go and examine your wardrobe! I have a suspicion that you will need a new day dress for this, as there are likely to be many eligible young men of good breeding. You must look your best for them—oh, just wait until I tell your father!"

Hustling her daughter down the hallway, Mrs. Smythe-Poole missed the heated gazes exchanged between her daughter and the butler. Her chatter filled the air as she and her daughter made their way upstairs to Louisa's room. Down the corridor, Rivers lingered in the shadows, the letter held firmly in his grasp. He watched as the two women disappeared, his eyes never straying from Louisa. With her obvious interest and lush figure, she was an unexpected bonus with this latest job. His eyes flickered briefly at the thought of his employer, fully aware as to what his opinion of the young miss would be. This thought was all the prompting he needed to move out of the shadows and off to find one of the servant boys to deliver the letter he still held. Glancing down again at the envelope in his hand, he noticed the address. It appeared, he thought, that there was more in store for the Smythe-Pooles than they expected.

Robert, one of the two boys employed to run errands, caught sight of Rivers' face as he entered the kitchen. The streetwise little urchin was perceptive enough to see more in his eyes than the efficient workings of a butler's mind. In a second, though, Rivers's face was impassive as he handed the letter to the boy with the necessary instructions and then walked away. The lad wondered, as he shrugged into his coat and gloves, if he had imagined the self-satisfied gleam. Shaking his head, Robert opened the door and set off on his journey, his mind already miles away. Rivers would have to remain a mystery.

◠

The twelfth of September arrived not in the blaze of sunshine Beatrice had ordered, but with a steady, drizzling rain. The sound of Beatrice's and Louisa's horrified moans echoed in the upper corridors as they rose that morning. Immediate consultation between the two produced an altered plan for hair and clothing that would, they hoped, avert the disaster of frizzed tresses and muddy gowns. With his wife and daughter and their frantically working maids secreted in their rooms, Roland fled to his den to avoid any inadvertent introduction into the mysteries of the feminine world. Closing the door behind him, he breathed in the masculine aromas of cigar smoke and brandy, the combined scents reminding him that, despite increasing demands from wife and daughter, he was still head of his home.

Walking slowly to the desk, the man frowned as he recalled the last of the business that had taken place in the room. Gerald's pale, drawn face flashed into his mind, the obvious haggardness reflecting what he knew was the unfortunate state of his own features.

"Roland, we much do something!" Gerald had cried. "It's all falling apart, everything! Sanders must have something up his sleeve, or he would never have forgiven our debt. It's not in his nature. Do you ... do you think he means to exact his payment in blood instead? Perhaps he means to catch us off our guard!"

"Off our guard? Are you an utter fool, man?" Roland remembered every word exactly as he had stated it. "We have no guard! There is no reason for what Sanders has done, nothing we can comprehend anyway. Just accept that we are pawns in his game, and it currently suits his purposes to release us from our obligation. I, for one, am not asking any questions."

Gerald had simply stared at him, fear crawling across his face. "If we were wise, brother, we would make arrangements to leave town immediately. You know this."

Roland knew full well that his brother-in-law was correct, but he also knew that there was nothing short of an army that would convince his wife and daughter to uproot themselves from Society and journey willingly into the obscurity of country life. Gerald was in similar circumstances himself, but his fear was great enough that Roland believed he might actually try to make a run for it.

"We cannot show such ingratitude to Sanders, Gerald. We must continue to play his game as long as we can, in the hopes that he would rather use us than …"

He trailed off, both men fully aware of the alternative. Seeing that there was nothing to be gained from staying, Gerald had left shortly after, his every movement betraying his disturbed thoughts.

Sitting at his desk, Roland laid his head in his hands. *Charlotte*, he thought. It was all her fault. If she had walked in at that moment, he could not have been held responsible for what he would have done. What had been dislike and resentment before had now become, in the blackness of his heart, a deep, abiding hatred for the young woman he called his niece. Long practice had him refusing to blame himself for any of his current difficulties, and the girl's very existence had soon grown from a minor irritation to the focus of his loathing.

Curling his lip in disgust, he thought of her behavior the night of Mr. Warren's visit. It had been astonishing that Warren had even wanted the dried-up, sallow-faced spinster—and she refused him! The ungrateful chit! She didn't deserve the air she breathed … well, he assumed she breathed. With Sanders, there was no guarantee of that. The thought of her possible demise brightened his face as he rose from his chair.

The sounds of rustling and chatter in the hall alerted him to the impending arrival of his wife and daughter on the main floor, and his stomach was reminding him he had not yet breakfasted. Perhaps this day, he thought, would bring something better than the last, a step higher in Society, a step further toward prestige and recognition. It could not very well bring something much worse, he thought, idly twirling a pen before setting it down on his desk. Crossing to the door, he inhaled one last time before bracing himself for the onslaught of gossip and perfume that would quickly chase away the calm of his study.

At the sight of his wife and daughter walking into the breakfast room, Roland reminded himself that they were worth it all. He hoped his worthless, sniveling brother-in-law realized that—or they were both doomed.

⮂

Seated in the parlor, Beatrice, Roland, and Louisa anxiously awaited their transportation to Lady Brooke's afternoon tea. Tensions mounted as the hour drew nearer, and the already sharp tongues of the ladies grew even more finely honed.

"Louisa, dear, stop fidgeting," said Beatrice, irritably. "You don't want to loosen the stays of your corset any more than necessary. This tea could be our opening into the upper echelons of Society, and who knows what eligible men will be there! Please, try to remember what I've taught you. You can display your assets, so to speak, discreetly, but you must not compromise yourself. Your virtue is a commodity we can use to bargain."

Louisa would likely have indulged herself in some well-chosen words for her mother had her mind not still been focused on Rivers's manly physique and her detailed plans for what she wanted to do with it. As it was, she barely heard the diatribe Aunt Beatrice had launched. Her silence further spurred her mother into the land of shrews, and the rant became even louder.

"And you," cried the woman, pointing at her husband, "sitting there, reading your newspaper as though this is any other day! Do neither of you understand how important this is?"

The sound of her labored breathing filled the room, and if the rising color in her face was any indication, the stays of Beatrice's corset were in more danger than her daughter's. Her hysteria could have reached unheard-of heights had Rivers not discreetly knocked and stepped into the room.

"The carriage has arrived, milady. Is there anything else you require?"

"Ah, Rivers, thank you. Come, Roland, Louisa—quickly now! We mustn't keep Lady Brooke waiting."

The maid in the hallway approached, cloaks already over her arm, overshoes laid out on the floor. Helping the ladies into their outerwear while Roland shrugged into his overcoat and took up his hat, she narrowly escaped being bowled over by Beatrice's determined beeline for the door. As soon as the ladies had passed outside, she fled from the hallway to recover from her almost injurious experience. Rivers opened the door and held it, watching the three figures made blurry by the rain as they approached and then climbed into the carriage.

As it pulled away, he was already turning to retrieve his own overcoat and hat, the carriage he had previously engaged coming into view as the other one disappeared down the street. Shutting the door firmly behind him, the butler quickly made his way to the waiting vehicle, ascending in a swift, graceful movement. With a slight jerk, the driver urged his horses onward, already informed of his destination. Rivers settled back on the seat, mentally reviewing his plan. Only time would reveal whether or not it would be successful.

Ahead of him, the Smythe-Pooles rode on, excitedly anticipating their entrance into high society, totally unaware of the web of deception now interwoven with their own. As the mother, father, and daughter drew closer to their destination, events were conspiring to bring long-buried secrets out into the open. Soon, there would be nothing left to hide. Soon, for someone, there would be nowhere left to turn.

Chapter

22

*T*homas had always admired his parents, but watching his mother as she supervised the preparation for their guests, he felt a fresh wave of affection wash over him. Lady Elizabeth Brooke was a small woman, with delicate features and the unconsciously regal bearing of an aristocrat. However, her appearance belied the apparently boundless reserves of energy she possessed. He could not remember a time when she had not seemed to flit from room to room, or person to person, like a good-natured fairy, her bubbly chatter adding to the sense of warmth that enveloped his childhood memories. Despite her sanguine nature, she had always had the ability to sense the emotions and undercurrents around her and was always willing to stop for a moment and listen quietly when someone needed her.

At the moment, though, she issued orders like a general, instructions liberally interspersed with encouragement when her wishes were carried out correctly. Hearing steps behind him, Thomas glanced back to see his father step into the parlor.

"She's extraordinary, is she not?" said his father, smiling.

"There is no one like her, Father," he said, grinning widely. "A good thing, since I think one whirlwind is terrifying enough."

His father roared with laughter, shaking his head at his son's insubordination. "You are fortunate she did not hear you say that, Thomas," he said, wiping tears from his eyes.

"Hear him say what, my love?" asked his mother, her small, quick steps making little sound on the carpet.

"I was only declaring how incomparable you are, mother," said a straight-faced Thomas.

"Of course I am, dear," said his mother, placidly. "And where is our guest of honor?"

Lord Brooke winked at his wife. "I believe Catherine cornered her and whisked her away to the conservatory to get to know her a little better. She was quite excited to meet Charlotte."

Both parents watched in amusement as their son flushed bright red, nervously fiddling with his cravat. "Perhaps I should go and join them," he said hesitantly. He was more than a little wary of his sister's interrogative powers, employed successfully since childhood, and did not relish succumbing to them in front of Charlotte.

"Splendid, Thomas! Do remind them that it is almost half past one, and our guests are due to arrive very soon."

At the reminder of their guests, Thomas straightened and sighed. He could not afford to be distracted by his feelings just yet. It eased his heart a great deal to have Charlotte under his parents' roof, but until the situation with her family was finally resolved, he knew the shadow over their life together would remain.

"I will remind them, Mother," he said, leaning down to kiss her cheek. "Thank you for everything you've both done. It wasn't necessary. I could have found another way, without putting either of you in harm's way."

"Nonsense, Thomas! Your mother and I are having the time of our lives. Not much chance for adventure at our age, you know," exclaimed Lord Brooke, throwing an arm around his son.

"Well then," said Thomas, "I'll go and collect the ladies so we can all wait together." He turned and walked from the parlor, pausing to select a small sandwich from under a silver lid on his way past.

Watching fondly, his parents stood silently until he his footsteps had receded down the hallway. "Adventure at our age?" inquired Lady Brooke, raising an eyebrow at her husband.

"I was simply trying to set him at ease," mumbled Lord Brooke innocently.

"I only hope you can manage to stay awake until our guests have left," she replied, "given your advanced years."

Lord Brooke smiled sheepishly and shrugged before giving his wife a soft kiss.

"We are doing the right thing, aren't we, my dear?"

"Of course, my love. He's our son, and Charlotte is a dear girl. She needs to know she is part of our family now." Turning, Lady Brooke caught sight of a maid setting a silver tray on a table next to a low-lying sofa. "No, Anne, not that one," she cried, already moving toward the girl.

Thomas's father took one last amused look before moving toward the door himself. Only time would tell what the afternoon would bring. He only hoped they were ready for it.

⁓

The London townhouse kept by Thomas's family was not overly imposing in appearance, but the nobility of the residents struck misgivings in the hearts of the arriving visitors. As the carriage rolled down the drive toward the door, Beatrice gave her husband and daughter a brief going-over to ensure they would make the best possible entrance. The tapping of her husband's cane as he stared out the window had nearly driven her mad, but she had appeased herself by noting his cravat was neatly tied in the latest fashion, and his gloves were spotless.

Louisa looked well, even if her dress was cut rather daringly for daytime. Beatrice normally encouraged her modiste to cut her daughter's gowns to display herself most advantageously, but she had observed that Lady Brooke and her daughters tended to dress in a more conservative fashion. Well, too late to do anything about it now, she thought, and besides … it was the young son of the earl, along with any of his close friends who might be present, that her daughter was meant to impress. Men were so predictable, she mused, glancing over at her husband. After all, it had not been her lively conversation that had gained the attentions of Roland Poole. The trick, she thought, was to catch the man before he realized it was not his own idea. It had infuriated her to no end when Lord Charles Edwards had practically tripped over his own feet pursuing her sister Amelia. Beatrice had never considered her slim, quiet sister to be much competition, especially after she had gotten involved with those religious fanatics and their open-air meetings.

Humiliation fueled Beatrice's fury when she recalled the way she had tried to lure Charles away from her sister, especially the outcome of her invitation for a moonlit garden tryst at one of the many balls they had all attended. After refusing to even escort her out for a breath of fresh air, he'd had the nerve to preach at her! The pitying, knowing look in his eyes was beyond endurance. Beatrice still fumed whenever she remembered his disinterest, preferring the nunlike dress and behavior of her sister. Well, she thought, he'd deserved the end he had received, as had her sister. It was only a shame that Charlotte had not been with them that night.

The slight jerk of the carriage stopping interrupted Beatrice's reverie. The rain had stopped during their journey, leaving muddy puddles as the only real danger to their apparel. A quick last look at her daughter assured her that every hair was in place, and Louisa confirmed that her mother was also in fine form. Fears allayed, the three alighted from the carriage and made their way through the remaining mist toward the entrance to the house.

The housekeeper and butler stood waiting to admit them and announce their arrival to the Brookes. Cloaks and coat quickly shed, the small party followed the middle-aged butler through a series of hallways into a bright, airy conservatory, where he stopped, drew himself up, and announced them as they followed him in.

"Mr. Roland Poole, Mrs. Beatrice Smythe-Poole, Miss Louisa Smythe-Poole."

Chapter 23

*F*rances Smythe gazed over her children with an air of smug satisfaction. They were, in her opinion, possessing of every virtue needed to succeed in their grasping climb to the highest levels of society. Though she was not considered a beauty, her strong features and forceful nature made her memorable, if nothing else. Frances had learned early on in her youth that her intelligence could be either her greatest asset or her greatest hindrance. Choosing to exploit this gift, she had cultivated a close friendship with the young Beatrice Smythe, whom she met at Miss Harrington's Finishing School for Young Ladies. The younger sister, Amelia, had not been worthy of her notice, as she correctly perceived that Beatrice held the most sway in the ambitious, faintly aristocratic Smythe family.

Obtaining an introduction to her dear friend's elder brother had been simple, and if she did say so herself, the poor man never had a chance. She had used every sly hint and subtle flattery necessary to convince him that she was the best possible choice of wife. It had helped that Gerald was sharp; as interested in growing finances through her connections as he was in romance. She had even managed to make him believe she was madly in love with him, a fine act indeed. It was not until the marriage ceremony had taken place that she allowed herself even a moment to let her guard down. Amazingly enough, she had actually come to love the fool over the past twenty years of life with him, and it appeared that he still loved her as well. Of course, that did not mean that she had any intention of altering her plans. Because his ambitions were so akin to hers, it had never before been an issue. Now, however, things had changed.

"Frances, you do not understand!" cried her husband. "He's just stringing me along, and Roland too! There's no telling if or when Sanders will decide that he does not need us any longer. We must leave the city and find a quiet place miles from here where he will not see or hear of us and be reminded of the debt we owed."

"Gerald, would you cease your whining? Now you said that someone paid your debt. Who? And why would Sanders have any cause to harm you now? You owe him nothing anymore."

Pretending that this was the first she had heard of Gerald's and Roland's debt to Sanders, Frances fixed an exasperated expression on her face. There was no way she and the children were leaving London.

"Frances, my dear," he began, his tone tense, "the man is not sane! For twenty-five years, I have lived under his shadow. I know what he is capable of! Think of my sister and her husband! That was his work, I am convinced! It was a warning, and it was received loud and clear."

Coming over to him, Frances sat on the arm of his chair and put her arms around her husband. Leaning close to his ear, she murmured, "Things are different now, Gerald. Twenty-five years ago there was no police force, no real accountability to the law. He would not dare do to us what he did to them—and besides, your account with him is settled. Please, my darling, we cannot leave because of what might be. Horace and the girls are poised for their entrance to Society! It is everything we wanted for them, and for us! Do not ask them to leave all this because of something that will likely never come to pass."

Gerald sighed and leaned into her. She smiled in triumph as she rested her chin on his head.

"Do you really think so, Frances? If you truly believe it … what you say makes sense. We will stay, for the time being. But any threats, and we go, do you understand me?"

"Of course, darling. You always know best."

⟡

The Smythe-Pooles had only just been seated and exchanged pleasantries with their host and hostess when the butler cleared his throat at the doorway.

"Mr. Gerald Smythe, Mrs. Frances Smythe, Miss Mariah Smythe, Miss Elsa Smythe, and Mr. Horace Smythe."

Looking up in surprise, Beatrice, Roland, and Louisa took in the familiar figures at the entry. Judging by their expressions, it was apparent that neither family had been aware of the other's invitation. Though bragging about social success was a hallmark of both families, both men's recent preoccupation with Sanders had distracted their wives so much that they had paid no visits since before their invitations to tea had been received. Smiling at the realization that his sister and family had made the guest list, Gerald temporarily forgot his fears and moved to greet them.

"Lord Brooke, Lady Brooke. Thank you sincerely for your kind invitation. Beatrice, Roland, and Louisa, it is wonderful to see you again!"

"Welcome to our home, Mr. Smythe," said Lord Brooke. "Please, you and your family be seated."

"We are truly honored by your attention," simpered Frances. "May I present my children? Mariah, Elsa, and Horace, Lord and Lady Brooke. We last met at Lord Dartmouth's ball last month, I believe?"

"Yes, it's quite possible," said Lady Brooke, "though we do not attend as often as we used to, now that our daughters and eldest son are married and settled. However, Lord Brooke and I do enjoy a ball every now and then, as do our children."

"And your youngest son? He is still unattached?" asked Frances, jumping on the opportunity to inquire about the eligible bachelor.

"Oh, he does not really enjoy Society," stated Lord Brooke, a slight grin on his face, as he neatly sidestepped the second question. "He prefers the company of his books and lives in relative obscurity. He is somewhat eccentric in that sense. However, he should be joining us shortly with Mr. Hayes, an old friend of his."

At his last bit of news, the ladies seated in the conservatory grew visibly more excited. Beatrice and Frances looked fondly at their daughters as all three sat up straighter, smoothing their skirts and patting their hair. Horace simply sat back, a practiced expression of boredom on his dissipated face. While the young ladies not so discreetly adjusted their dresses and their practiced coy expressions, Lady Brooke gave the order for Anne to serve the tea. Moving gracefully among the guests, the young maid began handing out a cup to each one.

At the sound of a throat clearing, everyone looked up. The butler, Adams, stood in the doorway once more. "Lord Thomas Brooke, Lady Charlotte Edwards, Mr. Jonathan Hayes, Mr. William Sanders."

Dead silence followed his announcement. It was broken only by the piercing sound of china shattering on the tile floor of the conservatory as Beatrice slipped to the floor in a limp swoon.

Chapter 24

"Anne, my smelling salts, please," said Lady Brooke, calmly, rising quickly and moving toward her unconscious guest. As her visitors watched, still stunned, she gently patted Beatrice's face to bring her round. With a small moan, Beatrice slowly opened her eyes to find herself face to face with her esteemed hostess. Color suffused returned to her cheeks as she spoke.

"I am most profoundly sorry, Lady Brooke. I have no idea what came over me."

"There is no need for apology, Mrs. Smythe-Poole. It appears you have had a shock. Please, allow me to help you to your seat."

Unnoticed by Beatrice, Lady Brooke's eyes were twinkling with suppressed mirth over the woman's response to Charlotte's appearance. Still, she was gentle and concerned as she helped Beatrice settle herself next to Roland on the sofa. Having seen to Beatrice's comfort, Thomas's mother turned toward the door where the most recently announced guests still waited.

"Thomas, Charlotte, please, come seat yourselves over here, beside me. Jonathan, if you and Mr. Sanders would not mind sharing this garden bench?"

Thus directed, everyone was seated and served within minutes. Gerald and Roland had shrunk visibly, eyes to the floor, as Mr. Sanders had passed by with a faint smile. Louisa, Mariah, and Elsa, while surprised at their cousin's appearance, were more interested in casting flirtatious glances toward the young men. Only Mr. Sanders responded, leisurely scanning the obvious attractions displayed by each of the three young misses. Beatrice and Frances were far too busy trying to determine Charlotte's relationship to the Brookes to notice Mr. Sanders's lascivious attentions to their daughters, though they would doubtless have celebrated the clear evidence of a man's interest in any one of their girls. Lord Brooke observed his guests with interest before addressing Charlotte's uncles.

"You, of course, know Lady Charlotte, daughter of Lord Charles Edwards and your sister, his wife, Amelia," said Lord Brooke, conversationally, "but may I present my son, Thomas, his dear friend Mr. Jonathan Hayes, and Mr. William Sanders. Thomas and Charlotte are just recently engaged."

"Engaged?!" cried Frances, completely losing her composure for the first time in over twenty-five years. "They are engaged to be wed? But she was to marry Mr. Warren! She must marry Mr. Warren!"

Her eyes flew to Mr. Sanders, the fire in her gaze almost palpable. Breathing deeply, she visibly calmed herself before speaking again.

"That is, I was given to understand that my dear niece was already engaged. My husband informed me of her impending marriage to her beloved Mr. Warren over six months ago. We believed she was in the country, for her health, as she prepared her trousseau."

Composure regained, she sent a look of affected confusion toward Charlotte that almost masked the hatred underneath. Twenty-five years of practice had made her the consummate actress.

Charlotte turned to her with a tight smile. "No, Aunt, it appears you were misinformed. I was only told of my 'engagement' when Mr. Warren, whom I had never met, came to dine at Uncle Roland's home on my birthday. When I refused him, I was told that I was to marry him anyway. I ran away, Aunt Frances, six months ago, to escape being sold by my own family into a life of servitude to an evil and lecherous man."

She paused, shuddering involuntarily at the memory of her would-be husband. Thomas reached over and took her hand, stroking it gently, and she managed another small smile at her aunt.

"Well, dear niece," exclaimed Frances, "I had no idea. Why did you not come to us? I cannot believe that your uncle could have been so cruel. Roland," she said, admonishingly, "what were you thinking, springing such a thing on Charlotte like that? You should have come to us, Charlotte. We would have protected you, my dear."

Though her voice hinged on sincerity, Charlotte's practiced ear could detect the disingenuousness underneath. She was especially impressed with the look of disbelief and censure that Frances cast at her brother-in-law. Her aunt, she thought, might have enjoyed a very successful career on the stage.

"Perhaps," came the voice of Lord Brooke, "we should take a moment to enjoy our tea before continuing? It appears my soon-to-be daughter-in-law may need a moment to collect her thoughts. After all, I understand she has been through quite an ordeal. It takes a woman of great inner strength to deal with such trials."

He glanced fondly at Charlotte, and she smiled shyly back. Thomas's parents had welcomed her with open arms, and his siblings were already very attached to her. Though they had only known her for a week, Thomas had written them regularly of his growing feelings for her, describing her strength of character in the most flattering terms. However, Lord Brooke was right—she needed to collect her thoughts before she continued. Giving a nod of acquiescence, she lifted her teacup to her lips, her other hand still tucked safely in Thomas's. Catching Louisa's eyes fastened on the expression of affection, Charlotte smiled inwardly. *No matter*, she thought. *They cannot hurt me anymore.* However, Louisa's were not the only eyes fixed on Charlotte. There was another pair, evil and hateful thoughts lying banked behind their placid stare. Not all was as safe or secure as Charlotte imagined.

⮎

After what seemed to be the longest tea time ever endured, Lord Brooke cleared his throat. "Well, it seems we are all refreshed and ready to unravel this mystery. Perhaps, Mr. Smythe-Poole, you could explain yourself? Or maybe Mr. Sanders could shed some light on the situation?"

The fear on Roland's face was apparent to everyone in the room. He opened his mouth to speak, but no words emerged. Looking at her husband's gaping mouth with disgust, Beatrice said coolly, "There is nothing mysterious about it, Lord Brooke. We were concerned about our niece's future, as no man had offered for her, and she showed little initiative in the area. She is, after all, twenty-seven years old, and her parents are long dead. We tried to raise her properly, care for her as our own, but, I hate to say, Charlotte was a difficult child, ungrateful and sullen, disappearing for hours at a time with no explanation. I hoped, once she reached womanhood, that she would become more ladylike, as my Louisa is." She beamed indulgently at her daughter, only to see her busily picking sandwich crumbs from her mostly exposed bosom, bored with what was going on around her.

Beatrice winced involuntarily before continuing. "As I was saying, we were concerned about Charlotte's future. Her odd and unsociable habits continued to emerge as she aged. When my husband heard that Mr. Warren was looking to take a wife, he went about arranging a comfortable situation for her. Everything was going so smoothly, but then Charlotte, ungrateful wretch as always, not only rejected Mr. Warren but ran away, taking most of our staff with her. We kept it quiet, hoping she would come to her senses. Mr. Warren had fallen in love with her at first sight. He was most distressed at her disappearance. So you see, she cannot be engaged to your son. She is already promised to another."

"Indeed," said Roland, finally finding his voice, faint though it was, "Mr. Warren has been most patient, but it is beyond time that you fulfill your obligations, Charlotte. Your parents, I am sure, would have wanted the same thing. It is tragic that they were killed in that carriage accident, long before you could remember them, but surely, as your guardian, I have a right to expect your compliance. I have paid for your upbringing, which was no little expense, particularly since you could not find a husband of your own. You are in my charge until you marry Mr. Warren. You should be appreciative of the lengths to which I went for you!"

The room was very still as the occupants processed this information. Charlotte's grip on Thomas's hand had tightened so much that her knuckles were dead white, her eyes staring unfocused at the floor. Though his muscles were cramped and painful, Thomas barely noticed. His rage was ice in his veins as he thought of Charlotte's unhappy past. He was about to defend her when she raised her head, eyes glittering. He thought she looked magnificent, her color high and her posture regal as she prepared to address her uncle.

Chapter
25

illiam Sanders was enjoying himself more than he had in ages. Prior to his invitation to the Brooke estate, his forays into Society had been limited to the lowest rungs. He knew, of course, that this one invitation would not smooth signal his entrance into the kind of circles the Brookes occupied, but it would raise his stock in the eyes of the so-called polite world. He would have far greater access to the pocketbooks of the gentry and the charms of the ladies. None were so easy to deceive as those men raised to believe they could not lose, and no women so easy to seduce as their bored, neglected young wives. Things were coming together very nicely indeed.

He watched, amused, as Roland and his wife dug themselves in deeper and deeper. He had been unwillingly impressed by Charlotte's courage, though he would have had her killed without blinking had it served his purposes. He had no fondness for either Roland or Gerald. In fact, he thought idly, perhaps he would have them removed, so to speak, as a wedding gift for the young couple. He eyed the two gentlemen, imagining creative ways to hasten them to that last, rattling breath he so enjoyed hearing before the silence of death was complete. Knives were so very versatile.

"While I cannot say I appreciate your plans or trust your motives, Uncle, Aunt, I would like to give you the benefit of the doubt and imagine that you simply wanted me off your hands. However, my abduction by Mr. Sanders's associates," said Charlotte, nodding toward the man in question, "and the subsequent events incline me to suspect that something more than simply ridding yourselves of the spinster niece was at the heart of your actions."

Charlotte's calm tone and frank gaze belied the increasing anger rushing through her. Though the hurt she had grown up with no longer held sway, fresh rage at the blatant cruelty of their plan made it difficult to keep from screaming and cursing at the man and woman who had, for lack of a better term, raised her. Her gaze moved to Gerald and Frances, and she shivered involuntarily at the pure hostility in Frances's stare. Though she had always known that Frances did not like her—really, none of her family did—the hatred her aunt was trying to mask seemed an excessive reaction to a thwarted engagement where the only benefit was casting off the unwanted family baggage.

On the other hand, it didn't surprise her that Gerald seemed more irritated than vindictive. Her uncle, though he possessed little fondness for her, had never seemed to hate her the way the other three did. She was just an imposition in his otherwise orderly world. A quick peek at her cousins showed as much confusion as interest, and more boredom than anything, at the unfolding drama.

Charlotte's reverie was broken by Gerald's plainly nervous voice. "I, ah, must admit that Roland, your aunts, and I may have seemed uncaring, my dear Charlotte, but that simply isn't so. You see—well …". He trailed off, embarrassed at his own inability to explain the situation.

"For heaven's sake, Gerald," cried Frances, "be quiet! It's time the truth came out." She addressed herself to the general company. "My husband and Roland Poole made a foolish mistake twenty-five years ago," she said calmly. "They borrowed a large sum of money from Mr. Sanders here in order to have enough capital to invest in Gerald's manufacturing plant. Though the plan has been successful, and they were paying back the loan as quickly as possible, needless to say, after twenty-five years of small payments, Mr. Sanders was getting tired of waiting. Only he can tell you why he was even willing to wait that long."

"I had my reasons," said Sanders, quietly. "They are none of your concern."

Frances, still cool and composed, continued. "So you see, when Sanders informed Roland that Mr. Warren desired to marry again and that, if Roland and Gerald would arrange the marriage to Charlotte, he would forgive the rest of the debt, the two men agreed. They really had no choice. The alternative was to come up with the remainder of the money within the week, and that was quite impossible. Besides, he seemed a decent enough man. We could not expect to find a better one, not for Charlotte. It was astonishing anyone wanted her at all."

Though Charlotte and her friends already knew about Sanders, it was a shock to hear it straight from Frances's lips. Not until after they had left Sanders's office had Thomas explained everything to Charlotte, including the fact that he had paid the remainder of the debt in order to convince Sanders to release her. He absolutely refused to tell her the amount of money involved, but she assumed it was quite substantial. It took the better part of the next day to convince her that he considered it well spent for him to have her as his wife and that her freedom was worth every farthing. By the time she had retired for the evening, safely ensconced in his family's London town house, she not only had decided to include her experiences, somewhat embellished perhaps, in the plot of her next novel, but also had acquired firsthand experience with swooning, abduction, blackmail, and the romantic embrace. The last one was her favorite.

She looked up at Thomas as he squeezed her hand, still in awe of the fact that she was finally loved, and by so fine a man. She could hardly wait until they were finally married. Though they had gone through a brief ceremony in Sanders's office, Thomas hadn't had time to procure a special license. By the time they had reached his family's townhouse, Charlotte knew that, despite wanting to be Thomas's wife more than anything, she wanted a real wedding, in a real church, not a second hurried ceremony just to make matters legal. She was relieved when Thomas said, with a broad grin, that his mother probably would throw a fit if they didn't have a big wedding anyway. She snuck a peek at him again, and, laughter lighting her eyes briefly, squeezed his hand to let him know she'd caught him sneaking a look at her too. The warmth of his touch made her feel safe, settled, and, finally, free.

Chapter

26

"It seems to me," said Lord Brooke, pinning Charlotte's guardians with a hard stare, "that, if you were indeed trying to find a suitable husband for your niece, you did a very poor job of it. My son informs me that his friend and associate here, Mr. Hayes, was aware of Mr. Warren's reputation long before he was connected with your family. It appears that not only is the man given to excess in drink, cards, and loose women, but his first two wives perished under rather questionable circumstances. I have no idea whether you can tell me honestly that you were not aware of his proclivities, but I am certain, given the information I have just imparted, that you would, of course, no longer deem him a suitable candidate for marriage to your niece, regardless of your debt or fear of retribution.

"I," he said, emphasizing the pronoun, "would not even give Mr. Warren the honor of meeting a daughter of mine, let alone marrying one."

Gerald, already pale and sweating nervously, lost what little color remained in his face as his eyes darted guiltily between his wife, sister, and brother-in-law. Roland managed to achieve a more convincing semblance of stoicism, though failing to affect innocence. The faces of the two aunts, however, appeared to be completely wiped clean of anything other than mild curiosity.

"I do wish we had been in possession of that information when the match was established," said Frances. "Of course, Charlotte would never have been given to Mr. Warren had we been aware of his flawed character. In any case, it matters little now, as she is obviously under your protection."

As she uttered the last sentence, she glanced at her companions, who were all expressing varying degrees of agreement through nods and murmured assurances. Though each of Charlotte's guardians seemed ready to agree to Lord Brooke's wishes, the resentment they felt was easily apparent to their niece. She couldn't understand why they were still so bitter. The debt was paid, and she was off their hands. That's what they wanted, wasn't it?—although the number of grudges she had watched her family hang on to was indeed substantial. Why, she mused, prosaically, would they begin treating her any better now? She had thwarted their plans, and if their past behavior was any indication, that should be enough to secure their rancor for the next twenty-five years.

"Now that it appears we have sorted out the … misunderstanding," said Thomas, placing deliberate emphasis on the last word, "perhaps we can take the rest of this time together to celebrate my engagement to your niece."

Charlotte decided to make one last attempt to clear the air and repair some of the damage. "I declare, I have had enough talk of Mr. Warren to last a lifetime. Let us agree, then, that I am to marry Thomas and am very happy. Be pleased for me, Aunts, Uncles, Cousins? I do so want your blessing.

Her erstwhile guardians nodded grudgingly, Roland mumbling an unintelligible affirmation.

"Come now," invited Lady Brooke, "let's forget about all this and simply enjoy a nice cup of tea together. Tell me, Mrs. Smythe-Poole, where did you get the fabric for your gown? It's such a charming shade of lavender."

At Lady Brooke's insistence, tea was resumed, and conversation turned to generalities and niceties. Charlotte's cousins, silent during the entire exchange between the Brookes and their parents, now came alive with all the latest gossip. They had been rather bored by the whole discussion, as it had little to do with their own ambitions. Horace was quite unconcerned about whether Charlotte had to marry Mr. Warren, and the girls rather hoped she would so that Thomas would be eligible once more. Since this did not prove to be the case, they cast their attention fully on Mr. Hayes and Mr. Sanders. They giggled incessantly anyway, gossiping freely while Horace devoted himself to the sandwich tray and wished it was time to leave so he could go to his club and win back the money he'd lost last night at cards.

"If you will excuse me for a moment," said Charlotte, rising at a lull in the conversation with a mischievous gleam in her eyes, "there is something I need to write down for my next novel before I forget it. Perhaps you have been reading my serials in the *High Street Gazette*? I understand from Lady Brooke and her daughters that they have become quite popular. Thomas is planning to publish them as a collection, once the paper is through running them and my first novel is printed." Charlotte grinned at the horror on Beatrice's face. It was probably petty, she acknowledged, but to see that expression was immensely satisfying. "Oh," she exclaimed, "in case I forget to mention it later, you are all invited to our engagement ball as well. Lady Brooke is planning it."

Thoroughly enjoying the looks on the faces of her family, she swept from the room with a dramatic air she had often practiced in her youth but never had the chance to use. Lady Brooke smiled behind her hand while her husband, her son, and the two gentlemen with them grinned outright.

"What …?" began Gerald in a bewildered tone.

"Have some more tea, Mr. Smythe," said Lady Brooke, calmly. "She will return soon enough, I imagine. We are all quite proud of her literary success, as you must be. She is such a talented young woman."

Lady Brooke's eyes sparkled as she began to chat animatedly with the ladies about plans for the upcoming ball. Lord Brooke followed suit, regaling the men with tales of his latest hunting expedition at the country estate. Realizing that nothing could be done to salvage their original plans for Charlotte, her family threw themselves into socializing with vigor, determined to milk the connection with the Brookes for all it was worth. The conservatory was soon filled with chatter and laughter.

Down the corridor, in the library, Charlotte was so focused on digging through the drawers of a desk for paper that she did not hear the click of the French door opening behind her. It was the soft swish of air as it shut that alerted her to the presence of another person. Whirling around, she saw the figure of a large man, outlined by the bright sunlight at his back, reaching for a solid silver candlestick. She hurled herself to the side just in time to avoid the candlestick that hit the desk with a heavy thud, splintering the wood.

"You!" she cried, looking up at her attacker as she lay on the floor. "But how …?"

Her question was cut off as the candlestick was again raised and brought swiftly down toward her head, forcing her to roll to the side, her heavy skirts trapping her legs, making movement increasingly difficult. She slid frantically backward, looking for anything that could be used as a weapon. Seizing the letter opener from the desk, she stabbed blindly in the direction of her opponent, eyes closing as the arm swung the heavy, silver candlestick unerringly toward her skull. The sickeningly feeling of metal slicing through flesh and muscle made her eyes jerk open, staring in horror at the blood quickly soaking through the fabric covering her attacker's right arm. The candlestick dropped with a thud, and her opponent, clutching his injured arm, gave her one last glare before slipping out the French doors through which he had arrived.

Charlotte huddled on the floor with her skirts a tangled heap around her. She was still staring unseeing through the open door after him when Thomas found her ten minutes later, bloody letter opener still held tightly in her white-knuckled grip. With a cry of alarm, he ran to her, and after making sure that she was unharmed, he moved to the open French door, noting the large footprints in the wet grass outside. Other than those, there was no sign of anyone. Charlotte didn't take her eyes off the doors the entire time.

"Thomas," she said, as he dropped to his knees next to her and pulled her into his arms, "I believe I've got another idea for my next story."

"That's wonderful, darling," he said, careful to keep his voice even, "but first, do you think you could tell me who you stabbed?"

Charlotte finally looked at him, color returning to her face as her eyes refocused and shock receded. Leaning into his chest, she smiled grimly.

"I believe I can, Thomas. I believe I can."

Chapter

27

*L*ady Brooke lobbied long and hard, after Charlotte's family had departed, for another celebration to follow the ball. She already had a list of guests the length of her arm for a weekend of shooting, riding, and all-around frivolity at the country estate.

"Wouldn't it be wonderful, Robert?" asked Lady Brooke, her eyes shining with enthusiasm as she turned to her husband, "A weekend house party at the country estate in honor of the engagement! Now we'll have to have Lord and Lady Durham, the Caterhams, Charlotte's family—sorry about that, Charlotte, dear, but it can't be helped. It would be a terribly slight if we didn't include them."

Charlotte watched in awe as Thomas's mother rattled on, busily striding around the conservatory, ticking names off on her fingers. Lord Brooke and Thomas merely watched with the kind of long-suffering amusement that betrayed just how often Lady Brooke ran ahead with her plans before they could rein her in. It was, she mused, like watching a tiny terrier who has found a bone and refuses to give it up, regardless of entreaty, threat, or coaxing. Her determination aside, the sheer speed of Lady Brooke's mind was daunting as she reeled off the names of people to be invited, tasks to be done, and plans to be made.

Charlotte, though she loved Lady Brooke's attention and enthusiasm, had finally escaped to the sitting room attached to her chambers, where she spent that afternoon and the great part of the following days writing. Thomas did manage to coax her out for walking and rides through the park—and for one protracted shopping expedition with his mother and sisters, who talked her into buying a complete trousseau as well as ordering a ball gown, all on his account. Though Thomas didn't mind in the least, Charlotte informed him that she was beginning to feel like a kept woman, especially since he was the wealthy son of an earl.

"Perhaps," she said, pertly, "I would not find it so galling if I'd had more time to adjust to your situation. Of course, that would have necessitated your telling me your true identity sometime before we became engaged."

"Charlotte!" he replied in an aggrieved tone. "I wanted to tell you, but with everything going on … it just slipped my mind until after you were taken. Besides," he added with a roguish grin, "my first three wives were so thrilled to discover I had money that they didn't even mind my kept women. Of course, all that's in the past now, my darling. You are my one and only!" He bowed gallantly to her.

Charlotte's only response was a rather unladylike snort of derision as she shoved her fiancé away in mock disgust. Her attempt at righteous indignation would have been a great deal more convincing if she'd managed to keep her small smile of amusement hidden.

During the fortnight before the engagement ball, Charlotte's family tried heartily to increase their involvement in her upcoming marriage. Beatrice, Frances, and their daughters came to call frequently, doing their best to ferret out information as to which eligible bachelors would be present at the ball and whether or not an introduction would be possible. They also exerted every wile to convince her to return to their care until the marriage was to take place, becoming more and more demanding until Lord and Lady Brooke finally stepped in. After that point, outright calls for Charlotte's return became veiled, biting comments, always phrased delicately enough that it was impossible to call the women to account. Although it infuriated Thomas and his family, Charlotte simply shrugged off the insults and said they were nothing to which she was not accustomed and that it did not matter now that she was acquiring such wonderful in-laws.

Hesitant to cause more trouble for Charlotte with her family, the Brookes held their tongues but began to make plans for departure to the country estate for a brief respite with a few guests after the ball was over. Lady Brooke had emerged triumphant once again, garnering Charlotte's unending admiration, particularly since she had, in the midst of planning a country getaway with guests, also had her personal dressmaker sewing madly to make sure Charlotte's wedding gown would be ready for the ceremony set only two months after the ball. Charlotte and Thomas hadn't wanted to wait even that long, but Lord and Lady Brooke prevailed, saying that no proper wedding could be planned in anything less than two months. Given what Charlotte already knew of Lady Brooke's determined nature, it was easier to simply give in, allow her free rein, and devote herself to enjoying the results.

The only thing marring her happiness—aside from that fact that someone was trying to kill her, she acknowledged—was the absence of her all but adopted family in Kennington. Shortly after her rescue, Charlotte had dispatched a letter to Violet Hill Manor, letting her friends know that she was safe and sketching her plans to marry Thomas. There was much more she wanted to say, but she wanted to tell them in person.

It seemed to take forever for the response to arrive, but it finally came the morning of the ball.

Dear Charlotte,

We are all so happy to hear that you are to marry Thomas. Of course, I could have told you that he was in love with you while you were both here with us, but you would not have believed me anyway. It is better that he told you himself.

Your description of your abduction read like something out of your stories! Both Betsy and Eliza were on pins and needles while Graves read your tale out loud and were most impressed with your attempt to thwart Mr. Sanders' plan by rendering Mr. Bailey unconscious. Though it did not work, Betsy wishes me to convey that she believes it would be a most thrilling situation in your next story, where the tactic would naturally have its desired effect.

We have a surprise for you, Graves and I. It turns out you were not the only member of our household engaging in a romance. As you know, I have admired Graves greatly for many years and have loved him for most of that time. He informed me, the day we received your letter and knew you were safe, that he is in love with me as well! I could scarcely believe it, but he has since proposed marriage and, due to the constraints of respectability and our own desire to live holy lives, has taken rooms at the inn. We plan to marry in a quiet ceremony here in Kennington soon, and would love to have you and Thomas come to join us in celebrating, along with Mr. Hayes if he is free. I will not write the details of Graves's proposal, but suffice it to say, it was worthy of your most noble hero and, had he not already won my heart, would likely have secured it then and there.

Now for one last surprise. By the time you get this letter, we will likely already be in London preparing to join you at your engagement ball. Betsy and Eliza are staying here in Kennington to watch over the house. Betsy wants you to know that she was offered a formal position at the village school, and has accepted. She is very much enjoying her role as schoolmistress and appears to have caught the eye of one of the local farmers. He is a good man, and time will tell if he manages to win her affections. She and Eliza find much enjoyment in village life and seem determined to stay on with us here at Violet Hill Manor after Graves and I are married. I am, of course, very satisfied with their decision. Graves and I look forward to seeing you very soon, my dearest Charlotte. There is something that Graves wishes to tell you regarding your parents, but he says it will wait until we see you in London.

All my love,
Mary Brown

"Thomas! Thomas! Read this!" cried Charlotte, running swiftly down the stairs from her room to the library. "Graves and Mrs. Brown are coming here to London, and they are to be married! Can you believe it?"

She stopped short in the doorway as she saw Thomas. She laughed in delight as she hurried to greet the couple standing next to him.

"Graves!" she exclaimed, "Mrs. Brown! You're here already! Thomas, did you know they were coming?" She threw her arms around Graves, laughing as he awkwardly patted her back, and then moved on to embrace Mrs. Brown.

"Yes, I knew, Charlotte," said Thomas. "My mother sent an invitation directly after our tea with your family, and it included an offer of lodging in our home while they are in London. However, she swore me to secrecy, as she wanted their presence here to be a happy surprise for you. Did it work?"

"It is a most happy surprise, Thomas! I must thank your mother immediately. Oh, have you met Lady Brooke yet?" she asked Graves and Mrs. Brown.

"Not yet, Charlotte," said Mrs. Brown, "but we are looking forward to it, and to the ball this evening. I've never been to a ball before. I do hope I don't embarrass myself too badly."

"You could never be an embarrassment, Mary," said Graves, his eyes softening as he looked at her, "and besides, I'm likely to be the one to shame us all with my two left feet."

"Never fear, Graves," said Thomas, chuckling, "if your dancing is that poor, I will be sure to call everyone's attention to it. Then you can relax."

"Thomas!" said Charlotte, trying vainly to suppress her amusement.

"I was just trying to help, Charlotte," he said with an innocent smile.

"Help, my foot," she muttered. "You are incorrigible. Of course, I have always been unwillingly attracted to such roguish charm. It complements my feminine wiles so nicely."

Graves and Mrs. Brown watched, amused, as the two bantered back and forth. It was wonderful to see them so in tune with each other, temporarily forgetting the danger they all knew still lurked in the shadows.

"I hate to interrupt," came a voice from the doorway, "but I need to speak to all of you regarding our plans for this evening."

Lord Brooke walked into the room, followed by his wife. After introductions to their guests were made, Lord Brooke bade them all sit down while they sorted out the strategy for the evening.

"Mr. Graves, I assume, from the information I received from you, that there are some facts about Charlotte's parents that need to come to light? Would you be so kind as to share them with us so that we know exactly what we are dealing with?"

"Of course. I shared some of this with Charlotte while we were still in Kennington, but I have come to the decision that she—along with you, as her soon-to-be family—should be in possession of all the facts. There are dangers, Charlotte, of which you are yet unaware, connections between your family and the underworld of London that have not been exposed. Your aunts and uncles have not given up, Charlotte. You must be continually on your guard."

He stopped, trying to decide how to proceed.

Charlotte cleared her throat. "But we already know about their dealings with Sanders and the money my uncles owed." She stopped, looking curiously at Graves's sober face. Sensing that what she was about to hear would be extremely unpleasant, she reached over and took Thomas's hand. "Please, Graves—what is it?"

Lord Brooke cleared his throat. "I have a suspicion," he said, "that this has to do with the deaths of Lord Charles and his wife?"

"Yes," said Graves, softly, "It begins with them."

Chapter

28

"Thirty years ago," said Graves, "I came into the service of your father's family, Charlotte. I was Lord Charles's valet when he was a young man, before he met your mother. At the time I arrived in the Edwards home, Charles had begun to frequent various religious meetings and open air revivals, which caused a rift between him and the rest of the family, who would have preferred he occupy his time at the club, frequenting balls and the theatre—more acceptable activities for someone of his station in life. As his valet, I sometimes accompanied him on overnight trips to these meetings, and he often invited me to attend with him. I soon felt the need to give my life to Jesus Christ and did so only two days before your father also gave his life to God. The decision he made seemed to dissolve the class boundaries between us, and Charles and I soon became like brothers, though I remained in his family's employ."

Charlotte nodded, encouraging Graves to continue.

"It was at one of the revival meetings, where Charles and I had begun to volunteer and serve, that he met your mother, Amelia. She was just completing her education at a nearby finishing school and had become a believer two years previously, through the influence of a school chum. Watching them together, I could easily believe in love at first sight. They arranged for Charles to call upon her at the school, where he met your aunt Beatrice and her best friend, Frances, the woman who later became your aunt. I was with him as well, and watched as the two young ladies tried their best to lure him away, but he only had eyes for Amelia with her gentle ways and quiet heart.

"Once she was back home with her family, about a month after they met, Amelia and Charles embarked on the type of courtship that society and family expected. He called frequently, and they were inseparable at balls and soirees. His parents were not thrilled with his choice of bride, but the Smythes did have a strain of noble blood, and seemed to have some money. Amelia's family, for their part, were overjoyed, not having expected much of a match for your mother, Charlotte. They rather thought she was prim, dull, and dowdy and frequently told her so."

Graves stopped and looked at Charlotte, "They were wrong. She was lovely and modest, my dear. Her faith was genuine and totally foreign to her family."

His gaze encompassed the rest of the room again as he went on. "They were engaged within three months of their first meeting and married quickly and quietly soon after the banns were posted. There was some talk of the reasons behind such a hasty marriage, but as you were not born until more than two years later, it quickly quieted down. Charles's family continued to disapprove from afar, but the Smythes saw Charles as their door into high society. Your parents still appeared in Society occasionally, but they devoted the majority of their time to philanthropy: overseeing new schools and orphanages and the like.

"Charles was not heir to the Edwards fortune, but he had a very generous allowance. It allowed him to paint freely, making a decent living as an artist, while Amelia oversaw the keeping of their house in Berkeley Square. I accompanied Charles and Amelia to their new home once they married, and was promoted to the position of butler. I enjoyed serving your parents, Charlotte, and was more than happy to stay with them."

"It was not until after you were born that things turned ugly. The Smythes had asked for small loans throughout your parents' marriage, and Charles occasionally obliged, though not often. Your birth, the first grandchild for Charles's parents, went a long way toward repairing the breach that had been widening since Charles married your mother. They came to see you frequently and were delighted with you, as was your father's elder brother, heir to the family money. Sadly, on a trip back from their country estate, their carriage was held up by a highwayman, and they were all three killed. The highwayman was never caught. Remember, there was no police force then, only the Bow Street Runners, and they were stretched thin in London already. With their death, the money, the estate—everything in its entirety went to your father."

Charlotte gasped. "You mean we were rich?" she asked in disbelief. "How rich?"

"Over thirty thousand pounds altogether," said Graves, "but a yearly income of around ten thousand."

Charlotte looked sickly. "You can't be serious," she murmured, softly. Her agile mind had grasped at once that great wealth was a powerful motive for abduction, blackmail—and murder.

"What happened to the money?" asked Lady Brooke, thoroughly intrigued.

"Once Charles inherited, requests from the Smythes for loans grew in frequency. He was finally forced to declare that they would not receive anything more from him or from Amelia. He and Amelia had decided to give the majority of the yearly income to charities and would keep only enough to live on. There was a huge row! Beatrice and Frances railed and cried, while Roland threatened that he would find a way to make Charles pay.

"I found out afterward that Roland and Gerald had just borrowed ten thousand pounds to start up the manufacturing plant, fully expecting to pay off the debt with loans from Charles. When they found out that the money was going to charity, they were furious. It was that very evening that your parents were to attend a ball given by one of Charles's old friends. Your aunts and uncles were also invited and planned to attend. Witnesses placed all six of them at the ball, and while your parents left around one o'clock, the other four did not leave until four o'clock."

"Why is the time they left important, Mr. Graves?" asked Lord Brooke, furrowing his brow in confusion.

"It is important," said Graves, "because that was the night Charlotte's parents were murdered."

"Murdered!" cried Charlotte. "What do you mean, murdered? Were they not killed in a carriage accident?"

Thomas slid over and tucked his arm firmly around Charlotte. When Jonathan Hayes had discovered that the Edwardses had been stabbed, he'd told Thomas that he was certain the carriage accident was simply a cover for murder.

"Jonathan Hayes came to me privately shortly before you were kidnapped, Charlotte," explained Graves, "with information that finally confirmed what I have suspected for the past twenty-five years but could never prove. His father was a Bow Street Runner, and some of his former associates proved most helpful in locating information.

"It turns out that there was a witness that night—a young boy who helped his family out by carrying messages back and forth between some of the less principled businessmen in operation. He was on his way home when he saw your parents' carriage stopped near an alley in his neighborhood. Being familiar with the area, he was able to escape the notice of both the coachman climbing out of the carriage and another man waiting on the street.

"The boy watched as the coachman raised the whip and snapped it at the horses' heads. They reared and took off, the carriage weaving precariously behind them. Suddenly, he said, the harness snapped, causing the carriage to overturn and skid several feet. Apparently satisfied with their work, the two men hurried away from the wreck, down the street and around a corner, after which the boy heard the clatter of another carriage departing. He made his way to the carriage to see if there was anyone inside. What he found were the bodies of a gentleman and a lady, both stabbed cleanly through the heart."

Both Charlotte and Lady Brooke covered their mouths in horror, the young woman's eyes filling with tears. Mrs. Brown hurried over to pull Charlotte into her embrace, as Thomas rose to pace the room.

"Please go on, Graves. We need to know. Why did the boy never tell anyone what he found?"

"He was afraid—terrified that if he came forward, his family would be harmed. Remember, he was already living in one of the seedier areas of London and was well acquainted with the fate of those who interfered in business other than their own. Besides, he was only ten years old at the time. It was only through Mr. Hayes' connection with the London police and their predecessors that the boy, now fully a man, heard that someone was looking into the deaths of Charles and Amelia Edwards. Ironically, years earlier, he'd told his younger brother, who in his turn at length became a police officer.

"This Sergeant Wilson passed the information along to Mr. Hayes, who himself confirmed the details with the witness. Unfortunately, he was not able to give a detailed description of the two men, having had to keep to the shadows to remain undetected. All he could say was that the one on the street was very large and the coachman, tall and slim. There was no knife in the carriage, so the killer must have taken it with him.

"Sergeant Wilson told Mr. Hayes that the police will certainly take action if he can discover the killer's identity, but they do not have the manpower to investigate further themselves. However, they would love to get their hands on Mr. Sanders. They've been after him for quite a while, but he keeps slipping through their fingers. Both Sergeant Wilson and Mr. Hayes are fairly certain that he is up to his neck in the whole business."

"Mr. Hayes is quite certain that Sanders is at the bottom of all this," said a dry voice from the library doorway.

Jonathan Hayes walked into the room, offering a general greeting as he found a seat. Thomas turned to him and asked, "Certain, are you? But have you found any proof yet?"

"I have my father's testimony and records from his years as a Bow Street Runner, though there is nothing conclusive there. However, I believe I have discovered a link that may explain Sanders's motivation in his extended involvement with your family, Miss Charlotte."

"Do go on, Jonathan," urged Charlotte, eager to piece together the facts, to try to make sense of what seemed so senseless.

"Graves was able to give me the information I needed to uncover your attacker's involvement as well, Charlotte. Would you prefer to continue, Mr. Graves, or shall I?"

"No, go on, by all means," said Graves. "My voice could use the rest."

"While in Kennington, I inquired as to Lord Charles's financial state before his death. Mr. Graves informed me that though he had fully intended to give the majority of his fortune, per annum, to charity, he had not yet made the arrangements with his solicitor. His former will stood, which left everything, property and all, in trust to Charlotte upon her marriage. Mr. Graves told me he wanted to leave it to you outright, but, as you know, the law does not allow the passing of property and fortune from father to daughter, except for providing an allowance for your care. It was the allowance that kept your aunts and uncles and their children in style, while you were made to think you were penniless.

"They knew if you found out about the money and left, the allowance would go with you. It appears that your uncles were starting to worry that you had found some way to leave, and that's why they arranged your engagement to Mr. Warren. They already owed Sanders, and by affiancing you to one of his business associates, they killed two birds with one stone. Your money would pay off their debt, and in the marriage contract they would no doubt have been assured the same allowance from your income that they currently enjoy, while Mr. Warren would have access to the whole of your fortune."

Charlotte's mouth had been hanging agape in a most unladylike fashion through most of this recitation, but none of the others noticed, equally stunned in their own ways. Jonathan glanced around, amused at the reaction, and then continued on.

"I also spoke in some detail with my father regarding Mr. Sanders and his business. It seems he emerged on the social scene shortly after your parents' deaths and maintains a front there as a respectable businessman. Because he has money and has not tried to assume airs beyond that of a well-mannered gentleman, most of Society prefers not to pay too much attention to the odd rumor of his involvement in less than respectable undertakings. It is likely that blackmail also keeps some silent who would otherwise object to his presence.

"However, my father long suspected that Mr. Sanders was, in fact, one of two very successful burglars who managed to steal over ten thousand pounds' worth of silver and antiques before retiring from that particular endeavor. During this time, Mr. Sanders began—pardon my frank speech, ladies—to buy up brothels, taverns, and gaming halls. By the time my father retired, he estimated that Mr. Sanders owned more than three-quarters of the unrespectable businesses in London and makes a fortune from them."

"I see," said Lord Brooke, amazedly. "I have tried to ignore Society gossip, in general, for so long that I am woefully uninformed."

"I told you, my dear," said Lady Brooke, in a condescending tone, "while you looked down your nose at my thirst for news, that there was indeed value in knowing the thoughts and deeds of our peers. Perhaps now you will join my afternoon teas with the ladies?"

The appalled look on Lord Brooke's face was answer enough. Charlotte coughed into her handkerchief, vainly trying to suppress her laughter while Thomas grinned widely at his father.

Jonathan smiled at the older man, completely sympathetic to his dilemma, before resuming the story. "When Thomas came to me with Charlotte's situation, I decided to dig deeper than my father, or the police, had been able to. I found, by methods I would rather not get into," he said, winking roguishly at Lady Brooke, "a man who remembered Sanders from his childhood. It seems that my witness, Mr. Firth, lived next door to Mr. Clark, who is Sanders's most trusted companion, when they were all lads.

He informed me, much to my surprise, that there was a third person who ran with Sanders and Clark."

"Well, who is this third man?" asked Thomas, eagerly. "Is he still around?"

"It was not a man," said Jonathan, as if imparting something vital, "but a young girl by the name of Frances—Frances Sanders."

"Frances? You mean—could it be ... my aunt?!"

Everyone stared in redoubled amazement at Jonathan.

"But—it cannot be!" Charlotte exclaimed. "I was told my aunt was formerly a Miss Frances Wilson, closest friend of my Aunt Beatrice from their finishing school. Although," she went on, rolling her eyes with a sigh, "why should one more lie surprise me?"

"Your aunt was not born Frances Wilson, daughter of gentry in diminished circumstances. It is a false identity she assumed to gain entrance to the finishing school, and from there, to Society. She is Frances Sanders, younger sister and long-time business associate of William Sanders. She, her brother, and Mr. Clark, from what I could discover, plotted from childhood to better their situations by using their wits and skills learned on the streets. Through pickpocketing and minor theft, they made enough to establish Frances at Miss Harrington's Finishing School for Young Ladies, where she befriended your aunt Beatrice. She purposely cultivated that acquaintance, knowing the Smythe family was her best hope for a springboard into Society, given her lack of noble ancestry. However, she also employed her sly nature to listen at keyholes and eavesdrop on conversations, feeding information about the families of other schoolgirls to her brother. Mr. Sanders and Mr. Clark then had all the information necessary to either blackmail or burglarize, whichever would most expediently increase their fortune.

"By the time Frances left the school to marry Gerald, Sanders was well on his way to his current position in the London underworld, their connection buried along with the bodies of anyone who attempted to stop them. Mr. Clark remained on as Sanders's right-hand man, serving as his protection as well as his assassin. Mr. Sanders and Frances are the brains behind the operation, but Mr. Clark is highly skilled with a variety of weapons and would do anything to protect the other two, which you obviously know. However, I believe Frances is the reason that Sanders gave your uncles so long to pay back their debt and has not yet had them killed. I do not doubt, however, that Charlotte is still in danger from them, as is Thomas."

"It's true," said Graves, urgently, "that until such time as Charlotte is married, her inheritance would become her family's property if she should die. From what you told me, Thomas, of the latest attempt on her life, Charlotte's aunts and uncles are well aware of that and are willing to resort to desperate measures to get their hands on her money."

"That's what we're counting on, Graves," said Thomas. "Their greed will not allow them to pass up a perfect opportunity to try again, only this time we are ready for them."

Charlotte, though her eyes were shadowed by sadness for her family, rubbed her hands together in anticipation of the outcome of the trap they had laid.

"May I ask exactly what you have in mind?" inquired Jonathan, curiously.

"I rather hoped you would, Jonathan," said Charlotte, archly, glancing at Thomas, "as we need your participation to make it work."

"Anything, Miss Charlotte," declared Jonathan, his eyes gleaming like a wolf's in the night at the lure of danger.

"I'm so happy you feel that way, because your first task is by far the most dangerous that we will ask of you."

"What is it? I am ready for anything!"

"Excellent! Louisa will be thrilled to hear it."

"Louisa? Your cousin? What does she have to do with this?"

"We need my aunts and uncles to believe that they have us completely fooled, Jonathan. It is absolutely essential that they think I trust them."

"Of course, but ..." Jonathan went pale as the realization dawned. "You mean, I'm—"

"Her escort," said Thomas, grinning widely at his friend, "You are engaged to accompany Miss Louisa Smythe-Poole tonight, to the ball celebrating our betrothal."

"Then it's a good thing I was already planning to bring my knife," muttered Jonathan. "This just isn't the form of self-defense I had imagined."

He smiled weakly as laughter broke out across the room.

Chapter

29

The night of the engagement ball was clear and bright. Stars glittered fiercely in the sky as carriage after carriage dropped off guests at the front door of the Brooke town house. The carriage that Jonathan Hayes had arranged for himself and Louisa pulled up directly after that of her uncle. Gerald, Frances, and their children were waiting in the hallway, having just divested themselves of their wraps.

Beatrice and Roland had declined Jonathan's somewhat desperate invitation to share his conveyance. He had hoped that the presence of her parents would keep Louisa's behavior in check, but, as Beatrice's husband-hunting tactics certainly did not exclude lures of the baser kind, a lengthy carriage ride alone at night suited her admirably. By the time he arrived at the Brooke home, Jonathan's legs were aching from the strain of moving from one seat to another in an effort to escape Louisa's overtures. He could not, however, escape the cloying embrace of her overpowering perfume.

Leaping from the carriage before it had stopped completely, Jonathan gasped in the fresh air before turning to assist his companion to the ground. Her well-practiced pout and breathy whining at his evasive maneuvers lasted only until they walked into the entrance of the Brooke manor. The delightful intrigue of the upcoming rendezvous in the garden with a man interested in her favors had her eyes sparkling and her lips curving upward in a sly smile.

"Louisa!" cried her aunt, "You look simply ravishing!"

The frothy lace that barely kept Louisa's impressive décolletage decent shifted even lower as she curtseyed to her aunt and uncle.

"Why thank you, Aunt!" she simpered, casting an eye back at her escort, who was trying desperately to look anywhere else. "I'm sure you remember Mr. Hayes."

"Mrs. Smythe, Mr. Smythe," said Jonathan, kissing the former's hand and shaking that of the latter. "Shall we enter the ballroom? I think I hear the musicians tuning up, and Miss Smythe-Poole informs me that she adores dancing."

Nodding their agreement, the couple turned and proceeded into the ballroom, the younger pair following closely behind. Jonathan thought, not for the first time that evening, that Thomas had better be prepared to stand in his debt for years to come. Should the feeling ever return to the arm to which Louisa had attached herself, he would, himself, fill up her dance card with the names of any man but himself.

The high-pitched chatter he had been ignoring suddenly caught his attention. "I'm sorry, Miss Louisa. What was that you said?"

"I should not blame you for being distracted, sir," breathed his companion, looking up at him through her lashes while stroking his arm, her bosom heaving in a practiced move.

Jonathan prayed for strength as he repeated his question.

"I only mentioned that my aunt, uncle, and parents seem determined to be introduced to everyone in the room."

"No, before that, please," said Jonathan, affecting what he hoped was a roguish grin. "You are correct. I was somewhat distracted by your … charms."

Louisa blushed slightly and tightened her hold. "I only said that even our butler was distracted this afternoon with all our preparation for tonight, but perhaps that's because he's only been with us for a few months, and Mother kept giving him messages to deliver. I'm not sure what they were about, but she would not allow anyone but Rivers himself to deliver them, not even the boy we usually employ for such matters. Sometimes she is very tiresome."

Louisa's expression of irritation at her mother was quickly smoothed over as she recalled her escort.

"Does that satisfy your curiosity, Mr. Hayes?" she asked, her tone and body language as she leaned even closer giving every indication of a double entendre.

"For now," whispered Jonathan, leaning close to her ear in order to be heard. His stomach twisted at the role he was playing, but he reminded himself that it was necessary. He knew enough gentlemen of high station and low character that it was easy to imitate their responses to a flirtatious young woman.

Besides, it seemed Miss Louisa Smythe-Poole was more than willing to enjoy the thrill of trying to entice a man into her arms with flattery and sensual behavior. Jonathan found any beauty she possessed eclipsed by the hardness in her face and the calculating look in her eyes. He was familiar with her type, not only from his investigative work, but because she was cast from the same mold as his mother. Mentally shaking his head to dispel the unwelcome comparison, Jonathan kept up his side of the light, flirtatious banter with Louisa. Spotting Lord and Lady Brooke, he guided his companion toward them while continuing to surreptitiously scan the room.

The room was filled with couples, everyone eager to dance, flirt, and gossip. Tomorrow, the parlors of the Society matrons would be the site of thorough deconstructions of the behavior and conversation of all the most eligible bachelors and desirable young ladies. The women would also take delight in recounting the various assignations, broken hearts, and outright scandals.

While there were men and women who actually believed in fidelity, just as many or even more greatly enjoyed embarking on any number of affairs. Most gentle ladies had perfected the art of extracting information from each other and their spouses, enabling them to enjoy pleasure wherever they found it, while maintaining a front of respectability. Insinuation, intimation, and allusion were skills crucial to any lady who wished to move in Society. While Jonathan found Louisa's behavior to be anything but ladylike, her actions were, sadly, typical of most of the young ladies of his acquaintance. He thought, not for the first time, that he likely would never marry. He was not afraid to take risks, enjoying the thrill of a certain amount of recklessness, but marriage was just too dangerous a prospect for him.

Lord Brooke looked up as he and Louisa approached. "Jonathan! Miss Smythe-Poole! I'm delighted to see you again. Are you prepared to dance until dawn?" he asked with a twinkle in his eye.

"I have a great deal of stamina," said Louisa in her breathy tone as she moved closer to the older man.

Pulling his wife over, with more desperation than finesse, Lord Brooke situated Lady Brooke between himself and Louisa.

"Look, my dear! Jonathan and Miss Smythe-Poole have arrived together. Isn't it almost time for the musicians to start playing? I'll just go and check on them."

Leaving Lady Brooke to deal with Louisa, Thomas's father backed away with a hasty bow and headed straight for the musicians.

"Miss Smythe-Poole, it's wonderful to see you again. You look lovely, and what is that scent you're wearing? It's quite … potent."

"Oh, it's the latest rage in Paris, Lady Brooke," bubbled Louisa. "This quaint little shop I found deals exclusively with the most recent trends from France. It's quite expensive, naturally, but worth the price."

Lady Brooke smiled while trying to discreetly distance herself from the cloud of scent wafting from the young woman. She suspected that the quaint little shop was more than likely making a fortune by selling extra potent lavender toilet water under the guise of Parisian fashion. She must remember to have the wall hanging and carpets thoroughly aired afterward lest they forever smell like Miss Louisa Smythe-Poole. She shuddered at the thought.

"I hear the musicians, Miss Smythe-Poole, Jonathan," she said, the soft strains of instruments reaching her ears over the chatter and laughter of the many guests. "Charlotte and Thomas should be making their entrance soon, and then the dancing can begin."

Louisa frowned involuntarily at the mention of her cousin, but her expression grew sultry as she turned to her escort.

"Perhaps later, Mr. Hayes, you would like to take a stroll through the conservatory where we met?" She batted her eyelashes skillfully once more and licked her lips, lowering her voice to infuse it with intimacy. "Wouldn't it be romantic, sir?"

Lady Brooke's sudden coughing fit saved Jonathan from having to answer. It would take all his skill and determination to stay out of any sort of compromising position with this young lady. However, he thought suddenly, if he passed her off to another gentleman, it was unlikely that she would come looking for him again. He had a sneaking suspicion that she would be satisfied to be on the arm of anyone in trousers. He was still trying to come up with a plausible way to lose his companion without her realizing that it was intentional, when a hush fell over the crowded ballroom. Lord Brooke stood before the musicians on the small stage and raised his arms to quiet the crowd.

"Ladies and gentlemen, I would like to welcome you to the ball celebrating the recent engagement of my youngest son, Lord Thomas Brooke, to Lady Charlotte Edwards. His mother and I are thrilled with his choice of a bride and are delighted to have the honor of introducing her into Society. Now, please find your partners, and take your places on the floor for the first dance of the night. Thomas, Charlotte, you must lead off!"

Turning to the musicians behind him, he exclaimed, "A waltz to begin the festivities, gentlemen, if you please!"

Louisa strained her neck trying to catch a glimpse of her cousin as Charlotte moved onto the floor. She passed over her on first glance, having expected Charlotte's gown to be elaborate and lavishly trimmed. Instead, Charlotte wore a simple gown in a lustrous, soft green satin trimmed delicately with the finest ivory lace. Though not ostentatious, the lines of the gown clearly indicated expensive, high quality tailoring. Her hair was upswept, accented with tiny ivory roses. A fine gold locket lay in the space between her collarbones.

It was her shining eyes and gentle smile, however, that caught Louisa's attention. She had never realized that her cousin could be beautiful, and the notion only served to embitter her further toward Charlotte. There was something in her face that Louisa knew was completely lacking in her own. It wasn't fair, she thought, mentally stamping her foot. That little nobody didn't deserve what she had!

Her angry thoughts were interrupted by a nearby voice. "Good evening, Miss Smythe-Poole. You look quite lovely. The effect of your gown is most alluring."

Louisa turned breathlessly at the sound to see a familiar figure standing a few steps away.

"Mr. Rivers," she exclaimed softly, "you flatter me! Might I say that you look rather dashing this evening? So very elegant and refined!"

She stepped smoothly away from Jonathan and Lady Brooke, who were still watching Thomas and Charlotte glide around the room. Inspecting the man thoroughly from head to foot, she found that Mr. Rivers was as impeccably turned out as any gentleman could be, from his finely cut formal jacket to the high quality of his black wool trousers. She wondered briefly how he had managed to acquire the obviously expensive apparel, then decided that there were more important matters at hand.

"I wondered if you would be able to meet me here," she murmured, placing her hand on his arm as he led her toward the edge of the ballroom.

"I found the lure to be utterly irresistible," he responded, eyes flaring briefly as he looked her up and down. Leaning close to her ear, he whispered softly. "The conservatory, Miss Louisa?"

Looking up at his dark eyes and rugged features, Louisa nodded. She found herself incapable of speech, her heart beating faster at the thought of being alone with him. His eyes scanned the room, then he tugged her smartly around the corner and down the deserted hallway toward their final destination.

The moonlight was bright as they entered the room, casting shadows everywhere. Rivers brought them to a halt next to a garden bench, moving closer to run his hands up and down Louisa's arms. As he looked into her eyes, which glittered with anticipation and excitement, Rivers felt the briefest sensation of guilt over what he was about to do. For all her antics, he knew that Louisa was, in fact, an innocent. Still—there was no helping it. An order was an order.

He cupped her face gently, his gaze dropping to her lips. They parted slightly, her breath catching, as he lowered his head. The catch turned into a gasp as his hands caressed her neck, their hold tightening. Her eyes stared, questioning, as she fought to breathe. Their light dimmed, and her gaze became unseeing as he relentlessly tightened his grip.

Just before everything faded into darkness, she heard his rough whisper: "It was necessary."

Rivers gently laid Louisa's limp body on the garden bench and, leaning down, softly brushed his lips across hers in an expression of regret. Then a wry smile crossed his lips. No kiss would awaken this young woman. Nothing would.

The figure watching from the shadows applauded slowly as he stepped into the moonlight. "An excellent job, Clark," he said. "You were believable to the last moment."

"Thank you," said Clark, alias Elliot Rivers, an air of grim satisfaction pervading his manner. "It was a pleasure."

Chapter
30

*C*harlotte's feet ached, her throat was parched, and she was tired of having people stare at her. One glance at Thomas told her that he was also ready to be done with all the socializing. The couple had been presented to the public and introduced to dozens of guests individually—and had not, since the moment they stepped into the ballroom, had a moment to themselves.

At first, Charlotte had very much enjoyed the romance of dancing the first dance with her intended, but she had since then come to view the ball as a task to be completed rather than an event to be enjoyed. On the bright side, she mused, she had only briefly seen her aunts, uncles, and cousins, and even though she knew that she would have a great deal more interaction with them before the night was over, she appreciated whatever opportunity she had to pretend that she belonged to Thomas and his family alone.

"And people wonder why I shun Society," muttered Thomas, drawing her away after they had escaped a trio of highly curious elderly matrons already well on their way to spirits-induced giddiness. "I vow, if I have to hear one more scarcely veiled hint that I can still throw you over in favor of one of their daughters, I shall not be responsible for my actions."

"Thomas!" exclaimed Charlotte, really laughing for the first time tonight. "You mustn't speak ill of those ladies. They're simply disappointed that such an eligible and desirable catch as yourself is now unavailable. Besides, I am fairly certain that if you send one more husband-hunting mother Jonathan's way, he will kill you himself. You missed the way he was glaring at you when he was obliged to dance with Mrs. Hewitt's youngest, Priscilla."

Thomas's eyes gleamed with laughter.

"Was she the one who brought her yappy little dog with her? And if so, where did she put that thing while they danced?"

Charlotte smiled widely as she caught Jonathan's eyes on them from across the room.

"I believe her mother held it and waved its paw at them every time they danced past."

Thomas started laughing just as Jonathan reached them. She remembered the aura of danger that had emanated from him when they had first met, and though she had long since become comfortable in his company, she was glad that she was not the target of his irritation. As the two friends stood next to each other, the rough edges and sharp eyes of the investigator were exaggerated by the innately elegant stance of the well-born son.

"I suppose you think sending tipsy Society matrons and their empty-headed daughters my way was a compliment?"

Thomas managed to smother his laughter long enough to shake his head solemnly. "Just wanted you to have a good time, old friend," he said, straight-faced.

"Of course you did. Out of respect for the lady, we'll finish this discussion at a later date." Jonathan's smile could only be termed deadly.

Thomas just laughed again, acknowledging to himself that he would pay for his fun later. Jonathan could be very creative when he tried. Charlotte watched the two, still unsure how to interpret the undercurrents she felt, but aware that this was not the first time that either had enjoyed himself at the other's expense.

"Actually, I came to collect your fiancée for a breath of fresh air," said Jonathan, proffering his arm. "Would you care to join me for a stroll, Miss Charlotte?"

"I'd adore it, Mr. Hayes," responded Charlotte, with a slight curtsey.

Thomas watched as his friend led Charlotte across the room and out into the hallway. He took a step in their direction when a gloved hand landed on his arm.

"Good evening, Mr. Brooke," said Frances. "I wonder if you would care to dance with you fiancée's favorite aunt?"

Though he would much rather have stolen Charlotte away from Jonathan for their own moonlit stroll, Thomas knew there was no acceptable way to refuse a lady's invitation to dance.

"I would be delighted, Mrs. Smythe," he said and offered his arm to lead her onto the dance floor. His attention diverted by his duty as a gentleman, Thomas did not see the pair of figures slipping out of the ballroom after his friend and his fiancée.

~

"A fine night for a stroll, is it not?" declared Jonathan.

"Indeed. The moonlight is so bright and lovely here in the conservatory. The air in the ballroom was becoming so musky and warm that I could hardly breathe. How do people manage to stay in such crowded rooms without feeling the need to escape?"

"I believe that for many ladies, this is their only time to practice the feminine arts on men, and for men, it is an opportunity to fall prey to those charms," replied Jonathan in a cynical tone.

"You may be right," mused Charlotte. "In fact, you are probably exactly right. It is certainly that way for my cousins."

The pair wandered among the plants, occasionally stopping to examine a blossom or shrub, their footsteps echoing in the still air.

"Thomas should be joining us soon," said Jonathan, after a few minutes had passed.

"Do not underestimate my aunt's powers of manipulation. She has thoroughly mastered the skill. I wouldn't be surprised if she has him dancing with my cousins as a last attempt to steal him away from me."

She tried to smile, making light of both her family's perfidy and her own hidden insecurity, but couldn't meet Jonathan's eyes.

"Charlotte, he would never leave you. I've known him for over ten years, and I've never seen him look at anyone the way he looks at you. It's you that he's been waiting for. No one else."

He shifted awkwardly as he spoke, his voice ringing true even though he was obviously uncomfortable with the subject.

"Thank you, Jonathan," she said, touched by his concern. "You're a good friend to him. You'll find her someday, you know."

"Find who?"

"The woman you're waiting for. She's out there. Waiting. Just as I was for Thomas."

Jonathan stepped away and abruptly said, "I'm never getting married."

Charlotte followed him. "Jonathan? I'm sorry. I didn't mean to offend you."

"You didn't offend me, it's just— What's that?"

He cocked his head, listening.

"What…?"

Charlotte stopped as he motioned to her to be silent. The sound of footsteps echoed in the stillness, followed by a voice. "Charlotte? Are you in here?"

Nodding to Jonathan, she gestured for him to stay put while she advanced. Charlotte moved swiftly around the foliage and through a flower-laden archway toward the familiar voice. Stepping into the wide area she remembered so well as the place where her family had first heard that she was in other hands than theirs, she realized that throughout their tour of the conservatory, she and Jonathan had only wandered the paths shrouded with foliage.

The obstruction of the plants, though, kept her from realizing that Jonathan was no longer observing her progress alone. Only the gun trained on his heart kept him from trying to warn her. She walked purposefully toward the voice she had heard and then stopped as the owner stepped into view.

"Good evening, Charlotte," said Frances. "Come say hello to your cousin."

Moving aside, she gestured to the figure lying motionless on the bench. Charlotte stared in horror at the unnatural stillness and awkward position of Louisa's body. She whirled to call for help and ran straight into the man who had crept up behind her. His right hand tightened around her, pinning her arms to her sides, while the left came up to clap a surprisingly strong hand over her mouth.

Frances smiled, pure evil emanating from her features. "May I introduce my brother?"

Chapter 31

M r. Sanders kept his hold on Charlotte's arms.

"It's a pleasure to see you again, Miss Edwards," he said, his soft voice sending shivers up and down her spine. "If you value your life, you'll keep silent when I remove my hand. Do you understand me?"

Charlotte nodded slowly, trying to calm her frantically beating heart. Her thoughts churned. It was clear that Frances had something sinister in mind, something that very likely included Charlotte's untimely demise. It was also clear that Frances was unaware that Charlotte already knew of her connection to Mr. Sanders. Charlotte knew that her life depended on keeping her captors talking as long as possible.

Thomas was supposed to meet her—oh, she hoped that he was safe. If something happened to him because of her, she would never be able to live with herself. She closed her eyes briefly, breathing deeply. She could not afford to be distracted by fear. She had a plan to follow, and she had to trust that everyone else would do their part. Glancing unwillingly at her cousin's motionless form, she felt her heart clench for yet another lost life in Sanders's pursuit. She took another deep breath before speaking.

"Would you kindly release me, Mr. Sanders? You have my word that I will not run. But please … is Louisa … You didn't … is she dead?"

"I will indeed release you, but we don't need your word. Frances never goes anywhere without her knives, and I never go anywhere unarmed. As for your cousin, she had an unfortunate encounter with Mr. Clark. You remember him, of course." He smirked at Charlotte's involuntary grimace. "Your uncle needed a little reminder of what happens when I am unhappy with him, and my sister was finding the competition between Louisa and her own daughters tiresome."

"But—Aunt Frances, you must know that Aunt Beatrice will never forgive you for having anything to do with her daughter's death!" Charlotte stared at Frances, her confusion readily apparent.

"Charlotte, you really are a little idiot, aren't you?" asked Frances in the sort of manner one uses when explaining something to a small child, "You'll be lying here dead with her. It will be easy enough to convince Beatrice that you, or perhaps Mr. Hayes, attacked Louisa. She is well aware that my brother has plans to kill you for your money, but the timing will make it appear as vengeance for Louisa's death."

Sanders let go of Charlotte's arms and pulled an ugly gun out of the pocket of his overcoat. Seeing Charlotte's gaze fixed upon the small, deadly object, Sanders elaborated. "I still carry a knife as well, but I find this to be a very effective second weapon."

Charlotte looked at her aunt, noting the wicked-looking knife lying on a table beside her. "I was not aware that you had any siblings, Aunt Frances. You always told us you were an only child."

Frances smiled gleefully. "It was so much fun creating a different past for myself. Those girls at the finishing school would never have spoken to me if they had known that my father was a drunk and my mother a whore who left Billy and me to scavenge in the gutters for food. Oh, how I laughed inside at those prissy little princesses with their ruffles and lace. They were terrified when the robberies broke out while we were at school, always walking around together, talking about when their families would be away and hoping they wouldn't be next. They never knew I was listening, or that I passed the information on to Billy and Clark so they could pick their next target."

Her look turned pensive as she remembered.

"Beatrice was the only one who caught on, but she would never have given me away. We had it all planned out—how to play the game so that we could marry into wealth and nobility. My new past gave me a hint of aristocracy, and I had some money from the robberies for a dowry, and you know what Beatrice had."

"It was obvious to any man what Beatrice had," commented Sanders, dryly.

Frances laughed shrilly, the sound echoing in the still air.

"It certainly was. By the time we left school together, Beatrice had seduction down to an art."

A change came over her features, fury burning in her eyes.

"Charles Edwards should never have been able to resist her! It was all worked out! I was engaged to Gerald, and Beatrice would marry Charles to secure the money for Gerald's manufacturing plant. Amelia was nothing! It didn't make sense!"

"My mother was not nothing!" cried Charlotte. "She was beautiful and gentle, and my father loved her more than anything! He would never have betrayed her, no matter how hard you tried to make him! It would have gone against his faith and his heart!"

"You silly chit!" exclaimed Frances. "Do you honestly believe that your Thomas will be able to stay true to you once my daughters have had a chance at him? I have them occupying his attention right now. He probably doesn't even remember that you exist. Your father was an aberration, a one-time failure ... but I dealt with him and your mother. They should never have gotten in my way."

Charlotte went white as she comprehended the meaning of her aunt's words, amplified by the madness in her voice. Glancing at Sanders, she saw nothing but satisfaction at his sister's scheming successes.

"What did you do, Frances?" she asked. "What did you do to my parents?"

Frances smiled dreamily as she picked up her knife and studied it as it gleamed in the moonlight. "I did what I had to, Charlotte. They were going to give it all away, you see. All that lovely money, and they were going to give it away. We needed it!"

She looked up suddenly, glaring at Charlotte. "I would have killed you as well, but it would have looked too suspicious. I thought about it a few years later, but by then, the police force had been formed, and it was far too risky."

She cocked her head to the side reflectively.

"Besides, we did have access to that lovely allowance of yours as long as Roland and Beatrice remained your guardians. Beatrice and I talked often, as you got older, about how we could gain control of your entire fortune. Billy here was obliging enough to allow our foolish husbands to pay back their loan at a much slower pace than he would normally consider. After all, I am his sister. We talked about your inheritance, and how to get our hands on all of it, didn't we, Billy dear?"

"A great many times, Franny," replied Sanders, content to listen to his sister's tirade as he lounged near Louisa's still figure.

The way he watched Charlotte while toying with his gun unnerved her. His eyes were ice cold, and though sharp, there was no hatred in them. In contrast to his sister, Sanders seemed to be simply tying up loose ends. For Frances, Charlotte feared, her death had become an obsession. Her only hope was to keep Frances and Sanders talking long enough for help to arrive. She prayed that Jonathan had made it safely out of the conservatory and that he and Thomas were on their way. They had known that Frances would have to make an attempt quickly, but standing in the wide open space as the focus of two deadly killers, Charlotte found her nerves beginning to fray.

"But I never knew I had an inheritance!" she exclaimed. "You could have gone on using it, and I would never have known. Why did you need to marry me off to Mr. Warren? Didn't you think I might resist?"

"You stupid girl!" cried Frances, free at last to let her true feelings out. "We could only touch the monthly allowance, not the whole! It was fine for a while, but then Billy came across the investment scheme of a lifetime, and we needed your inheritance to buy into it. It was either marry you off to someone involved, or kill you outright. You should thank my brother for finding you a husband. My idea was to dispatch you in a mishap similar to what carried your parents away, but I was outvoted."

Frances's look of disappointment made her resemble a petulant child who has just been told she cannot have another piece of candy. Though Charlotte was disgusted by the indifferent attitude her aunt had toward her parents' deaths, she swallowed the bile rising in her throat and prompted the madwoman further.

"What do you mean, dispatch me? What, precisely, did you have to do with my parents' deaths?"

Frances giggled as she exchanged conspiratorial glances with her brother.

"Oh, tell her, Franny," he said at last. "I sent Clark to deal with Mr. Hayes, so no one is coming to save her. She won't live long enough to tell anyone what she knows, and besides, my connections and status in the darker side of London are too great for anyone to touch either of us anyway."

Charlotte's eyes slid shut as her hope for rescue died. Sanders was right. Whatever the outcome, she thought miserably, she had to know what had happened to her parents that night so long ago.

"Please," she whispered, "please tell me. You owe me that courtesy, if nothing else."

"Very well, I will tell you," began Frances, obviously enjoying herself. "The night your parents died, we were all invited to attend one of the many balls of the season. Gerald and Roland were in a state of near panic when they realized that they would get no more money from your father. They were in no mood to attend the ball, but Beatrice and I convinced them that it would take their minds off their troubles. We pretended ignorance when it came to finances, and thus, our husbands thought we had no idea how deeply in debt they were.

"Beatrice had discovered, through conversations with Amelia, that Charles intended to legalize his plans and change his will when he saw his lawyer; his appointment was set for two days after the ball. We needed to move quickly. I got in touch with my brother and arranged for Clark and himself to help us. The night of the ball, Billy took his first opportunity to test the identity he had created for forays into polite company, escorting an ambitious fallen gentlewoman named Madeline from one of the brothels he owned. Between Billy, Madeline, and Beatrice, Roland and Gerald never noticed that I slipped away for a time. No one else paid attention to the comings and goings of one more middle-class woman."

She stopped, a faraway look in her eyes as she relived the event.

"It was child's play to have Madeline occupy Gerald's attention while I followed your parents' carriage. They kept much earlier hours than most, so I knew I would have plenty of time to return before Gerald even began to think of leaving. My husband never was able to keep from making a fool of himself when fussed over by a beautiful woman.

"Billy had arranged for their regular coachman to fall conveniently ill earlier in the day, and the replacement was, as you may suspect, Mr. Clark. He drove them into one of the worst areas of London, the neighborhood we grew up in, while I followed, driving a carriage of my own. I had exchanged my gown for trousers and a man's shirt and coat, tucking my hair up under a cap. No one spared me a second glance, and Billy had let it be known amongst our former neighbors that anything they saw that was out of the ordinary should be quickly forgotten."

Charlotte held her breath, willing Frances to keep going. Her aunt's voice took on a singsong tone as she recalled her actions.

"Clark had stopped the carriage in front of an alley, and I, quickly tying the horses to a lamp post, ran over to meet him. He already had the door open, and was brandishing his knife, but I didn't want him to spoil my fun. I made him move back and then poked my head into the carriage to greet your mother and father. Oh, the looks on their faces!"

The sound of her mad cackling filled the air. She wiped tears of mirth from her eyes as she went on. Charlotte hung on every word, despite her growing horror.

"I killed your father first, before he had a chance to react. One thrust through the heart with my trusty blade, a quick turn to ensure death, and so much blood! More flowed with every inch of knife I pulled out! It wasn't my first kill, you know, but it was the first one really up close and personal. I watched his eyes as the light went out. Your mother tried to run, but Clark blocked her way out. She kept crying, saying things like 'Please don't do this' and wailing, 'Charles, Charles!' I would have stabbed her just to shut her up by then. Same as your father, knife straight through the heart. I remember watching her eyes too, thinking it was taking a lot longer for hers to dim. They did, though. I thought she was dead when she breathed suddenly, and said 'Charlotte.' After that, her eyes stayed dead."

Frances shook her head, returning to the present.

"As if she could have saved you anyway! Those two were so weak, with their religion and their faith, always trying to 'share the gospel' with us. Fools! I never needed anything but my own wits to make it! Billy and I pulled ourselves and Clark out of the gutters, and look how far we've come! All your parents left you was money you don't deserve and beliefs that won't get you anywhere in life! And now, you'll join them in death. At least you have something to look forward to after, don't you?"

She laughed madly again, bloodlust filling her eyes as she gripped her knife more firmly.

"What do you think, brother? Straight through the heart, just like Mother and Father dearest? Or maybe one quick swipe across the throat— something special, just for you, Charlotte."

Frances advanced toward her niece. Charlotte tried to back away but was blocked by Mr. Sanders. She stood, no way out and nothing between life and death but the hand of God. Tears pricked her eyes at the thought of never seeing Thomas again. He would never know just how much she loved him. They would never have the chance to make a life together. She couldn't let that happen.

Charlotte knew if she was going to act, she had to move quickly. Cowering to make herself as small a target as possible, she whimpered and looked up with pleading eyes. They widened briefly in surprise as she took in the full perimeter of the room, but she quickly lowered her head and whimpered once more.

"Please, Aunt Frances, don't kill me!" she sobbed. "I won't tell anyone, I promise! You can have my money, I swear it! I didn't want it anyway!"

"Oh, shut up, you sniveling little idiot!" roared Frances, now out of control, knife flashing wickedly in her hand as her brother moved back to give her full access to her prey. "I want you dead! Dead, do you hear me?"

Her attention fixed on Charlotte's shrinking form, Frances failed to notice the stiffening of her brother's posture or the faint whisper of cloth on swiftly moving limbs.

"I heard you, Frances," said a calm voice from behind her, "but the only ones dying today will be you and your brother."

Chapter
32

Frances whirled about but did not move swiftly enough. Charlotte hurled herself to the floor in a futile attempt to pull herself out of danger. Lying there, she was unable to keep her eyes from following the graceful upward arc of a knife as it was brought to Frances's throat. Still in shock, she tried to comprehend the scene before her as the woman she had presumed dead traced a delicate, taunting line across the front of her aunt's neck.

"This," she said, "is for trying to have me killed."

Charlotte watched, horrified, as Louisa jerked the knife in and across Frances' throat in one quick movement. The fountain of blood that spurted from the wound was unavoidable, and though Charlotte scrambled away, the splotches of red soaking into the skirt of her dress bore testimony to the vile act that had just taken place.

Louisa watched dispassionately as the body of her aunt dropped face down on the hard tile floor of the conservatory. She glanced at the weapon still clenched in her fist, then looking at her aunt again, crouched down and began to clean the knife on the skirt of the dead woman's gown. Satisfied with the restored cleanliness of her weapon, Louisa looked up. Her eyes glittered in the semidarkness of the room.

"Hello, Cousin. Your concern for me was touching, but as you can see, I am not in need of it. Elliot, do you need any assistance with Mr. Sanders?"

Charlotte turned around, rising to her feet as she did so. Sanders stood motionless, a murderous fury in his eyes. His weapon was no longer pointed in her direction, but was held in the left hand of the man behind him. The gun trained on Sanders' heart never wavered as the man holding it addressed Charlotte.

"Miss Edwards, it is a pleasure to see you again. I hope the events of this evening have not overtaxed your nerves?"

The polite, refined accents in which he spoke belied the coarseness of Elliot's features and build. They were very different from the common accent he had employed the last time they had met, but Charlotte recognized him immediately.

"Mr. Clark? But I thought …?"

She flicked her gaze toward Sanders, who was visibly livid at his associate. Clark followed her gaze and smiled coldly. "You mean you thought I was absolutely devoted to Sanders? So did he, and I was, so long as it suited me. However, I am through playing the ignorant lackey to his crime lord, doing the dirty work and getting nothing in return. I have been planning this for some time, and your situation has played perfectly into my hands. Billy and Franny, here, were so focused on you and getting revenge that they never noticed me building up my own following amongst our associates and issuing orders on my own. When Billy ordered me to apply for the position of butler at your uncle's home, with the object of seducing and killing Louisa here, I went along with it to allow myself more freedom of movement. As soon as I met Louisa, however, I knew I had found my perfect partner. Isn't that right, my sweet?"

The look he sent Louisa spoke volumes more than words could have expressed. She returned his gaze steadily, intense emotion burning in her eyes. It surprised Charlotte to see the obvious commitment to each other evidenced in the exchange. Apparently, she mused, murderers had feelings too. How intriguing.

"Absolutely, Elliot. It became a game for us to play— - daughter of the house and the butler as well as Elliot and Louisa, plotting against those who would keep us apart. I found Elliot's plans to be very clever and most … enticing." She smiled seductively at her lover.

Charlotte's mind reeled with questions. "When did you know that he was sent by Sanders? How did you know you could trust him? Do Uncle Roland and Aunt Beatrice know who he is?"

And when, she thought desperately, will Thomas come to save her? Hasn't Jonathan gotten away? If Clark was here, where are they?

"So many questions, Cousin Charlotte! You always did bother me so with that curious look of yours. All those years with Mummy and Daddy, and you never spoke more than two words at a time. I thought you quite stupid, you know. It's not fair how everything has just fallen into place for you when I had to work so hard to secure my future."

She glared briefly, her bottom lip stuck out in a petulant pout while Charlotte stared at her in amazement. She hardly thought twenty-five years of life as the unwanted appendage of a vicious, sharp-tongued family constituted having everything fall into place for her, but she wasn't about to argue with the woman holding the bloody knife. She watched as Louisa's gaze moved to Elliot, who still had Sanders at gunpoint, her expression becoming positively sunny.

"Are you going to shoot him now, Elliot?" she asked, excitedly.

"Actually, Louisa," said the man, "I had rather hoped you would. If you shoot him from where your aunt was standing, we can make it look more like Billy attacked Franny, and she was defending herself. I imagine that Mr. Hayes has gone for the police. He had notified them that an attempt was likely to be made on Miss Edwards's life soon, but he had no evidence as to when. They will be here within a half hour, if I am not mistaken. We will need to be gone by then, Louisa, so if you are willing …?"

Elliot, keeping his own gun trained on Sanders, offered the one he had confiscated from his captive to Louisa. Eyes shining with excitement, she took it and moved back to stand just behind the lifeless body of her aunt.

"Is this right, Elliot?" she asked, anxiously.

"Perfect."

Moving away from Sanders, gun never wavering, Elliot gave the order.

"You may shoot him now, Louisa. Aim for his heart - though it is unlikely he has one."

Smirking at his own joke, Elliot Clark gave one last long look at his former partner in crime.

"Good-bye, Billy."

Louisa pulled the trigger, her aim impeccable. Though Charlotte was prepared, the sound of the shot still made her jump. It was as though she was stuck in some horrible dream. She watched as Sanders raised a hand to his chest, staring at the blood that came away on his fingers. He crumpled to his knees; then, slowly, he fell forward onto his face. The look of surprise never faded, even as the life in his eyes did. Charlotte felt herself becoming hysterical and fought the sensation. The scent of death surrounded her, and the sight of the blood pooled under her aunt made her ill. She felt a scream building up in her throat and struggled to keep it inside. Clark and Louisa did not need any more motivation to kill her too.

"We must leave now, Louisa. Hurry!"

Elliot strode over to Louisa and took the gun from her reluctant fingers. If the wide smile on her face was any indication, Charlotte's cousin had none of the inhibitions about murder that Charlotte felt. Elliot placed the gun in the limp hand of the dead woman, then pried the knife from her cold grip and placed it beside the still warm body of her brother. Rising, he looked at Charlotte one last time.

"I hold no ill will toward you, Miss Edwards. You have nothing to fear from these two any more, and may rest assured that I consider the matter closed. As long as you keep your mouth shut, you need fear no reprisal. After all," he said, amusedly, "I do believe we're family now."

With a brief wave from Louisa and nod from Elliot, the two departed swiftly. Charlotte wondered briefly how they would escape notice, then realized that it likely did not matter. A man with Elliot Clark's newly established rank in the London criminal underworld would be practically untouchable, as would his lover. No doubt there would be a plethora of individuals willing to alibi both Elliot and Louisa for the time the killings took place. The police would be hard pressed to build any sort of case. The statement of a lone, frightened woman would hardly stand up in a court of law.

Charlotte's already battered nerves suddenly got the better of her as she realized that she was standing alone with two very dead bodies, their mingled blood soaking the hem of her gown. Hysteria rose, and strong though she was, panic and shock from the nightmare she had just experienced overwhelmed her. Staring blindly at the gory scene before her, unable to move, she began to scream. The last thing she heard before the darkness claimed her was the thunder of running footsteps in the corridor.

Chapter

33

homas's heart stopped at the sight of the three bodies lying in the middle of the conservatory. Heedless of the shouted warnings from Jonathan and Graves, Thomas ran straight to Charlotte's side and looked frantically for signs of life. When his fingers detected a steady pulse in her wrist, he wanted to weep with relief.

After a quick check for obvious injuries, he lightly patted her cheeks. "Charlotte! Charlotte! Wake up, please!"

Moaning slightly, she turned her head away. "Go away," she mumbled, "leave me alone."

"Charlotte!" said Thomas, sharply, "Wake up!"

She groaned and slowly opened her eyes. Blinking, she stared at him. "Thomas? You came! Oh!" she exclaimed, shutting her eyes quickly and turning her face into his arm, "are we still in the conservatory? Are Frances and Sanders here? I don't want to see them again, please! So much blood …". Her voice trailed off as she shuddered.

Thomas looked up, his eyes focusing on Jonathan's grim face. The man shook his head slowly and said, "They're dead, Thomas. I'm not surprised—Clark assured me they would be."

Charlotte spoke into Thomas's arm. Realizing that he couldn't hear her, she turned her head slightly and repeated herself. "Clark was here. He pretended to kill Louisa to follow Sanders's orders. Then, once Frances had me trapped between herself and Sanders, Louisa snuck up behind Frances and, and …"—she swallowed—"slit her throat."

There was a marked difference, she thought, in writing the words and in actually seeing the blade slice through the neck of a living woman. In writing them, there was a thrill. In living them, there was only the bloodstained memory of an empty life meeting an empty death. Charlotte knew that what she had seen would leave its imprint on her soul forever.

"After Frances ... expired," she said, choking on the word, "Louisa and Clark explained their plans to me and to Sanders. I think they wanted to brag about it. Clark is taking over Sanders's role in the underworld, has been planning it for some time. Louisa is joining him. I know the police won't be able to prove anything, and Clark told me as much. Then he got Louisa to shoot Sanders and put the gun in Frances's hand. She wanted to. It doesn't make sense to leave a witness, so I'm not sure why they didn't kill me too. Louisa would have done it in a heartbeat."

Charlotte looked up at Thomas, Jonathan, and Graves, who had just returned from checking the rest of the conservatory.

"Something in my cousin is truly evil," she said, her eyes far away. "She enjoyed it, and so did Clark. I suppose they might truly be made for each other. The killing was almost romantic to them."

She sighed, tired, but too tightly strung to calm down.

"Anyway, after that, they left me here alone with the bodies. I meant to leave and find you, but when I looked at Frances and Sanders one last time, I just fainted. How pathetic of me. I honestly thought I was past such nonsense. After all," she said, squaring her shoulders, "I write about these things all the time. They are the basis for my stories!"

Charlotte grew more animated with every sentence, completely forgetting herself in her rising frustration.

"What kind of self-respecting writer can I be if I faint at the sight of the horrors I write about? And where were you three?" she demanded, glaring. "I thought we had a plan. We'll trap them, you said. Thomas will be watching, you said! Between Graves, Jonathan and you, Thomas, I would always be protected, you said! And here I was, alone! Do you have any idea how terrified I was?"

To her complete mortification, she burst into tears. Valiantly attempting to regain control of herself, Charlotte accepted Thomas's handkerchief, sniffling with as much dignity as she could muster. Her anger dissipated when Thomas wrapped her tightly in his arms and pressed a kiss to her hair. Strong as she was, Charlotte couldn't keep from melting into the comfort of his embrace.

"Do you have any idea how terrified I was?" he whispered. "There I was, trapped in the ballroom by your cousins and good manners, trying to believe that Jonathan and Graves would keep you safe. Then I burst in to find you lying so still in what appears to be a pool of your own blood? I thought I'd lost you!"

His hold tightened even more.

"I couldn't bear losing you, Charlotte. My heart stopped until I realized you were only unconscious. Please, never frighten me that way again! The thought of not having you in my life—" He swallowed hard. "I've never loved anyone the way I love you, Charlotte. It would be like losing a piece of myself if I lost you."

"You won't, Thomas," she replied, nestling closer, reveling in the safety of his embrace. "It's over now. It's over." She reached up and cupped his cheek, drawing his ear close to her mouth. "I love you too," she whispered softly before pressing a kiss to his temple.

She turned her head at the sound of shouts and footsteps approaching.

"How are we going to explain this, Thomas?" she asked solemnly. "Jonathan? Where's Graves?"

"He's the one who went for the police," said Jonathan, "and you don't need to worry about explaining anything. I'll take care of the police; my father and I both have connections in the force. The powers that be, I suspect, will want this kept quiet and dealt with as soon as possible. Graves and I will tell them what they need to know, and if and when they interview you, it will just be a formality."

"The scandal, though," said Charlotte, mournfully. "Thomas, how will your parents ever forgive me? There's no way to keep this from getting out, and once the gossipmongers get ahold of it, it will be all over town."

"Charlotte," Thomas replied, grinning, "haven't you learned anything about my mother yet? She's going to adore the notoriety of having a double murder in her very own home, especially one that took place during our engagement ball. Once the society matrons realize how much she's enjoying herself, talk will die down. Beside, there's always some sort of scandal brewing among the nobility. You'll see."

Still unsure, Charlotte smiled weakly while Thomas and Jonathan chuckled over the mental picture. The shouts and footsteps grew louder as Graves led the police into the conservatory and toward what would now become a crime scene.

Suddenly unutterably tired, Charlotte leaned into Thomas and sighed. "Can we leave now, please?"

"Soon, darling. Just as soon as I inform the police that you and I will be available for questioning tomorrow afternoon. One of the perks of nobility is that people seldom dare to refuse you."

Setting her down on one of the benches, facing away from the bodies, Thomas walked over to Graves, Jonathan, and Ramsey, the detective in charge. After a brief consultation, he returned.

"Come on, Charlotte. I'll see you to your room."

They walked slowly past the policemen who were examining the bodies, then Jonathan, Graves, and Ramsey, whose sharp eyes took in the evidence of tears and strain on Charlotte's face and then focused on the stiffening dried blood that coated the hem of her gown at least six inches deep. The splatter reached almost to her waist, with irregular droplets scattered across her bodice as well.

Eyes returning to the scene as the pair made their way into the corridor, Ramsey found the keen gazes of Jonathan and Graves fixed on his face. He cleared his throat, eyes serious as he directed his attention to the gruesome scene in front of him, tucking the observations he had just made into the back of his mind. He would pull them out to examine and piece together later. He had no doubt that Jonathan would give him the pertinent information, if he asked, but he trusted the private investigator enough not to ask, if Jonathan did not offer. Some things, he knew from experience with the force, it was best not to know. As the three men stood watching, the two officers Ramsey had brought with him gathered what evidence they could before the doctor en route took the bodies away for post mortem examination.

Thomas and Charlotte took the back stairs up to the family rooms on the second floor. After holding her close, softly kissing her brow, and making sure she locked the door behind her, Thomas left Charlotte upstairs with Mrs. Brown, hoping that the woman would be able to bring his fiancée a measure of comfort. He doubted, however, that it would be more than a quarter hour before Charlotte found some way to send the woman away so she could be alone. He saw in her eyes that the terror of the night would not soon fade from her mind and wished there were some way he could ease her pain.

Though Charlotte had not completely shut him out, she still automatically tucked her feelings away to deal with alone. Thomas knew that she would have to sort everything out herself before she would let him into her pain. As much as he wanted to force his way in, he had to respect her need for the familiarity of grieving alone. He shook his head and moved reluctantly down the hall.

He headed toward the ballroom to inform his parents of the tragedy that had taken place in their home and warn them of the scandal that would soon descend upon them. He thanked God as he walked into the still-crowded ballroom that it was noisy enough to have kept anyone from noticing the grim proceedings in the conservatory and the arrival of the police shortly thereafter. Servants' entrances, he decided, were an ingenious invention.

He spotted his mother and father standing near the refreshments, looking slightly bedraggled after hours of dancing, socializing, and worrying about the outcome of the trap he had laid for Charlotte's enemies. Seeing him walking toward them, his mother nudged his father, rousing him from what seemed to be a standing sleep. He looked around, blinking owlishly, then spotted his son. It was obvious that, despite Lord Brooke's foray into dreamland, both parents had been waiting anxiously to hear the news.

"Well, Thomas?" asked his mother, nervously. "Did it work?"

"Mother," he said calmly, "Charlotte is safe and sound, Sanders and Frances are dead, and you're about to get your greatest wish."

"What's that?" inquired his father, clearly curious for details of the outcome. His relief over Charlotte's safety warred with the thousands of questions now filtering through his mind.

Thomas began laughing, the tension that had been in his frame since early that morning finally lifting. "A scandal, father. A great, big, messy scandal."

Chapter

34

As the ball ended in the early morning hours, rumors of flirtations, affairs, and murder began. Though the majority of what had happened remained unknown, the prying eyes of various guests had noticed the police presence in the front corridor, and even though the servants' entrance was used, the removal of the bodies could not be kept secret.

The extreme discretion Graves employed in locating the rest of Charlotte's family and gathering them in the library still gave way to talk. More than one inquisitive gaze followed them out of the ballroom, just as more than one curious ear overheard the sounds of shock and grief emanating from within. Many an exhausted husband was treated to speculation and gossip about the identity of the dead and the behavior that had precipitated murder, as they and their wives travelled home.

Though Lord and Lady Brooke were aristocracy, they were not immune to the damage that could be caused by a breaking scandal. That said, they did not often move in Society and had little concern for stories of murder in their home, as long as it would be eventually known that they were not the killers. In fact, true to Thomas's assessment, Lady Brooke was far too excited at being the source of such notoriety to be remotely concerned about its effect on the number of invitations she received. She rose after only a few hours' rest and dressed carefully in a stylish, high-quality day gown that fairly shouted old money and respectability.

By midmorning, she had sent brief notes to seven "dear friends" who just happened to be the major sources of most of the speculation floating around high Society. The invitations to a session of tea, cakes, and gossip planned for late afternoon would be unanimously accepted, she was certain. Though they would likely hope to gather in the still bloodstained conservatory, or at least be led on a tour, the matrons would have to be satisfied with meeting in the parlor. At eleven o'clock, she knocked on Charlotte's door, a maid with the breakfast tray standing slightly behind her.

"Who is it?" came Charlotte's voice, immediately.

"It's Elizabeth, Charlotte. May I come in? I've brought Susan with your breakfast as well."

"Yes, certainly. Please come in."

She opened the door, and, gesturing Susan ahead of her to arrange the tray on the bedside table, she stepped into the room. Charlotte sat at the small writing desk, staring out the window at the bright, clear morning. She was surrounded by sheets of paper covered with neat, straight writing. Her fingers were ink-stained, and though the satisfaction that writing always brought was visible on her face, the dark circles under her eyes and the pale cast to her cheeks bore witness to the sleepless night of a greatly troubled heart.

Lady Brooke thanked God that Charlotte had not been present when the news of Frances's deception and death had been broken to Gerald. The pain etched on his face was too sharp, too clear to be anything but genuine. Though her daughters and son seemed shocked, they did not appear to mourn their mother's death so much as find it an inconvenience. Lady Brooke had little doubt that the girls' thoughts concerned the style of mourning gowns they would need more than the loss of their mother. As for Horace, she figured he would find solace in sports and the life of dissipation already evidenced by the florid cast of his young face even as he lifted a second snifter of brandy to his lips.

Roland and Beatrice had been informed that their daughter had run off, but Graves kept the details to himself. Beatrice had crumbled under the strain of losing her best friend and her daughter in one fell swoop, especially when she'd had such high hopes for an advantageous marriage. Lingering while the others left the library, she had requested that Graves tell her everything. The uncertainty and pain that lurked in her eyes had belied her imperious tone, and so, this morning, while Lady Brooke planned her strategy for besting the ladies of Society, the men, her husband included, had gone to meet Beatrice in her home in Berkeley Square. Though she wondered briefly how they were getting on, Lady Brooke quickly returned her attention to Charlotte's disheartened air.

Dressed in a flattering striped day gown the color of cinnamon and cream, Charlotte looked impeccably ready for the day, aside from the ink stains on her fingers. If Lady Brooke had not been observant enough to note the slight pallor and purple shadows under her eyes, she might have been convinced that Charlotte suffered no ill effects from the night before. However, her trained mother's eye was still sharp, and Charlotte, still unused to concern directed at her, was not able to hide the dimness in her usually clear eyes. Susan, having finished setting out the tray, curtseyed low to Lady Brooke and Charlotte and then left the room, shutting the door behind her.

"Tell me, Charlotte. Have you slept at all?"

Charlotte turned her face away, her gaze unseeing as she stared out the window.

"I couldn't," she said, flatly, "Every time I closed my eyes, all I could see was blood and death everywhere. I finally got up and started working on my next serial. I thought if I used what happened and wrote it into my story, that might get it out of my thoughts."

"Did it work?" inquired Lady Brooke's soft voice.

"I don't know," replied Charlotte, her shoulders slumping. "I still can't sleep—but at least blood and bodies don't appear every time I close my eyes."

"Oh, my dear, I'm so sorry you had to go through this. I wish I could take away the ugliness and horror you experienced." Soft arms came around Charlotte's shoulders and a gentle hand cupped her chin, turning her head to meet sympathetic eyes. "I can't make it go away—but I can be here with you as you face it. Tell me about it, Charlotte, dear. Let me help shine some light into the darkness."

Charlotte swallowed hard against the lump that had risen in her throat. She was afraid that if she gave in to the tears again, she might never regain her composure. It was one thing to be alone and afraid, but quite another to allow someone else to share in her vulnerability. Still fighting for self-control, she tried to find the right words. The kind eyes holding her gaze never faltered. Finally, she spoke.

"I can see them lying there. Less than a minute from alive to …" She stopped.

"Death is always difficult, Charlotte, but what you saw was far more violent and unnatural than most. It's not surprising that you can't sleep. Did Mrs. Brown stay with you last night?"

"She wanted to, but I sent her away," said Charlotte. "I needed to be alone to think and to write. I love Mrs. Brown, but as long as she was here, all I could do was think about how guilty I feel that the people I love are involved in this whole mess. I couldn't think about what actually happened until I was alone, and then"—she shuddered—"well, then I was too alone and too afraid to sleep, so I started writing."

"Charlotte, this isn't your fault!" said Lady Brooke. "Thomas has shared this entire matter with his father and me. You and I both know this started long before you were even born. It's your tender heart that makes you want to protect those you love, but you can't carry the weight of responsibility for events beyond your control. Your family did wrong by you for twenty-five years. I would imagine you might be relieved to have them out of your life, and that is understandable."

She looked at the expressive green eyes filling with tears.

"Charlotte, nobody expects you to be strong all the time. Lean on us. We are your family now. While Lord Brooke and I would never expect to replace your own parents, we are thrilled that God has blessed us with another daughter, through your marriage to Thomas. Come now, do as my own dear girls used to: lay your head on my shoulder, and cry it all out. That's what mothers are for."

Charlotte's face crumpled, and she did just that. Lady Brooke rocked her back and forth, stroking her hair. Her breathing evened and became the slow, regular rhythm of sleep. Though she knew her arms would soon fall asleep as well, Lady Brooke didn't move. Instead, she bowed her head over the sleeping girl and prayed. A half hour passed before a quiet knock sounded on the door.

"Come in," she called in a hushed tone.

"I've just come for the tray, milady," said Susan, curtseying.

"Here, Susan, help me carry Lady Charlotte to her bed and get her settled."

The two women easily lifted Charlotte's slight if sleep-heavy frame and tucked her into bed without her stirring a bit. The exhaustion and strain of the past few day were smoothed from her face by the magic of sleep. Susan picked up the tray, and Lady Brooke, after stroking Charlotte's cheek one last time, led the way from the room.

"Let her sleep through lunch, Susan, and I'll come and wake her later this afternoon in time for tea."

"Yes, milady."

Watching Susan's progress down the hall, Lady Brooke sent one more prayer up to heaven for Charlotte's welfare—and, if she was honest with herself, for vengeance against those who had caused her such pain. Sighing ruefully at her own vindictive nature, Lady Brooke made her way down the corridor, a smile lighting her features at the thought of the tea yet to come. Perhaps she would have a chance for her own small vengeance. She wondered, as she reached the stairs, if she should pray for forgiveness before or after the tea for what might come out of her mouth. Knowing her, she thought wryly, she had better do both.

Chapter

35

hough Graves, Lord Brooke, Thomas and Jonathan arrived at the Berkley Square manor a few minutes early, the door opened immediately upon their knock. The haggard, strained face that poked out before opening the door fully was so at odds with Beatrice's usually rested though still ill-tempered features that she was almost unrecognizable.

"Please come in," she said shortly.

It appeared that what little sleep she had managed to get had done nothing to improve her spirits. If anything, the stiff set of her shoulders and her slow, measured steps spoke of resignation to the information she was about to receive. She led the small party into the front parlor, not even waiting until they were seated before demanding that Graves begin.

"Where is your husband?" he inquired.

"In his den, as always," replied the woman, shrugging carelessly. "He doesn't care to know any more than he has to. He never knew about Frances's brother, and his main concern is Louisa's fate, though he is not overly concerned about that either."

She sniffed indignantly. It was obvious that she felt Roland was taking the events of the previous evening, particularly the fate of his only daughter, much too lightly, and that his aversion to discovering more of the truth grated on her.

"I suspect that he cares more than you think, Beatrice," said Graves. He had no desire to begin this encounter with the woman's formidable ire already raised. Though he had detected honest fear and concern for her daughter, he had worked in the household long enough to know that Beatrice was aware and responsible for almost as much as Frances in regard to Charlotte's fate. She saw little beyond her own desire for wealth, power, and respectability. Though her love for Louisa ran deep, most likely the shame of having a ruined daughter concerned her more than the actual fate of that daughter.

"He is a stupid fool!" cried Beatrice, not caring if her husband heard her. "For years, Frances and I worked and worked to gain footing in society, and all for nothing! Roland never appreciated everything I did for him, and now ... well, he just retreats into his den as always and leaves me to face whatever comes from Louisa's disgrace.

"He hates Charlotte, you know," she said, her tone turning conversational. "He will never admit it now, but he's always hated her. We only kept her because of the allowance from her inheritance—and because I knew what Frances had done to her parents. I wanted to send her away to a boarding school, but we couldn't because we were never sure what could happen if someone began looking into her past."

She fixed Graves with a grim look. "For twenty-five years I had to look at her weak, insipid little face, so like my sister's, and know that we would never be rid of her! Now Frances is dead, and it's all Charlotte's fault! Why couldn't she have taken the scarlet fever or some other childhood ailment and died long ago? Why was I cursed to see my sister's eyes staring at me every day?" She began weeping uncontrollably, her sobs angry and frightened.

The men exchanged glances, shifting uncomfortably in their seats until the sobs quieted to the occasional muffled sound in her handkerchief.

"Beatrice, it wasn't Charlotte's fault," said Graves, quietly. "You and Roland may hate her, but none of this was her doing. She is innocent, and you cannot keep laying the blame for others' decisions on her shoulders. It's a miracle she has borne it these past twenty-five years without crumbling, but it just shows what a remarkable young lady she is. Thomas loves her and will marry her, and there's nothing you can do about that. Louisa would never have stolen his affections, no matter how much you plotted and planned to that end.

"Yes," he said, wryly, catching her surprised look, "your attempts were more than a little obvious."

"More fool, he, then," she muttered, darkly. "My Louisa would have been a far better choice, but I won't say anything more on the matter, as it's beyond repair now."

"You know Frances and Sanders are both dead, but what I have not yet disclosed to you is that the man who organized their deaths is the man with whom your daughter has run away. It is Mr. Elliot Clark, new head of the London underworld. You would remember him as Rivers, your new butler, now missing."

"What?!" exclaimed Beatrice, "You cannot be serious! That man ... But how—and why?"

Her voice faded as she comprehended the position the man now held, as opposed to the one she had known him to occupy. "You mean he's in charge of everything Sanders was involved in?" she asked, surprise giving way to a shrewd look.

"Yes, he is," said Jonathan, speaking up for the first time. "Frances and Sanders stood in his way, and that was why he had to bring about their deaths somehow. It was logical to choose last night's engagement ball. That way, it would look as though any one of the guests attending could have slipped away and done it. Everyone knows, especially the police, that blackmail and illicit liaisons are the norm in the upper echelons of society. He knew Frances and Sanders planned to kill Charlotte there, and he had been ordered to kill Louisa as well, and so he decided to make his move."

Though it was Louisa who had actually killed the two siblings, the men did not intend to tell Beatrice unless it became necessary. Despite her avid dislike for her niece, it would serve no great purpose for her to realize that her beloved daughter was little better than a psychopath.

"If what you say is true—then Louisa is not without hope!" cried the woman. "She certainly has the resources to restore her reputation, especially if she marries Mr. Clark! This is good news indeed! I had feared that all was lost, but now ... well, now she may achieve far more than we had planned anyway."

Beatrice smiled, the tension in her features easing as the reality of wealth and power, albeit illegitimate, sank in. No longer interested in the men sitting before her, she rose and moved toward the door.

"You may see yourselves out," she announced, arrogance quickly restored to her voice. "I must discuss this with my husband."

Glancing at each other, the men rose and followed her out the door and into the front hallway. They were reaching for the overcoats they had tossed on the coat rack upon their arrival when a shot rang out.

Beatrice, already on her way toward the den, began to run, with the men following close behind her. "Roland!" she shouted, "Roland! Open the door, please!"

She knocked, but there was no answer. When she tried the knob, it became apparent that the door was locked from the inside.

"If you would step aside, madam?" requested Jonathan.

Beatrice moved out of his way, shock radiating from every feature. Jonathan stepped back a few paces, then ran at the door with his shoulder braced for impact. On the third try, the door flew open. The sight that met their eyes confirmed what all had suspected. Roland Poole sat at his desk, staring at them with eyes that would never see again. The bullet hole through his temple and the blood still oozing from it were quite visible.

Jonathan suspected that, once they searched his desk, they would find a note declaring his inability to live with his daughter's disgrace and his financial problems and stating that this was the only honorable way out. Suicide among the disgraced nobility and financially crippled was something quite familiar to Jonathan. He moved forward to do just that when there was a commotion behind him.

"Bloody fool!" cried Beatrice, starting angrily into the den. Then her eyes rolled back, and she crumpled to the floor.

Jonathan turned around to find the other three men bent over the fallen figure, now stretched out on the floor of the corridor. There were, he thought mournfully, so many better ways to start a Saturday. Murder was not objectionable. Fainting women certainly were.

Chapter 36

Duty constrained Thomas to offer his family home as temporary lodging to Beatrice. Once she had been revived and thought about it, however, she decided to stay in her own home. It seemed, if she could be believed, she would rather stay where her daughter could easily find her once news of Roland's death became public.

While Lord Brooke went to fetch the police, Jonathan and Graves assured Beatrice that they would have some men come to take care of the mess in Roland's study. Though she was obviously shocked and angry at her husband's suicide, Beatrice did not seem to feel his death to be a great loss. She informed Graves that her husband's will stated that she would inherit everything that was his, which was likely not much, but that she knew dear Charlotte would see fit to take care of her poor aunt. Graves, sickened as he was by her presumption, knew that this would indeed be the case. It had always been impossible for Charlotte to see need without wanting to alleviate it, and she would feel responsible for her aunt's well-being.

Having dealt with the police to everyone's satisfaction and seen to the removal of the body, the men departed. Beatrice seemed quite content to be left in the care of the two maids that remained in her employ. The grieving widow she was not, and would never be, not for Roland Poole. She had married him for his position and money as a banker, and that was all. If the overtures she had not so subtly made toward Lord Brooke the previous evening, and during the removal of her husband's still warm body, were any indication, her attitude toward men and money had not been affected by either her daughter's abandonment or her husband's death.

❧

When Lord Brooke and company arrived back home around one o'clock, Lady Brooke had luncheon ready for them. She had left Charlotte to sleep, planning to wake her only when it became necessary to prepare for the tea that afternoon.

"Are you quite sure she is well, Mother?" asked Thomas for the fourth time.

"She will be, Thomas, as I told you before. She just needs to sleep, and then she and I will take care of the stories that are sure to spread like wildfire, given last night's events." Lady Brooke rubbed her hands together as she anticipated the upcoming tea.

"But you said she hadn't slept?" repeated Thomas, obviously unable to shake his anxiety over Charlotte's well-being.

"Thomas! If your mother says she's fine, she's fine," said Lord Brooke, carefully hiding his grin behind his napkin. He was finding far too much enjoyment in watching his hopelessly besotted son. "Come, we will visit the police while the ladies gather," he said, nodding to Graves and Jonathan, "and find out what we can about Roland Poole's affairs and the official conclusions regarding Sanders and Frances. Jonathan, you mentioned something about a contact you have that could confirm what we know of Mr. Clark and Louisa?"

Jonathan nodded. "I've sent word to him already, and we're meeting this afternoon. He can find out anything, provided the price is right."

"Pay whatever you have to," replied Lord Brooke, forgetting his wife's presence until he caught sight of the avid interest on her face. Mrs. Brown looked on in interest as well.

"Elizabeth, my dear, you have your own web to weave," he reminded her, shaking his head in mock chastisement. He well knew that Lady Brooke was equal to any task and loved her confidence. It amused him to see similar traits in Charlotte and to watch his own son learning to support and encourage. A lifelong process, he knew from experience, but it was inevitable that his son would end up with a woman as magnificent as his mother.

"Come, gentlemen, we have much to do, and the ladies must prepare to do battle with their own kind," declared Lord Brooke, leaning down to

188

exchange a sweet kiss with his wife. Graves followed suit, abandoning his innate sense of propriety long enough to make his recently acquired fiancée blush. Seeing the wistful look on Thomas's face, Jonathan slung a friendly arm around his shoulders and tugged him toward the door.

"All right, Thomas," he said, jovially, "let's get this all sorted out so that you can come back home, marry the girl, and live happily ever after, while I go back to my cold, dark office, alone and forgotten until the next time you get involved in the criminal underworld."

Thomas smirked at his friend. "You poor man. I'll be sure to send one or two of Charlotte's cousins to brighten your spirits, if you do not perish of loneliness first."

Lord Brooke and Graves, turning around swiftly at the sound of a loud thump, were treated to an expression of utter innocence on Jonathan's face as he stood observing the lanky figure sprawled on the floor. He often found a well-placed foot in front of his opponent's shin to be supremely satisfying. Dusting off his trousers as he scrambled to his feet, Thomas had the good grace to laugh over his well-deserved if unexpected communion with the floor.

Lady Brooke watched the men depart, special affection in her heart for the two younger men. Her son, she knew, would be fine, particularly now that he had found his soul mate in Charlotte, but Jonathan ... she worried about that boy. His character was as solid as they came, but there were carefully hidden wounds behind those dark eyes and charming smile. Turning back to Mrs. Brown, she smiled a roguish grin of her own.

"Shall we wake Charlotte? It's time to hold a council of war."

Laughing, the two women headed upstairs to make their final preparations before descending to face the dragons disguised as the matrons of Society.

⌒

Charlotte had awakened on her own shortly before Lady Brooke and Mrs. Brown came upstairs to find her. She had lain silent for a while, eyes closed, willing herself to face everything that had built up and become so overwhelming. The deaths of Sanders and Frances were the climax, she thought, to the unhappy tale that was her family. Their evil had not surprised her so much as confirmed what she had always known about her aunt, anyway. As for Sanders, she could remove herself somewhat from his actions and death simply because she could recognize that it had little to do with her and more to do with his sister and his business.

It was Frances' bone-deep hatred of her that wounded her most deeply, even more than the attempt to kill her. Though Charlotte knew that Frances was responsible for her own death, in her heart, she still struggled with guilt over not being able to make her family love and accept her. It was one thing to write heroines who were confident and always did the right thing, even under duress, and another to try to convince her heart that the weight of guilt it bore was unnecessary. Perhaps, she thought cynically, that was why she found such satisfaction in writing the unfortunate ends of her villains. It provided the release she needed but could not find outside her work.

Sighing, she rose and changed her gown, as she suspected that the one she had been wearing was hopelessly creased. She sat down at her desk once more and began to go over what she had written so frantically the night before. Grinning, she read more intently, almost missing the sound of knocking on her door. It sounded again.

"Come in," she called, distractedly, her head still bent over her papers.

"Did you sleep well, Charlotte?" asked Lady Brooke, entering the room, with Mrs. Brown close behind.

"I did, Elizabeth, thank you," she replied, a little embarrassed as she recalled her breakdown a few hours before. She shuffled the papers into a more organized pile and turned to face her visitors.

"Excellent! We have much to settle before the ladies arrive."

"Ladies?" asked Charlotte.

Mrs. Brown smiled at her question. "Lady Brooke has invited some of the most ... inquisitive high Society matrons to tea this afternoon."

Charlotte began to laugh, quickly grasping Lady Brooke's intent. "I assume, then," she began, "that you are planning to satisfy their curiosity as to the tragedy last night?"

"In a creative and, perhaps, somewhat biased manner, yes," replied Lady Brooke, grinning.

"This should be most enjoyable," said Charlotte, with a growing smile of her own, "shall we get our stories straight?"

"Stories, indeed. I have an idea about that." Eyes sparkling, Lady Brooke gestured the other two closer and began to scheme.

"Oh, how scandalous!" cried Lady Compton. "You mean to tell me that those people that died in here last night were here to attack Lady Edwards? How deliciously thrilling!"

"How did you survive? Was it terribly frightening?" cried Lady Barrington, her eyes pinned to Charlotte's face.

"Oh, I couldn't tell you," said Charlotte, with the air of someone imparting a great secret, "because when I saw the knife and gun, I fainted dead away and was not revived until Thomas woke me."

At the words *knife* and *gun*, the women gasped in horror, clearly hanging on Charlotte's every word. Lady Brooke stepped in, providing even more titillating information.

"If turned out, if you can believe this," she said in a low, intimate tone, "that Mr. Sanders is not a gentleman of Society, as we all thought, but was actually involved in the criminal underworld. He wanted to get his hands on Charlotte's inheritance and was part of a conspiracy long ago to murder her parents, Lord Charles and Lady Amelia Edwards."

The ladies gasped in unison, then sipped their tea, exchanging looks of excitement. It was evident that they each wanted nothing more than to leave and spread the news far and wide.

It was Lady Barrington who asked the question that her hostesses dreaded most. "But was not your aunt the other person murdered? I heard from my husband that Mrs. Smythe was dead and was found with Mr. Sanders in the conservatory. What was she doing there?"

"Well," said Charlotte, carefully forming her phrases to guard her uncle and cousins against unpleasant backlash, "she came to find me, and then Mr. Sanders appeared. Things happened so quickly that I cannot be certain of the details, and then I swooned. When I awoke, I was lying next to two bodies, and blood had soaked into my gown while I was unconscious. It is a tragedy that my aunt was murdered last night, perhaps as an indirect result of Mr. Sanders's nefarious plot against me."

The gory details of the murder scene and black description of Mr. Sanders were enough to distract the ladies from Frances's possible involvement. They were satisfied to believe that she might have been an innocent bystander, though, Charlotte thought sadly, that was certainly not the case.

"Oh my!" cried Lady Aylesbury, who had been silently digesting the information, "then who was the murderer?"

The women leaned forward, their gazes piercing and intent.

"That is the mystery," replied Lady Brooke, carefully phrasing her answer. "No one has been charged with their deaths. My husband has spoken with the police, and they have not yet discovered the identity of the killer. They have concluded that Charlotte is too traumatized to give evidence, and the killer was already gone by the time Thomas and his friend Jonathan arrived to find her."

"How shocking! Oh, how utterly terrifying!" cried Lady Compton. "You mean, there's a murderer on the loose?" Though her words would indicate fear, she appeared far more excited at the revelation than afraid.

"It would appear so," murmured Charlotte, trying her best to appear fragile yet resilient, if such a thing were even possible, "and no one knows who will be his next target." She glanced over her shoulder with a shudder, as though the killer was somehow present with them.

"My dear Lady Edwards," said Lady Barrington, "you have been through a terrible ordeal! I do hope you will recover soon. After all, you and Lady Brooke have a wedding to plan." She opened her mouth to launch into the many wedding questions bouncing around in her head, but stopped short as she remembered there was juicier gossip to spread at the moment.

"Now," she said, turning to Lady Brooke, "I'm afraid that my husband is expecting me home, so I must depart. Thank you very much for the delicious tea and cakes and for the lovely company."

"I must leave as well," declared Lady Compton, a sentiment echoed by the rest of the ladies. Though all knew that they were more anxious to spread the news than return to their homes, it was also understood that their delicate untruth would not be exposed.

As they watched the carriages driving away, Lady Brooke turned to Charlotte and Mrs. Brown, who had listened silently at the door through the whole exchange.

"What do you think, my dear?" she said, addressing Charlotte. "Did we satisfy their curiosity?"

"I should say so," said Charlotte, thoughtfully, "and I believe that they will leave my aunt's involvement out of it, for the most part. Uncle Gerald and my cousins should be able to grieve in relative peace."

Mrs. Brown came alongside Charlotte and slipped an arm around her waist. "Your care for them is remarkable, Charlotte," she said, quietly. "It shows the beauty of your character."

Charlotte leaned into the woman, thanking her softly, and extended her hand to Lady Brooke. With an air of satisfaction, the three ladies strolled back into the house. Only time would tell if their plan had been successful, but all three hoped that it was finally possible for life to go on and for the dreams of Charlotte and Thomas for their life together to become reality. Besides, as Lady Barrington had pointed out, there was a great deal of wedding planning to do.

⌐

The wedding of Lord Thomas Brooke and Lady Charlotte Edwards was predicted to be the event of the season. The bride's and groom's plans for a small, intimate ceremony were quickly and masterfully altered by Thomas's parents, Graves and Mrs. Brown, who wanted to give Charlotte the kind of wedding she had always dreamt of, including a ball to follow at which no one would be killed.

To ensure this would indeed be the case, Lord Brooke sent Jonathan to have a friendly chat with Mr. Clark, whose position in the underworld had been solidified by the fear created by Sanders's execution and the fact that Frances had also been removed from the land of the living. The police never even bothered to interview him, knowing full well that witnesses could easily be bought and paid for with fear as well as with money. The investigation ground to a halt and was shuffled aside to free up manpower for new cases. It was unlikely that the case would ever be revisited.

Louisa was thrilled with her position as his mistress, and Clark had placed her in charge of the brothel industry while he focused on the gaming hells and taverns. From what Jonathan's sources told him, both sides of the business were flourishing. It was not difficult for him to obtain assurance from Mr. Clark that he and Louisa would behave with all propriety at Thomas's and Charlotte's wedding. After all, his position was established, but his entrance into Society was only beginning. He and Louisa would need her connection to Charlotte and the Brookes in order to capitalize on the many possibilities of the polite world. They were planning a quick trip to Gretna Green to formalize their own union before appearing in Society to bolster Mr. Clark's new reputation and identity as Elliot Rivers.

Beatrice never recovered her modest standing in Society, her reputation now tainted by her husband's financial ruin and suicide. She quietly disappeared from the public purview, a virtual recluse in her home in Berkeley Square, which, in truth, belonged to Charlotte. Perhaps it was only coincidence, but Charlotte, Thomas, and the others found it highly suggestive that around the time Beatrice retreated, a woman named

Madam Trixie showed up to manage Mr. Clark's least profitable brothel. Within three months, she had the place turning a generous profit, and rumor had it that she and Louisa were often seen together. Though it saddened Charlotte, she knew that her aunt and cousin were actually very well suited to the work they had chosen, and she held out hope that the tenuous connection they had would someday be enough to open their eyes to the evil of their ways. She doubted that either would give up their occupations and position, even for the social standing for which they had so long wished. The great deal of money available in their work went a long way toward keeping them happy.

Gerald never recovered fully from the scandal surrounding his wife's death. Though whatever love he had for her had died with her the night her murder had revealed her double nature, he still had to live with whispers and innuendo alongside his own doubt of her love for him. His children, recognizing that their standing in Society was precarious at best, moved quickly to secure their own futures. Their dowries still intact and their minds as sharp as their late mother's, Mariah and Elsa had little difficulty finding themselves suitable husbands. Mariah married an elderly widower who died within the year, leaving his entire fortune to his young widow. Both his death and his money suited her.

Elsa was not so fortunate. Her husband used her dowry to invest in a scheme that bankrupted everyone involved—the very scheme that Mr. Warren and Mr. Sanders had devised. Elsa and her husband retreated to their country estate, where her husband soon met with a tragic hunting accident when he was out on the estate alone. No one but the nearby village doctor, paid handsomely for his silence, ever knew it was not a rifle shot that killed the man but a knife wound straight through the heart. Elsa immediately returned to London to take up residence with Mariah. Perhaps it was only coincidence that Mr. Warren, shortly thereafter, met his demise in the same manner as Elsa's late husband.

Horace began working at the manufacturing plant with Gerald, grooming himself to take over when his father retired. Instead, he ended up marrying the daughter of a fellow businessman and going into trade with him. The result was an immensely profitable and extremely unethical venture into so-called herbal cures that caused more illnesses than they cured. Gerald's business continued to thrive, as did his fledgling relationship with Charlotte and Thomas and with Lord and Lady Brooke, who made a point of reaching out to the devastated man. The result was his spiritual awakening—and then a most pleasant surprise for all when he fell head over heels in love with the chaperoning spinster aunt of a young lady entering upon her first season in Society. The new Mrs. Smythe was a welcome addition to the family, particularly because she was not likely to try to murder any of the remaining family members.

Chapter 37

C harlotte sat at her desk in her second-story room, watching the pale, early morning light chase the night fog from the grounds outside. She rested her chin in her hand and sighed as she let her mind wander. The manuscript in front of her was nearly complete, but something was missing. Her heroine, the beautiful Serafina, had been forced to seek employment in a gloomy, mysterious castle as a governess after her wicked uncle had stolen her inheritance. Mysteries, phantoms, and innumerable secrets, and a growing attraction to Rudolph—a deposed German nobleman and tutor of the two almost-grown sons of the widowed, and wicked, Lord Craven—had her confused, frightened, and excited all at once.

Frowning, Charlotte pondered Serafina's latest dilemma. Trapped in the well-hidden, nightmarish dungeon underneath the castle with the lecherous lord, she had no hope for rescue but her love, Rudolph, whom she had last seen unconscious, being carried to his death by drowning in the castle moat by Lord Craven's two equally evil sons. Of course he would not die, she would be rescued, and, once his aristocratic heritage was made known to society, the two would be wed and welcomed into the polite world, carefree with the treasure they would discover hidden in the castle.

But how could she rid them of Lord Craven and his sons, while protecting the innocent young daughter to whom Serafina was governess? And more important, how would Serafina use her wits to escape Lord

Craven's grasp and the dungeon? Refusing to admit to any trace of writer's block on the morning of her twenty-eighth birthday, she furrowed her brow and began to jot down ideas. A knock at the door caused her pen to leave a trail of ink splatters across the fresh page as she jumped.

"Come in," she called, still distracted as she patted her hair and smoothed her gown.

"Breakfast tray, ma'am," said a respectful voice from the doorway. Footsteps crossed the room, and the tray was set down next to her papers as gentle lips nuzzled her neck.

"You are awfully impertinent for a servant," she murmured as she tilted her head back to kiss her husband good morning. "I don't believe I've ever had my breakfast brought in quite that way before."

The week that she and Thomas had been married had brought out a degree of playful mischief that had surprised them both. So much of their courtship had been spent fending off disaster that the relaxed pace of their married life was an unexpectedly pleasant change. As she turned her gaze back to the green field visible from her window, she felt a sense of rightness in her heart. It had begun when she saw Thomas standing at the front of the church in London on their wedding day. She would never forget walking steadily toward him, eyes shining as Graves escorted her, her father's Book of Common Prayer and a single blush-colored rose in her hands. The kiss Thomas had given her after the vicar pronounced them man and wife had been filled with such a promise of passion that she was blushing deeply when their lips finally parted.

"Perhaps that's what this story is missing," she mused aloud, turning the idea over in her mind.

"What's that, my love?" inquired Thomas, looking over her shoulder.

"More passion, gazes filled with longing, hearts beating faster..." She stopped, giggling at the look of wry amusement on her husband's face. "What sort of writer of the 'horrid novels' would I be if my heroine did not have a thrilling romance along with her dangerous adventures? Of course," she said, affecting the look and attitude of world weariness, "I shall try to keep from infusing too terribly much of my vast experience into my writing."

"I suppose," he said, sighing with feigned resignation. "Mercy, what a danger it is to marry a woman who thinks for herself, and—worse yet—writes for a living. What was I thinking?"

Narrowly dodging the slippered foot she aimed at his shin, he quickly moved a safe distance away from his wife, grinning naughtily. Only because she knew how much her husband actually treasured her uniqueness did she stay seated at her desk rather than pursuing him with another kick in the shins.

"I actually came in to see if you would be interested in a morning stroll with your charming husband. I hear it is customary for spouses to occasionally be seen in one another's company."

She arched a brow at him. "How strange. Are you sure of this?"

"Indeed, my lady."

"Well then, we had better adhere to custom. I would hate to do anything improper."

She cast a sidelong glance at him as she rose. Laughing, he held out his hand and began to draw her toward the door.

Suddenly he stopped. "Your breakfast! I completely forgot!"

He led her back to the desk and gestured for her to sit down. Moving the unfinished manuscript into the top drawer, he slid the tray directly in front of his wife. Charlotte stared at him in bemusement. Smiling slyly, Thomas lifted the silver lid from the tray.

"Thomas! Is this …?" Charlotte leapt up and threw her arms around him.

"Fresh from the presses," he said, swinging her round. "I had my uncle send us the first copy as soon as it was ready."

He set her gently down and then cupped her face between his hands.

"I love you, Charlotte Brooke," he said, his eyes clear and bright as they gazed into hers.

"And I, you, Thomas Brooke," she replied, "more than I ever thought possible."

She thought of the day, one year ago, when she had poured out her heart to God, asking for someone to love, but not able to believe her prayer could be answered. A year filled with extreme danger and complete safety, steps of faith and revelations of long-hid secrets, tragedy, and the sweetest, truest love of all was certainly not what she had expected. She only hoped that God had allowed her parents a peek into the happiness that He had brought her. Everything she had desired for so very long, and had almost given up hoping for, was hers.

She lifted her face to Thomas as he reached out to cup her cheek. Gazing into the depths of his eyes, she sighed, a sound of soft contentment. Sunlight filled the room, chasing away the shadows, as he laid his lips on hers. It was perfect—a perfect beginning.

CPSIA information can be obtained at www.ICGtesting.com
Printed in the USA
LVOW08s1630090614

389247LV00003B/860/P

9 781449 704186